# GEORGE SCA

# AN EYE FOR EVIL

Luke's desires were simple - to enjoy a normal family life and to indulge in his real passion of wildlife watching and photography. That sometimes-involved excursions in the dark. But circumstances went against him. The darkness dealt him an evil and sinister hand.

One night he saw too much, or did he? He certainly wasn't sure. A new boss brought additional unwanted stresses into his work life. That was bad enough but his reporting of suspicions to a disbelieving Police Officer resulted in him having to completely re-assess his predicament. One thing was certain. Because of the stressful possibilities and consequent impetuous actions, he was now entirely on his own.

Even though he wasn't quite sure what he had observed, ominous people believed he was a danger to them, and they wanted him silenced, by whatever means necessary. How was Luke going to deal with his changing circumstances, survive the onslaught and prove something really was afoot before his luck ran out?

Having to deal with the problems of work and a Police force that doesn't know what to make of his claims, was bad enough, but as gangland intimidation becomes more frantic, Luke's problems really begin to mount up. Eventually, through frustration, this graduates to unambiguous determined assassination attempts against Luke. Due to a combination of luck and pre-conceived anticipation, Luke survives these attempts, but there are lethal consequences. How did his situation become so messy, convoluted and out of control? Which will kill him first - the evil mob, the righteous mob or the stress caused by the realisation that he cannot defend his reputation or himself? The domino effect of the events has left him standing alone, looking a very guilty man indeed. And the fact is that no-one seems willing to believe his side of the story.

***A Crime Thriller novel with hints of humour.***

***Best experienced with a suitable glass of wine, such as a nice Chianti.***

# CONTENTS

## Prologue

It was a twenty-minute journey to the old railway line. Luke parked up off the road and walked along the old track line until it went over a bridge above a river. Immediately after the bridge was a bare rock surface where the line continued into a disused railway tunnel. The tunnel was at least ten metres high and the same wide, lined with arc shaped stonework.

As Luke reached the three hundred metre mark inside, the light from the tunnel mouth disappeared altogether. He was now in complete darkness apart from his torch.

Outside the tunnel, a dark Mercedes car parked up close to his parked car, with another one parking near the other tunnel mouth, one mile away. Two men then entered the tunnel at each end.

Luke didn't know it, but he was trapped between these four men with ominous intentions, inside an old railway tunnel in jet black conditions and what was coming was not going to be friendly in the slightest.

## Chapter One – Luke's Background

**Ten years earlier** - Scotland.

Jumping into his car, Luke pulled away and drove fifteen rolling and scenic miles to a farm where he found Grant, in one of his farm sheds. Grant was a typical thirty-something farmer, stocky in build, with a weathered face from working outdoors, strong in arm and with tough skinned, calloused, dirt ingrained hands showing he had done lots of hard physical outdoors work. He had been a valuable asset on the rugby field, aggressive, skilful and tenacious, always keeping up with the action. He also had a wicked sense of humour.

"Thanks for coming to photograph my tup (ram)" he said.

"That's ok" Luke said, "is it close by?"

"Ah well, I meant to have him in, we'll have to go and get him."

"Alright", Luke said, "where do we have to go?"

"Well, you see that cairn showing at the very top of the hill – if we walk up to it, there is a stone walled field about three hundred yards further on – that's the field where he was last night."

"Oh great" Luke said to Grant "that means he could be anywhere on the far side of that hill."

Grant laughed at the discombobulated expression on Luke's face.

"That's why I brought him down last night, he's over in the shed," said Grant.

“Ah, very funny, Grant” Luke said as he let his head shake from side to side in an imitation of the old nodding plastic dogs that used to be left in the back window of cars. In doing so he acknowledged being taken in by his friend’s mischievous humour.

Grant, like many farmers was very fond and indeed proud of his animals. Start talking to Grant about his animals’ and he could go on at very great length about them. In fact, at very, very, great length indeed.

Farm livestock photography remains uniquely old fashioned. There is no desire for close ups, no wide-angle shots or inventive new compositions. Instead, consistent with paintings produced before photography was even invented, the desired composition is to have a trophy animal with a very regular stance, the legs straight, evenly dispersed, with the head held up proud and the back straight as a ruler. Of course, few self-respecting animals stand like that naturally, and especially when close by, strangers are moving about with equally unfamiliar devices in their hands. A camera is too reminiscent of vets’ tools, associated with pain or discomfort, so the animals are very rarely cooperative.

To achieve the required stance, Grant used a special stick with a pointed end and another backward facing point. This allowed him to gently tease the animals’ individual leg backwards or forwards until the perfect position was achieved. Then the other three legs would be attended to, until in theory they were all perfectly aligned. Of course, the reality, probably due to spite on the part of the subject animal, was that one leg always seemed to be out of the correct position. By the time it was adjusted, the animal invariably moved another leg, just to keep the game going. Once the perfect position was achieved,

Luke had to be quick enough to catch the moment. In his own mind, Luke felt sure the tup was playing it like a game, perfect stance, then move quickly just before the photograph was taken.

Grant was telling Luke about the latest rugby tour trip. "You know, Luke, I don't know why you don't come along on the next tour. They're great fun. There are a lot of hardy annuals come along every year, you know."

Luke smirked at Grants botanically orientated referenced joke. "And like hardy annuals, they'll be resistant to all sorts of poisonous concoctions like huge amounts of alcohol. Not me, not anymore. The time I went on a rugby tour to Copenhagen, because I was Irish, I was given a large shot of illegally sourced Irish poteen to drink. The whole team took a step back like a moving enlarging circle because they thought I would throw up. When I didn't, the bastards then gave me another shot of Poteen and I still didn't throw up. I almost did, but I kept it down, much to their annoyance, but I was gaga for the rest of the day" said Luke.

"And now you've had an addled brain ever since" added Grant.

Luke laughed at Grants sardonic humour.

At one stage, Luke's mobile phone rang. Luke just pressed the message button discontinuing the phone call.

Grant said "Could that have been important. You could have taken the call. I wouldn't have minded."

"No, it's just a friend," said Luke. With a twinkle in his eye, he continued "he's probably just wanting to know does he cut the red wire first or cut the blue wire first. If he gets it wrong, it'll be bye-bye time. I'll phone him back shortly, just in the nick of time. We'll let him sweat for a moment or two, while the countdown continues. He shouldn't have forgotten which is which, anyway."

"Sounds pretty urgent to me" said Grant with a wry smile and chuckle, catching onto the bombed-out humour.

After a while, Luke was up to the job and photographs were taken that he felt would be up to the required standard. It was all good fun whilst they tried to get the perfect picture, with good banter between Luke and Grant and even the animal looked as though it had enjoyed the entertainment.

Mission accomplished, Luke said goodbye to Grant and started to head home. Within a mile, he was stopped by a policeman on the country road.  Rolling down the window, Luke asked what the problem was. "We have an escaped prisoner on the loose – there were two, but we've recaptured one. Have you seen anybody who may have been an escaped prisoner or was acting suspiciously?" he asked as he eyeballed the inside of the car. Luke shook his head whilst muttering "No, nothing at all."

"Well, if you do see anything, you'll be sure to let us know," said the officer.

"Of course," Luke said. He pressed on, this time with heightened alertness.

As he came to a road junction, he saw two police cars go whizzing past and even in the fields, two dog handlers with their German Shepherd dogs searching for scent clues to the whereabouts of the prisoner. "They'll be lucky to find him if they work like that" Luke thought to himself.

Luke pulled the car into a spot where he could survey a very wide arc of the surrounding hill slope and countryside. Luke knew the way to do it is to be in the right spot, which is an area with a wide arc view but unnoticed and then repeatedly scan for any signs at all. It's a technique he used to find all sorts of wary wildlife when he wanted to locate and then photograph them."

"If he's about here, he'll be sticking to cover, unless he's a complete numpty" said Luke thinking aloud. He felt the competitive urge to outdo the security services. Luke felt he would have the edge in the situation as finding animals that preferred to stay unnoticed was his speciality. And now he had the opportunity on a runaway human. It was a rare occasion indeed.

"Right, I'll check the hedges, those woods, and that big patch of gorse" Luke thought to himself. Luke grabbed the binoculars he kept in the car. Within a few minutes, he thought to himself "I've just seen something move in that patch of gorse!" In less than a minute Luke confirmed he had seen the blue shirt of a young man moving in the gorse. "He'll be making himself comfortable in that gorse" he said with a wry laugh. "A bit jaggy, is it?" Luke muttered this so low that he barely heard his own words. "All I need to do now is to tell the police exactly where he is." Of course, even though there had been police cars zooming about in all directions five minutes before, when he needed to contact a policeman, there were none to be found. A police dog handler could be seen heading away from the spot about half a mile away, but there was no way to contact him. After a few minutes though a police car came racing up the road. Luke got out and waved them down. "I've found your escaped prisoner for you" he said.

“Oh yeah, well where is he, then?” came the slightly fractious reply from one of the bobbies. Luke described and pointed out the exact spot and soon all the dog handlers were headed in the right direction.

“And what’s your name” asked the copper in a not untypical brusque way, “oh and your address, as well?” It seemed to Luke that policemen very rarely have the greatest social skills.

“How did you find him up there” asked another of the policemen, this time in a slightly more amenable tone.

“Oh, it’s just something I do, finding and watching wild animals – I do a bit of wildlife photography. It looks to me that I could teach you guys a thing or two about searching for and locating runaway humans” Luke said, getting a little rub in against the first policeman’s initial prickly manner.

Shortly after, the radio crackled into life – “yep, he’s here” said one of the dog handlers. With the dogs at close proximity, he would have been a foolish guy to have tried to have made a break for it. With the job done, Luke got back into the car. By this time, the policemen were otherwise engaged and barely noticed as Luke slipped away in his car.

Luke had grown up as a policeman’s son in Northern Ireland during the troubles. At that time, trouble could come from either side of the religious line as there were hardliners on both sides with some very nasty characters indeed. Assassination attempts were regular, with shootings or by using bombs under the cars of the policemen. Luke had been old enough to fully appreciate the threats against his father and indeed even the family, as terrorists declared Police families as fair game. This meant Luke had developed extreme sensitivity to suspicious behaviour.

Over the years, his heightened alertness helped spot many other live crimes and even on one occasion, Luke saved a drunk from dying of hypothermia. Lying at the side of the road with only a clothed shoulder showing as he lay becoming hypothermic and comatose with drink, in a ditch. Luke only just caught a glimpse of his shape, as he drove past at four in the morning. Luckily, his curiosity made him turn his car around and go back to find out what it was. Still breathing, but only just, the heavily drunk young man was distinctly cold and not a pleasant colour, even in the high contrast brightness of the headlights. Luke phoned in to the services and within five minutes an ambulance had arrived. If he had fallen in the wrong direction, he could have easily been lying on the road and would probably have been hit by an oncoming car in the gloom of the predawn light. If he had fallen flatter, he may well have not been noticed at all until too late.

Luke's interest in wildlife photography meant he not infrequently got up very early on many weekend mornings, usually before dawn, which in the summer could be as early as three in the morning. Night-time is when many wild animals are active, but it's also when the less considerate and unruly members of human society do their unsavoury work.

As a result, Luke encountered a disproportionate number of active criminals because the vast majority of people sleep right through these quiet hours. One morning he came across three guys, all dressed in identical outfits, walking in a line along the road. He phoned in the details and a squad car was despatched to investigate. A policeman friend came back to him after the event. They had done a burglary, but their vehicle had broken down, so they were forced to abandon the van and walk out – before they were arrested. The identical outfits were an attempt to confuse any witnesses, as they all would look the same. Not that that mattered, as they were now under the tender care of the authorities.

JCB diggers were regularly stolen in the countryside as at that period, they were easy to start. Heading down a country road early one morning, Luke noticed a JCB heading his way. The frustration on the face of the driver willing it to go faster was comical but also suspicion arousing. Combine that with the time of only three thirty in the morning and Luke knew instinctively that the JCB digger had been almost certainly borrowed without permission from its legal owner. The sight of the thief with a desperate, wide eyed, tight cheeked expression, swaying back and forward as though his body movements would force the vehicle to go at a higher speed, gave him a chuckle, even disregarding the seriousness of what he was doing. Needless to say, the thief didn't travel too much further before he was apprehended. It wasn't much of a runaway vehicle – more of a "crawl away at 25 miles per hour vehicle whilst making lots of excessive noise and black exhaust fumes" type of vehicle. It was little wonder he looked anxious.

Being a light sleeper, Luke didn't even escape his social duties at night. When he had first met Kim, his wife, he was living in a flat at a crossroad junction. There were several shops close by, which meant the place buzzed during the day but at night, after midnight, often it became very quiet. One of the shops was a newsagent and it sat further away than all the others with a railway line and bridge beside it.

One night Luke awoke to the sound of breaking glass – not loud, but as muffled as somebody could possibly make it. Luke knew straight away that somebody was breaking in somewhere. The sound had not been like a bottle being broken against the road. Luke looked out but could see nothing at all. However, he knew something was amiss, so he got onto the phone to the police. The police came around to find a shop door wide open with cigarettes missing and the till tampered with. There was no sign of the burglar or indeed burglars. The guilty party had been in and out very quickly. Three weeks later, he was awoken again, but this time to the clatter of a door being knocked in. In doing so, the burglar managed to break some glass as well. After the previous experience, that was the first place that he looked to check out what was going on. Sure enough, in the shadowy entrance of the shop, there was a guy complete with a balaclava. This time the police sent around a dog handler. There was blood on the door, where the guy had cut himself on the glass. The dog was sent to catch him but after a long chase, he got away again in the darkness of a local park.

After that, the owner of the shop got a metal grill fitted on the front and he stopped getting problems. The police told Luke that on both occasions, he was the only person who had phoned. Luke wondered did that mean other people slept much deeper and didn't stir or did they just choose to ignore the sounds or even not get involved in any way?

There was a humorous event to one unintentional rendezvous with night-time criminals. Luke went up into the hills early one morning, intending to go and photograph at a hide. As he drove, it suddenly began to pour heavily with rain. Not wanting to proceed if he was going to get soaked, Luke pulled into a lay by and adjusted his seat to have a short sleep, hoping the weather situation improved. If it did, Luke would resume his journey. After falling into a light doze, Luke became aware of a vehicle pulling into the lay by. Next thing, a face was pressed up against his driver side window. Out of shock, Luke sat straight up. The guy looking in, grunted in horror at the sudden appearance of Luke's face, one foot away and nearly jumped five feet backwards and out of his own skin in shock. Then he immediately leapt into his white van and drove away as close to breakneck speed as he could. It was obvious, the white van driver was checking out the car to see if there was anything of value inside the car, as breaking a window so far away from any habitation would have been child's play and almost certainly completely risk free. For some reason, though, Luke himself, didn't see the funny side of it at the time.

All these were interesting little anecdotal indications of Luke's unintentional biproduct skills from his fascination with nature, his all-absorbing curiosity to investigate and learn, plus his suspicious nature from his Northern Ireland experiences. They say "curiosity killed the cat" so maybe Luke should have considered that motto as applicable to himself. But then young men are "bulletproof" - aren't they?

## Chapter Two – Turbulence at work

Luke considered his job to be about as good as they came - well almost. If he had the perfect job, he would have been a full-time wildlife photographer who made enough money to have no financial worries. The reality was that the trouble with being a wildlife cameraman was making sufficient income as it was a limited market with too many people wanting to be one of the top dogs, but he would have settled for having somebody to pay him to do it. He had resigned himself to dabbling in it, making a little bit of money, as and when the opportunities allowed.

Wildlife photography was unlikely to keep the financial wolves from his door. His day job was working for a multi-national company as an area manager, covering Scotland. Luke occasionally ventured south on business to London and other areas but most of his time was within Scotland. Working within towns and cities and across the whole spectrum of countryside Scotland had to offer, he became familiar with nearly all of Scotland.

As with many other hardworking, but uncommonly non-political types, Luke's job was only spoilt by the political movers, shakers and hustlers, which exist in every multi-national organisation. So many of the players wanted to climb the management ladder, that it sometimes left him wondering if he was the only one who was content to work at ground level. Luke enjoyed getting around seeing the countryside and his clients. He had also developed great relations with most of his clients. There was no doubt that many of his work compatriots deluded themselves as to their capabilities, but that would never stop them trying and sometimes, even more frighteningly, succeeding in getting a promotion to a position beyond their true abilities. A small proportion amongst them, were more than just ambitious, they were also quite capable of being prepared to back stab and shaft their workmates, as Luke was to find out.

Bosses came and went. They ranged from the good to the hopeless but often they lay in the quagmire of distinct mediocrity. The first level middle managers were mostly manageable people. Luke always believed a worker should aim to guide their manager, using humour, common sense suggestions, and flexibility. However, some of the highest managers could be a law onto themselves. Often, these types exhibited more psychopathic or sociopathic characteristics, which was half the reason they made it to the very top level of management. More difficult to reason with on a logical level, their decisions and moods could be volatile and far less predictable. Luke was just one of many who had to see if he could adjust to the many and varied management strategies employed by these people who not infrequently had difficult, somewhat complicated personalities. For years, there had been no problems with senior management - laughs, good times, high morale and productivity amongst the workforce were the norm. But like good weather, sooner or later it was going to come to an end. A very dark and threatening cloud loomed closer and closer. Behind the higher management doors, a sinister individual called Damian manoeuvred himself into the General Manager position, disposing of some well thought of and competent managers in the process.

Luke's job rating meant he was normally a maximum of only two levels away from the managing director, so any changes there would definitely affect him. Like many of that character type, Damian, a small, unfit, somewhat portly man, with a passing resemblance to Stalin without the moustache, came with a reputation for being highly ruthless, extremely conceited, capable of very devious acts but always self-serving. He was a man that believed the rules only applied to others. It was widely accepted that it was inadvisable to get on the wrong side of him. Unfortunately, his character make up was the very antithesis of all that Luke stood for and believed in. As soon as the news broke that Damian was going to be the new boss, Luke, along with quite a few others, knew that the future was going to be a bumpy ride.

---------------------------------------------------------------

On an October day in 2001, not long after the infamous 9/11 incident, Luke was working around Edinburgh. At lunchtime, he crossed the Forth Road Bridge heading to see clients north of the Forth. At the northernly Fife end of the bridge, Luke noticed three men on the east side of the bridge. All three looked to be of Asian or Arabic origin. Two of them were leaning over the fence pointing specifically at the structure of the Rail bridge, half a mile to the east. The other guy was looking upwards at the CCTV as though keeping an eye on where it was monitoring. As Luke drew alongside, the two guys turned around off the bridge fence. They were about 150 metres onto the bridge. Being very suspicious about this, Luke realised that their behaviours were highly unusual as in many hundreds of trips over the Forth Road Bridge, he had never seen anybody lean over the fence to point at something on the Rail bridge. Luke pulled into the layby only several hundred metres on and called the Police. He dialled 999 and explained the situation and his reasoning for suggesting that the guys he had seen, needed to be checked out. After a minute or two, the bridge control team came back to say that they could not see them on the bridge. Luke stated they were definitely there. They were right below the CCTV pole but they explained to Luke, the camera at that time, could not look straight down. This only heightened his suspicions further. He asked if the police wanted him to stay, but he was told to leave and not to hang about. If necessary, they would get back in touch.

Ten minutes later the police phoned him back as a team from Glenrothes was despatched to the bridge. They asked for exact details of the location of the guys on the bridge. Luke supplied the information and then offered to come back, but they said it was unnecessary.

Luke had no further contact with the police. He just carried on with the day's business. There was nothing about the incident in that evenings televised news. But the very next evening, the police announced that they had arrested four men on terrorist charges. The Golden Gate Bridge in California was closed just after that for a few days to make security camera changes, so whether there was any tie up with his observations, he was unsure. There was no thank you note or indeed, even acknowledgement of any sort from the police forthcoming. Luke felt very sure that the guys he had seen may have been on a terrorist reconnaissance mission, but that thought would lie unresolved, for some time.

---

Two weeks later, Luke had to go down to London for a meeting at Head Office. He had only told his own adult members of his family about the Forth Road Bridge situation. Damian was now the Managing Director, and the rest of Luke's team were there as well. During a break in the proceedings, Luke informed Damian and a marketing officer about his experience at the bridge and how he believed that it was his information that had led to the arrest of a terrorist team. Naively, he thought that because his boss was in a position of high responsibility, that it must ultimately mean, despite his gut feel about his new boss, that he would be a responsible type of person. In that case, he would undoubtedly approve of what Luke had done and so would win some respect and brownie points with his new boss. The reality was though that as two men, they were so markedly different in their viewpoints on life, that each could barely understand the way each other man thought. As time went on, this disparately split view on morality caused increasing distrust and the mutual contempt only grew.

In his own mind though, Damian had registered the details of what he had been told and stored it away in the back burner department of his memory, with a stamp note on it - "retrieve for use at a future date." Somehow or other he knew he would find ways of using that information against Luke. Damian had already decided that Luke was going to be next on his staff elimination list. When you have been successful at removing many smart managements people from the company, as Damian had, then getting rid of someone like him, situated several rungs of the ladder lower, would surely just be child's play.

Several more months passed and during that time Damian upped the pressure on him as much as he possibly could. Being Luke's direct line boss as well as the managing director, the performance appraisals were unkind regarding him, to say the least. His work pattern was closely monitored and criticised at every opportunity. Predictably enough, the other members of the team were overlooked when it came to criticism, despite his work performance record being markedly superior to the others. Luke had no real release valve for the enhanced pressure. He considered moving on but being a dogmatic individual, Luke decided to just try to ride it out. Unrealistic call rates were set and scrutinised but only for him. Target jumps were always highest for him. Behind his back, Damian backstabbed and made highly derisory statements to his team of middle managers, creating a tense and negative atmosphere. They saw the type of fear management that Damian employed and fell in with his tactics. Most were afraid not to, as they worried, they may have been targeted for removal too. Damian knew he would win, it just depended upon how much misery could be heaped on Luke before he cracked. Indeed, Damian fully intended to pile it on, the more the better as far as he was concerned. Damian preferred to dish out a "death by a thousand cuts" method rather than by a single cut. The more misery he could inflict, the happier he was with life.

On his side, Luke began to lose his cheery, humorous side. He no longer shone in company as he had before the arrival of Damian as Managing Director. His appearance became less polished. Damian could see this, and the truth was that he was enjoying every little moment of it. The power he exerted seemed to charge him more and more, whilst steadily sapping the life out of his victims, including Luke. He regularly metaphorically, patted himself on the back for his ingenuity. Damian was on a roll, and he knew it. But would Damian make even one major critical error?

Luke noticed that he had received three phone calls on consecutive Sundays on his business line number. When he checked for the number, he found the numbers had been withheld. Luke thought little of it, nor of the fact that they all happened on the Sunday lunchtime, always about one thirty in the afternoon. On the next two Sundays, he chanced to be in the vicinity of the phone when it rang. Luke answered. "Hello". There was only silence. Then after fifteen seconds, the phone on the other end was hung up. Once again, when he checked for the number, the number had been withheld.

After a few more weekend mystery calls, Luke asked the phone service provider to organise to have withheld numbers barred. However, despite this being done, the calls continued, regular as clockwork, at Sunday lunchtime. Each time, a twenty second silent message and the noise of a phone being hung up was recorded by the machine. There was one change – the number was now being revealed. The number came from the same area code as his work Head Office. Luke had no idea at all who the number belonged to. Then, one Sunday, the message recorded a man's voice speaking in an unidentified language using a highly aggressive tone. The message sounded like an Arabic type of language, but whatever it was, it certainly sounded highly threatening in tone. Luke listened to the message. Luke's wife, Kim, wanted to call the police in, but Luke was more self-assured. He wiped the message as he didn't know what language it was or indeed what was being said. What was very clear though, was the highly aggressive tone. Despite his laid back and unconcerned appearance to Kim, privately Luke was beginning to get somewhat rattled by these phone calls. The pressure from his relentlessly persecuting boss at work and these possibly disturbing developments were beginning to take a major toll, both on him and on his marital relationship.

Luke started phoning the number at all times of the day and night to see if he could get a reply, but with no success. It always just rang and rang and rang. It was never answered, ever.

On the next two Sundays, more messages were left. The first was a recording of a woman, ranting in a highly aggressive tone. The message, although in a foreign language, certainly sounded very threatening. Luke allowed Kim to listen to the message, which ironically started with the English word "right" before proceeding in the foreign language, suggesting it was a bi or multi-lingual person leaving the message, but whose first language would be English. Luke wiped the message.

The next message was another rant by a man in a foreign language. Luke dismissed Kim's concerns, flippantly declaring they had got the wrong number and wasting their very obvious vocal talents on their phone line. Again, Luke wiped the message. Privately though, he was becoming mildly concerned.

By now, Luke's wife, Kim, was becoming quite upset about the messages. Kim and Luke listened to the next message several times. Once again Luke wiped the message and dismissed Kim's pleas to call the police.

On the next Sunday, Luke lifted the phone when it rang. Someone grunted at the other end and promptly hung up. Luke phoned the number back but only got an engaged tone.

By now, Luke decided Kim was right. Luke went to the Police, gave them the details and asked the officer to determine the identity of the registered owner of the number.

After a day, he returned to see the officer. He told him the name – a double barrelled name – James Shistere-Aylott. It meant absolutely nothing to Luke. The address was quoted too. It was only a few miles away from the Head office, but again Luke had never been there or was aware of anyone that lived in that vicinity. At home, Luke checked the employee list, but there was no-one of that name. He phoned directory enquiries, but although there was one Shistere-Aylott, he was ex-directory. Luke had come to a dead end and was uncertain what to do.

However, Luke had a plan. He had his business line number changed and told only Damian, the Managing Director and the Human Resources officer about the change of number. Luke was highly suspicious that Damian and probably the Human Resources Officer were somehow behind the phone calls. He explained to Damian that he had been receiving sinister phone calls and that was why he wanted to change the number. Deliberately, Luke laid it on thick, saying it was affecting his wife as well. Damian sounded sympathetic down the phone, but Luke felt sure he was smirking at the other end of the phone. Luke assured Damian that he would take care of disseminating the new phone number to all the relevant people at his end, but of course he didn't. Only Damian and his Human Resources officer had been notified about the number change.

On the next two weekends, more silent but sinister phone calls came through, right on cue at one thirty in the afternoon. No other phone calls came through on the new number at all, at any time. Luke now knew that somehow Damian was irrefutably involved with the phone calls. The only number showing as having called was the exact same number that had been associated with all the prior malicious calls. Having satisfied himself of Damian's involvement, Luke simply unhooked the phone each Sunday, for months thereafter, to avoid any more calls that might upset Kim. Or even him for that matter.

## Chapter Three – A wander in the dark

Luke's sleep pattern was now very erratic. The pressure of the bullying at work and the history of the malicious phone calls were beginning to take their toll. Deprived of sufficient sleep, everything in his life began to suffer - his mood, his ability to concentrate, his reasoning and work efficiency all declined. Luke began to feel the stress and the first signs of depression, anxiety and heightened emotionality, with Luke often feeling as though he would be liable to uncontrollably burst into tears at any moment. This was most upsetting to him as he always believed he belonged to the "stiff upper lip" brigade and felt he was letting himself down. When he went to see customers, Luke yawned uncontrollably in their presence and his responses were stuttered and invariably very slow. On a couple of occasions, he actually nodded off whilst talking to clients. Luckily, the clients were forgiving, especially when Luke told them he had barely been sleeping for a few weeks.

Luke and his wife now had a daughter and a young son, both below the age of seven. They were taking the normal exhausting toll on both parents, but because of his state of mind, Luke seemed permanently cranky with them, giving his young kids an unrealistic impression of their father. Kim, although stressed, refreshed every night by managing to sleep like a baby. When Luke did manage to sleep, he did so very lightly, with the slightest noise or disturbance waking him. Luke had always been a light sleeper because of the scarring experience of the Northern Ireland troubles. He had grown up as the son of a Policeman and during that time many were killed on duty, some were killed by gunmen just appearing at their homes, whilst others had bombs placed under their cars which blew up shortly after driving off, if they had forgotten to always check under the car. Any suspicious sounds at night provoked a wake and investigate response in Luke. As a result, Luke grew up with heightened senses of all going on around him and developed a very suspicious nature. It was almost as though his brain was hard wired that the slightest clue might need to be picked up on to save his father's life, or indeed other people's lives and as a consequence of that, Luke rarely achieved the benefit of a really deep sleep. At that time, a restoring slumber would have been the ultimate unachievable luxury for him.

For whatever reason, Sunday nights always seemed to be the worst, with the result that at the start of the week, Luke felt like a half-shut knife and for the rest of the week, the situation didn't improve at all. Damian's efforts were working well, and he would have been smugly congratulating himself, if only he truly realised how effective his "behind the scenes efforts" were. Luke put on a front, to cover his real state of mind, but it was about to take a crashing dive in the next few days.

Kim suggested that Luke should invest in a night vision monocular and go out at night to spot wildlife. The added benefit was that it would help tire him out, possibly helping him to sleep better at night. Luke thought it was a good idea, so he ordered one which duly arrived on the next Friday. It was then close to mid-winter, with darkness prevailing for the majority of hours in the day. Kim suggested going out on the Sunday evening, as that seemed to be the hardest night for him to get to sleep and also the night that would be expected to be the quietest. If Luke got back by eleven o clock, then he might just sleep well, for a change. It seemed to be a sensible plan with him.

Luke headed out on the Sunday night, driving to a remote spot up a lonely glen he knew well. The tenant farmer had given him permission to take his vehicle there. Although there were a couple of inhabited farms once out of the glen, the rest of the glen was devoid of population, making it a great place for wildlife of all sorts, especially at night.

Luke drove his car right to the very end of the tracked road, going through the semi-derelict farm steading at the very top of the glen. He got out of his car, opened the gate, drove through into the hill park, stopped and shut the gate again. He then drove on another 150 metres up the rough track. Luke parked at the edge of a wood. Collecting his night vision gear, he switched off the interior light, so that when he got out there would be no illumination. The light would spoil his slowly developing night vision. Immediately he could feel the night air was chilly, with an icy wind blowing up the glen. A three-quarter moon was shining down through the large gaps between the few clouds in the sky. This glen was far away from the light pollution of any towns, the stars twinkled all the colours of the rainbow in the night sky. Luke shivered but he knew that the walk ahead would start to warm him up.

Initially, he experienced difficulties in using the equipment, getting focused was not as straightforward as he had hoped but as he walked quietly onwards, he began to get the hang of the gear. During his hushed progress he saw the usual suspects of the country night. An owl flew by and landed in a conifer tree. Not the Tawny Owl, he thought it would be, but a Long-Eared Owl, a rarer, slimmer and even more attractive bird. The view of it, fleeting as it was, made the trip more than worthwhile in his opinion. Rabbits bounced about and two Hares came running past quite close to him. But the real prizes, the Pine

Marten and the Scottish Wildcat had eluded him that night. Luke checked his watch. It was by now 11.35pm. Over three hours had just zipped past without him realising how late it was. He was about to head back to his car when a fox let out some screams nearby.

Spooked by the wailing noise, Luke uttered a hushed expletive as a means of reassuring himself. Luckily, it was just what he had been hoping for. Using the last bits of power left in the night vision binoculars, Luke quickly got onto the animal to find there were two of them.

Luke watched the foxes, enjoying the short personal show they unknowingly laid on for him. One major weakness of wildlife photographers is that they always want to be as close to the action as possible. Luke was not photographing them or videoing them, so he had no actual need to get closer to the action. He decided to try to bring these foxes in closer to him by squeaking. This impersonates the noise made by voles, tempting them in to hopefully catch a mouthful of food. Within less than half a minute, one of the foxes had caught his scent and the wildlife watching for him was over for that evening.

It was now getting close to midnight. Luke had stayed out far longer than he had originally intended. A twenty-minute half-mile walk back, in the darkness to his four x four vehicle, lay ahead for him.

At that very moment, six miles away, two cars stopped together in a lay by in a quiet country road. The first signs of frost were appearing on the road, making it appear as though it was coated with icing sugar. One man stepped out of a black Range Rover and made his way to the Navy-blue coloured Mercedes parked behind his vehicle. The driver in the Mercedes wound down the window.

Bending down and looking into the car, the first man spoke in a gravelly voice "Have you brought my stuff?" He grimaced slightly, suggesting he was possibly mildly sniggering to himself.

"Yes" came the reply.

"Any problems?" said the man outside.

"Nope, none at all" came the Glasgow dialect resonating from the car interior.

"Good," said the first man, "right Shaun, you come in my car." The man in the passenger seat quickly vacated the Mercedes. Leaning into the window again, the big man said "Right, channel thirteen, but only if you need it, and be careful what you say, understand."

"Channel thirteen, understood".

"You give us three or four minutes first before following, just in case. OK."

"Not a problem" came the reply.

"Right Shaun let's go" said the big man and then the two men jumped into the Range Rover. The wide tyres spun as the car started away, kicking up some small stones, one of which clanged off the front of the Mercedes.

It was now 12.15 am. Luke was still cursing from taking a muddy fall. He had just arrived back to his car and got in. It was parked one hundred and fifty metres away from the farm buildings. Suddenly, Luke noticed the lights of a vehicle coming up the glen. He had not anticipated this annoying development. Reaching for his night vision equipment again, Luke monitored the approaching vehicle. The car headed straight into the mainly derelict farmstead. From what he could make out, it looked like a big dark coloured Range Rover type of vehicle. He was able to see there were two men in the vehicle, but one jumped out, once in the farmyard and went into the buildings. Luke was befuddled and wondered what he should do. The tenant farmer drove a Toyota pick-up truck, so Luke knew that the vehicle was not his. His concern was that if it was the local laird, he might give him some verbal abuse or even tell off the farmer for allowing a wildlife photographer to be on his land with a vehicle, without his knowledge. As Luke contemplated his options, he noticed yet another vehicle coming up the glen.

"Shit" he muttered to himself, "what the hell is going on now?" The vehicle progressed right up the lane. He watched using the night vision binoculars. He could see it was a big car, probably something like a Mercedes or a bigger BMW. It continued right up to the derelict farm and parked in behind and facing the Range Rover type vehicle. Because of his angle of view, Luke now couldn't see much of the car except its edge.

Both drivers got out of their respective cars, and they opened the Mercedes boot. They struggled with something heavy and cumbersome in a big black bag, to the extent that the other guy came out and helped them. Luke believed he could see them carry the huge package into one of the sheds, but of course it was very dark and difficult to see in the shadowy portions. They then repeated the operation with yet another equally bulky bag. Luke sat bemused within this unforeseen situation and wondered to himself what to do. He sat on quietly.

He knew that to drive out now, he would have to open the gate right at the farm and then drive past the two cars, if indeed there was enough room to get by. He wondered to himself "why the hell are these guys meeting in a place like this?" Luke checked his watch. It was 12.35am, now far later than he meant to be out.

Luke decided to take a closer look. Double checking the interior light was still switched off, Luke quietly got out of his car and walked to within thirty metres of the farm. He could now see that it was indeed a dark Range Rover and the number plate, all by the light spillage from the single electric light switched on, partially lighting the farm. Luke tried to memorise the number and as he could see or hear nothing else of interest, he just made his way back to his own vehicle. As he sat in the car, he tried to think if there was any other way out for him, but there wasn't. His only way out would have to be through the farm.

Within a couple of minutes, one of the men came back out, jumped in the Mercedes car and turned the car past the Range Rover, driving back down the farm lane and then down the glen road, until he was out of sight. Luke breathed a sigh of relief. Now he only had to wait until the other two guys drove off. He really hoped that would be soon.

As it turned out, time dragged on. Luke drifted to sleep as he sat in the cold compartment of his car. He was aware of a sawing noise coming from the farm shed which still showed bright by the electric light outside and one inside amongst the overwhelming darkness of the countryside. He was confused. Luke couldn't think what type of work they would be doing or why were they doing it in the middle of the night. Luke drifted off to sleep again.

Suddenly, a very loud crack woke him with a start. The scare from the noise caused him to bang his head. Adrenaline surged through his body, setting his heart racing. "What the hell was that?" he muttered to himself. Then again – crack, crack. Instantly Luke identified the sound in his mind. It sounded like bones being broken by being smashed with something very hard. Were they cutting up the carcase of a deer? Or was something else even more sinister happening? Surely not! Luke dismissed that idea and yet it kept coming back into his head. If they were poachers, maybe he should phone the police. He looked at his mobile phone. There was no signal for his network and the battery was showing it was on its last legs.

After what seemed like an eternity but was actually only about another fifteen minutes, the two men emerged from the shed carrying several heavy black bags. They opened the boot of the Range Rover and noisily seemed to dump the bags into the car boot. After a few more minutes of collecting more bags and other stuff, they switched off the light. One of them said "that was a good job we done tonight, tonight eh?" just before they both jumped into the car. The sound carried so much better and clearer once they were out in the farmyard. The driver quickly turned the vehicle around and started heading away from the farm.

Luke finally breathed a true sigh of relief. At last, he could actually start to head home without these guys knowing he had been there. When the Range Rover was away in the distance, Luke started up his own vehicle. The headlights came on automatically, because of the settings he had left when he departed the vehicle earlier. Luke grimaced with concern as he wondered if his vehicle's lights may have been spotted by the guys in the Range Rover. "You twit, you should have waited just another twenty seconds" Luke declared to himself in a highly agitated way.

In the Range Rover, the man seated in the passenger seat wheeled around and said "Eh, I think I just saw car lights coming on, up over in a field over there", as he pointed back in that direction.

"Really" said his companion.

"Yes, what should we do, will we go back and see who it is?"

"No, we'll get Mike to check him out. Get on the walkie talkie and tell him we'll be with him in a couple of minutes."

Very soon they pulled up beside the Mercedes and the driver wound down the passenger window.

"What's happened" asked the driver of the Mercedes.

"We think there has been some guy near the farm. He may not have seen anything, but you wait until he comes past, then get his car make and registration and if you can, get a look at him" said the Range Rover driver.

"Do you need me to do anything else?" asked the driver of the Mercedes.

"No, not now, just make sure you get the details. We'll see you later" said the driver in the Range Rover. With that the two men departed into the black night.

Back at the farm, Luke was keen to get away and homeward bound as quickly as possible. He drove to the gate beside the farm and got out, opened the gate, drove through, got out again and shut it. Luke could just make out the only door they could have used, by the light from his car headlights. Curiosity meant he couldn't stop himself. He walked over and looked in the window. He could see nothing. Then he went to the door and turning the handle, opened the door. There was a slightly damp, musty but also a sickly-sweet smell, but he couldn't see anything yet again. His hand collected some gel like substance, which felt unpleasantly tacky. Pulling his nose up on his face in disgust at whatever the substance was, he took out his handkerchief and wiped his hand. He felt around for a light switch, but he couldn't find one.

Closing the door, Luke jumped into his own car. It was time for him to go home. As he drove down the road, he wondered what had been going on at the farm. Surely his senses were just playing tricks with him. He had four and a half miles to travel down the glen road before he got back to the main road which would then eventually take him home.

Suddenly as he came around a corner on the glen road, there was the dark Mercedes parked in a gateway. "Oh fuck" Luke thought "it looks like he was waiting for me." Within seconds, the car was behind him and continued following for almost a mile. Luke watched it in his rear-view mirror, wondering if it was going to flash him to indicate for him to stop. Instead, it just pulled over and Luke continued on his way home uninterrupted.

Luke arrived home four hours later than he was supposed to. Not surprisingly, the house was in complete darkness. He locked the house front door and went upstairs. Luke felt filthy after his night trekking about and his fall in the mud. He took all the contents out of his pocket and placed them on a shelf above a radiator. In the gloom he misjudged the height level. Luke caught the edge of the shelf dropping his rolled-up handkerchief containing coins. Other coins cascaded downward towards the floor, dispersing them all over the floor. Too tired to care, Luke stripped off and put all his clothes in the wash basket. A hasty ablutions session and Luke slipped into bed beside Kim. She mumbled a protest briefly in her drowsy state about how cold he was. His skin was very cold and he knew it. Luke kept away from body contact with Kim, waiting to warm up and until he felt sleepy. Gradually, despite his normal sleepless state, Luke did eventually slip into a sleep of sorts, but not without going over in his mind about the possibilities of what had been going on at the old farm steading. Luke did feel that whatever it was, it was almost certain to have been on the wrong side of legal. Or just maybe, thinking rationally, there would be a perfectly sensible explanation which would come to him in the next day or so.

## Chapter Four – Suspicions to report

The next morning alarm came far too early for Luke who had again only got a couple of hours of restless sleep. It was the usual run around, getting the kids ready for school. Luke felt very groggy as sleep had been patchy. He had been particularly restless from five o clock onwards. His mind kept churning over the events of the previous evening.

Kim, as all wives seem to be, was ultra-efficient at getting the kids rounded up in the morning and ready to go to school. Luke volunteered to drive the kids to school. He told Kim he would be staying away that night, not an uncommon situation with his job. She asked "did you see anything unusual, last night?"

"Well yes I did, I watched two foxes for a while, but there was something really weird went on at the farm last night."

"How do you mean?" asked Kim.

Luke paused with a slightly confused look on his face and a fogged brain delay to his answer. "I aaah, I don't really know" he said.

Kim really wasn't that interested anyway. "Look, I'll speak to you tonight on the phone and you can tell him about it then" said Kim, putting on her coat. A quick kiss on the cheek and she was off to work.

Because of sleep deprivation and mental grogginess, Luke was now in slow motion mode. He rounded up the kids and duly delivered them to the school gates. All day, the possibilities rolled around slowly in his mind. His mind was only chugging, almost to the point of stalling. Could he have got the possibilities about the cracking noises wrong? What could have caused that? What had the men carried into the farm shed? Why were they there at that time of night? What were in the bags they carried out later? What, why, who? Despite his chugging mental state, the questions still came thick and regular, unlike the answers, which just weren't coming at all, at least seemingly rational possibilities.

Luke through stress and lack of sleep, like everything else was slowed down quite a bit. So were his communication skills and ability to make a decision. Eventually, by that evening, Luke decided he would have to phone the police and report what he had seen, regardless of whether he was completely off target in his assessment.

Staying away from home, Luke phoned the nearest large police station to his home using his mobile phone. The duty sergeant took the call. "Can I speak to the most senior officer on duty" Luke asked.

"I'm the duty sergeant – Sergeant Brown - can I help you?"

Luke tutted, "I need to speak to the most senior officer available please. I have something very important to let him know."

The irritation showed in the sergeant's voice. "You will have to speak to me first, sir – how can I help you?"

Luke took a deep breath, thought to himself "well here goes" and said "Look, I'm not sure but there is a slight possibility that I may have seen, that is, I think I watched some guys possibly disposing of a body last night. It may have just been a deer."

“Is that right, sir” said the sergeant whose tone suggested he had already decided which side of the psychiatric hospital walls this caller should have been.

Luke realised he was already digging a hole for himself, and he had only just started to explain his story. “No really”, Luke said, “I was up a glen last night and there were two cars with three guys, and I heard noises that were just like smashing bones”

“Is that right, sir” came the Sergeants reply, whose tone transparently exposed his thoughts – “why always on my shift?”

Inside, Luke realised his stress and lack of preparedness had meant it was likely he was not going to be taken serious at all.

“No honest, I took note of one of the cars number plates” he said.

“All right sir, what was the number?” Luke recited the car number and after further questioning gave his name, address, and mobile phone details. At last, the officer seemed to be taking his information and would at least check it out. Luke thought the details were far too brief, so he offered to drive up and give a much more comprehensive statement. The duty sergeant said it would not be necessary. Luke didn’t know it yet, but hell on earth was just about to begin for him.

As soon as he was off the phone, the duty sergeant drove round to his house to speak to his wife.

Kim was slightly shocked to see a policeman at the door. “What’s happened?” she asked.

"Nothing to worry about," said the Sergeant. "Can I come in; I need to ask you a few questions about your husband?"

"What's he done?" asked Kim in a slightly anxious tone.

"Nothing, except claim he has watched a body being cut up! "

Kim was taken aback. "What today" she asked?

"No, last night, apparently" came the policeman's reply. This was enough for the sergeant who could see the bafflement on Kim's face. "Is your husband suffering from some sort of mental illness at the moment" asked the policeman, intently looking into Kim's eyes.

"Well, I suppose he has been under a lot of stress with work lately."

"So would he harm anyone?" The question unnerved Kim – she knew it may mean Luke could be taken into custody.

"No, absolutely not!" "What have you been saying, Luke" Kim thought to herself.

"Because of his report, I now have to drive away to a location many miles away and check it out" said the sergeant whose face gave away his true feelings of annoyance.

"Well, I'm sorry", said Kim, "I didn't realise he was getting quite so stressed out."

"It's not your fault" said the officer as he started to make his way to the door. He jumped into the police car and headed off into the night.

---

Luke was frustrated. He knew he had made a complete mess of the phone call. Luke phoned back to offer again to drive up and give a more complete statement. "Can I speak to the duty sergeant, please?" he said to the lady on the other end of the phone.

"He's out of the building at the moment" was her reply.

"Oh right" he said, as he mentally stumbled over his options, "ah, when will he be back?"

"We're not expecting him for quite a few hours" said the lady, "who's speaking?"

"Ah, my name is eh – Luke, Luke Walker" was his reply. After a slight hesitation, he said "it's just that I......." Luke suffered another satellite delay on his decision as to what to say next. "I'll maybe try and phone him later. Bye."

His second phone call hadn't gone anywhere close to plan either.

---

The duty sergeant radioed into the station. "I'm on my way to the location, have you guys got anything on that number plate?"

"Yes, Sarge" came the policewoman's reply "it's registered to a Mr. Henderson and his home is down in Devon. It's a red Range Rover Discovery, but he says it hasn't been driven by anyone for four days."

"Has he got anybody to vouch for that" asked the duty sergeant.

"His wife said they had guests round for dinner on last night and they all saw the vehicle sitting on the driveway when they arrived and departed," said the policewoman.

"Just as I expected, what a waste of time. Right, I'll speak to you later". His tone suggested a man who was now thoroughly pissed off.

After arriving at the old farmstead, Sergeant Brown got out of his car and walked across the cobbled stone yard to the main shed. His hand torch made little impression in the darkest corners of the rundown buildings. After a few minutes of looking around the derelict buildings and through the cobweb infested windows of the farm building, he jumped into the police car and headed down the glen.

"Sergeant Brown to base" - the message crackled over the radio.

"Base here – go ahead" answered WPC MacDougall.

"I'm going in to see the farmer at the bottom of the glen to find out what he has seen, if anything." Within ten minutes, Sergeant Brown knocked on the farm door. A dog barked aggressively from a nearby shed. The farmer's wife appeared at the door. "I'm sorry to bother you at night, madam. My name is Sergeant Brown. Can I ask you about some possible activity at the top of the glen?"

"Oh right, I'll get my husband, I'll just be a minute." At that she disappeared into the house. The dog continued to bark.

Donald McLean, the farmer, looked groggy, tiredly blinking his eyes, which Sergeant Brown took to mean that he had probably just been woken up. "Shut up, dog" he shouted in a grizzly voice. The dog instantly obeyed. Turning to the policeman, he nodded and grunted an acknowledgement and said "you'd better come in."

They walked into the main sitting room. A real fire with a couple of cut logs on it, beamed intense heat across the room. Sergeant Brown thought to himself "it's little wonder he was asleep in this heat." The furniture was sagged, well-worn with a scattering of equally well-worn cushions. The wallpaper was old fashioned, garish with flowers and multi-coloured, but it had faded with time. Farmer McLean indicated to the policeman to take a seat.

"How did you know I look after that farmstead" asked the farmer.

"I didn't" said Sergeant Brown "Can I ask do you know a Luke Walker?"

"Oh, the guy that does wildlife photography, yes I know him."

"We had a report from Mr Walker of some vehicles up there last night and that he was there himself. Did you know Mr. Walker was up there last night?" asked Sergeant Brown.

"Well, I didn't know he was up there last night, but he did tell me he was going to be up, he just didn't say exactly when," said the farmer.

"Do you know anyone else who may have been up there close to midnight?" asked Sergeant Brown, as he brushed some coarse short white Jack Russell dog hairs which had found their way from the seat, onto his uniform.

“No, I don’t,” said farmer McLean, ”I suppose it could have been the laird but that’s not very likely, not at that time. Sometimes though, because it is at the very end of that glen road, people drive up and it’s only when they get to the farm that they realise they can’t go any further. Then they turn around and go back down.”

“Yes, you are probably right. Oh well, sorry for bothering you” said the sergeant, standing up and making his way to the door. “I’ll need to call on the Laird and check he wasn’t there last night. How do I get there?” he asked.

“Head back down the main road for half a mile. His house entrance is on the left, it has two small stone lions sitting near the verge. You can’t miss it. The big castle is his,” said Donald.

“What’s his name” asked the sergeant. “Angus McFadzean” came the reply.

Five minutes later, Sergeant Brown pulled up on the gravel front to the castle house, his car tyres displacing and crunching the rounded stones. There was no obvious doorbell, instead just a big, discoloured brass knocker. He over zealously knocked on the door. A very deep voiced dog barked in reaction to the doorknob shattering the peace of the castle. “Fuck me, that sounds big” muttered the sergeant to himself.

The castle door was divided into squares, each bearing a thick black knob of steel centred on each projection. It creaked noisily as it was pulled open. A Great Dane jumped out barking at the sergeant who jumped in alarm. “Don’t worry, he won’t bite you, you know”. The laird delivered his words like an actor, emphasizing them with all the clarity that several marbles in the mouth would allow and at a volume that suggested his audience was a hundred metres away.

You could have fooled me" thought Sergeant Brown to himself, "if you weren't here, he would have had me then".

Regaining his thoughts, Sergeant Brown diverted his gaze away from the slobbering huge mouth of the Great Dane and looked at the rosy cheeked man with an oversized purple nose in the doorway who was standing with a glass of whisky in one hand. "Angus McFadzean, I presume?" said the sergeant.

"Yes" came the reply.

"My name is Sergeant Brown. Sorry to call on you unannounced, but we had a report of some activity on the old farm steading at the top of the glen late last night. Were you up there last night or aware of anyone that would have been" asked Sergeant Brown.

"No, not at all. What, what do you mean by activity?" asked the laird.

"Two cars met at the top of the glen for a while," said the sergeant.

"Do you know some silly buggers go up that road thinking it will be a short cut, only to find out it's a dead end. Serves them bloody right for being so damn stupid," said the laird.

"Could there be anything of value to steal there" asked the sergeant.

"Nothing any more mouth-watering than some mouldy old hay" said the laird, spluttering high speed drops of alcohol laden spit out with the force of his answer. Sergeant Brown blinked, rubbed an eye and wiped a couple of droplets of saliva off his face. "I'm sorry to have caused you disturbance, Mr McFadzean," said the sergeant.

"That's ok" said the laird, "come in, get warmed up for a while and have a drink before you go".

"Well as much as I would fancy a coffee, I'd better get going," said the sergeant.

"Oh no, I meant something a little bit stronger than that" said the laird winking at him.

"Thank you, sir, but I can't whilst on duty. And anyway, I'm also driving. Goodnight, sir".

With that he turned to his car and thought to himself, "a waste of a bloody journey and my time. I've that bloody report on traffic statistics to do for tomorrow as well". Sergeant Brown jumped into the police car and headed back to his base, having spent enough time on an obviously pointless errand.

---

## Chapter Five – Counteractions

In Glasgow, CID Chief Inspector Michael McGregor was tidying up his paperwork on the Monday early evening before setting off for home, when a text came through on his personal mobile phone. He had hoped to watch the big match that night on TV. Now all that would have to be postponed or at the very least delayed.

Mike, as all his closer compatriots knew him, was a grizzled officer with a prickly demeanour but who was generally respected, whilst not entirely trusted or indeed even particularly liked by his fellow police officers. He had seen it all at some stage of his career and was battle hardened to almost all crime. With a clean police record, he did though have one major skeleton in his closet, which he wanted no-one to know about.

At one time he had pocketed a major bribe from one of the city's top criminal heads. It was only minor information he had released, and he had been paid a disproportionately high amount. But he had taken the money when his wife had wanted an extension built in their house and now because film had been taken of the handover, he was at the beck and call of his creditor. If he didn't play ball, the truth was liable to be out and he knew how hard jail could be for former policemen. To keep things quiet, he would supply minor details for small payments but mainly for that most precious commodity – silence.

The text asked for information on the name, address and details of the owner or driver of a vehicle. McGregor asked a policewoman to check out the details of five suspicious cars he had seen near a possible incident. It was unlikely to reveal anything, but, explaining to her, just in case. She discreetly researched the owners on the police databank and scribbled the details down on a plain piece of paper. The name of the driver he really wanted, meant nothing to McGregor. He also noted down that there had been a report from the very same person of suspicious activity, which after investigation, had been dismissed by the duty sergeant who had looked into it. McGregor knew there must have been a dubious connection, but he just didn't want to know. He didn't even want the money he would get. But he knew he was locked in, with no way out as he saw it, other than to deliver the information.

The transaction took place with not a word being said on a park bench. As always, it wasn't the boss but one of his many anonymous generic gangland men who placed the envelope and then lifted McGregor's envelope, which had been discreetly positioned between the two men. McGregor waited a minute and then moved on from the parkland bench. He might just get back in time to see the last quarter of the big game. McGregor cursed his impetuous, ill-advised greed, which had embroiled him with the criminal boss.

---

The feedback from McGregor did not bring good news. The gangland boss, known to his dishonourable friends as "Bloody Thumper" or "BT" for short, had believed he had picked a suitably isolated spot for the job. He knew his man would have spotted any activity coming up the glen but hadn't considered someone actually being in the fields and woods beyond, unseen, especially late on a freezing winter Sunday night. He needed to move fast on the situation and change a few things.

The next night, he had one of his men go up to the old farmstead and play with the electric wiring to set the building on fire. It had to look like it was probably rodents had eaten through the wire causing the fire. If there were any bloodspots or other forensic clues, these had to be destroyed. The stack of old hay and straw in the adjoining farm buildings guaranteed the fire would be quick to spread. The whole place was razed to the ground, the old metal girders of the barn bending and collapsing under the intense heat. Nobody saw the fire, because no one was up the glen after nine o clock at night. It was discovered by farmer McLean on the next morning when he arrived to load some hay bales to feed his hill ewes.

Although it was highly suspicious, the local investigating team from the fire brigade and police could find no evidence as to how the fire started. It was suspected that the electrics were involved. It was believed it might have been caused by mice or rats, that had chewed on the old electric wires, but there was nothing conclusive.

Thirty-five miles away, unaware of these developments, Luke was still showing impaired capabilities due to the stress and lack of sleep. Kim told him he had to go see a doctor and the end result of that was that the doctor signed him off for one month.

Damian, his boss, took great delight with the news that he had taken time off as he knew he could use this development to further discredit him within the upper echelons of the mother company management. It also showed his little campaign was working. As far as Damian was concerned, it would now just be a matter of time before he could notch up another successful staff character assassination. It really didn't pay to give Damian anything to use, but by now Luke was completely overwhelmed by all that seemed to be happening to him.

Luke was not going to get a restful period, despite being signed off. After school on the Friday, he took his kids to the swimming baths.

On coming out to the car park after the swim, he noticed that he was being watched. A tall but stocky figured man with silvery hair seemed to be watching his every move. When Luke stared at him, he backed off round the side of a van. Luke got the kids into the car and reaching for his binoculars, he tried to view the stranger. His response had been registered and again the stranger put the van between him and Luke. The road system was one way only, so when Luke started his car, he had to go right round again to get back to see this character who had seriously unsettled his nerves. By the time he got round again, all the vehicles were still there but the stranger had disappeared. Luke felt a hundred percent sure the stranger had been monitoring him. Who was he? Why was he there? Luke had no idea, but he wondered whether his presence had anything to do with the Sunday night episode.

When Luke got back home with Kim, he told her about the man watching him. "Should I go to the police and say about him?" he asked her.

"No, the police have decided your mental state is not good – they could end up sectioning you. You don't really have the police option anymore."

In that one sentence, she had conveyed the true reality of his dilemma – he had a boss that was looking to use anything against him, and mental instability would be a gift of a weapon, the police had already taken a decision that Luke was suffering some sort of mental breakdown, so everything he said was to be treated as suspect and now he had a sinister stranger monitoring him. Kim was the only person who knew the history and who seemed prepared to stand by him.

As the days passed, Luke noticed new people about that he hadn't seen before. Some of these started to appear as regular as clockwork. Maybe Luke had just overlooked them before, but he felt one hundred percent sure that because of his normally suspicious nature, he wouldn't have done that.

A few days later as Luke drove away from his house, he noticed a small white van pull out quickly and fit in tight behind him. When he got to a junction, he pulled out with just enough room for him to comfortably drive onto the road without being reckless, but the van driver just pulled out as well as though the two vehicles were connected by a short, strong piece of rope. The oncoming car had to brake firmly, and its driver registered his annoyance by honking on the horn at the white van as it continued on its way behind Luke's car. Luke was trying to reassure himself that it probably meant nothing more than that he had an idiot driver close on his tail. The van driver stayed close behind him, even though there was no reason for him to have done that. Luke thought he had better just check the situation out.

On arrival at a set of traffic lights, there were two lanes – the left lane to go straight ahead and the right lane to turn right. There were three cars in the left lane and two in the right lane. Luke sat in the left lane with the van right behind his car. He waited until a car started to arrive in the right lane, then promptly and with just adequate time, pulled in to fill the space as the approaching car came up behind his car. The white van now couldn't get into the right lane regardless of what he did. Luke watched as the driver of the white van, holding a big spliff between his fingers, very obviously uttered expletives, nodding his head with the force of his words. As the traffic lights changed, the cars ahead of the white van moved on, whilst the right-hand lane of traffic waited to turn after the oncoming traffic cleared. This left the white van driver sitting trying to get into the outside static line of traffic, but the other cars behind him started honking their horns, so he had no option but to move on. The van driver was not a happy man, and he didn't hold back on visibly expressing his annoyance. Luke had got rid of him without resorting to a high-speed chase or other dramatic means, on that occasion. The fact that he was smoking a big spliff suggested strongly that he was certainly no policeman. It also began to seal his belief with further circumstantial proof that he was being monitored and needed to keep his wits about him. Who were these guys, and did they have anything to do with the reporting of his suspicions to the police?

Later that night, Luke heard the distinctive hum of a Range Rover engine several times. By the time he managed to look out, the vehicle was too far away to see the number plate. All he managed to do was confirm was that it was a dark Range Rover just like the one he had seen on that night.

Luke set his daily routine so he could be very cautious, not venturing outdoors unless absolutely necessary, because he really felt he may have put himself in serious danger. Now extremely alert, Luke would see shady looking characters loitering at the nearby street corner or sitting in a car up the street. Which of these were innocent was hard to judge for Luke, but some showed up regularly over time, exacerbating his concern. Luke began to be even more affected by the perceived pressure. His gut instinct, which over the years he had learnt to trust, told him that there was something very ominous going on and some of these people in the vicinity of his home were not concerned about his wellbeing or his health or indeed connected in any way with the police. A social night was coming up soon, so Luke decided he may have to be extremely wary when he was walking up and coming home, especially as his family were going to be with him.

Soon enough, the date of the invite arrived. On the day Luke had some hard decisions to make. He felt he needed some extra self-protection, as if he got it wrong, that night may become his very last alive. If he got it incorrect the other way, then he might end up on the wrong side of the law. However, the police were not going to protect him, just list his demise as an unfortunate unexplained murder or that he had mysteriously disappeared. Luke was on his own and it was entirely up to him to decide what to do. His gut instincts told him he had some hard decisions to make, he had to create a self-protection plan on what to do that evening. Luke had his wife and kids to look after as well.

Unknown to him, hard men in Glasgow had been told to be ready to travel up at short notice to Luke's address, in case Luke came out of his house. Two, two-man teams in cars were to ensure Luke had a short sharp lesson, whatever it took, with all eventualities to be allowed, up to and including lethal actions. They were instructed to do it quickly and quietly as possible.

Luke, on his part decided to carry a couple of extra implements to protect his family and himself just in case his instincts really were correct. He packed a three-inch bladed penknife hidden in his pocket and a two foot long, sturdy metal Maglite torch. By this time, Luke was now a man on the very edge. If outsiders had known what was going on in his mind, they would have been concerned but Luke knew he was not delusional or suffering from any actual mental condition, other than extreme stress. He was a man who couldn't afford to miss any clues, no matter how small they might be. Luke had become fuelled by adrenaline and anxiety with hardly any sleep credit to talk of. The net result, of course, was that he was incapable of being his normal sharp and happy self. He knew the party was going to be socially difficult to say the least, because of his agitated, stirred-up state.

On the walk up, Luke had the torch on, suggesting to his kids that it was to avoid any dog waste being trekked into their host's home. At that time, dog owners were not legally obliged to lift any waste presents left by their dogs. The reality was Luke checked each shadowy hedgerow or entrances that could conceal a man. He stayed away from the edges to give himself maximum time if anyone did happen to jump out. The family reached the hosts house without any mishaps or suspicious happenings at all.

Unfortunately for him though, Luke's manoeuvres had been noticed though and the message was relayed that he had left the protection of his house. The hit was on. Four men set off in two cars to set themselves in the ambush position. One parked up the road from the house they had gone to, facing downhill. The other car parked downhill, facing uphill, close to his house. Luke was to be the proverbial rat in the trap, caught in the middle. Once in place, all they had to do was wait for his reappearance.

Meanwhile at the party, Kim needed a break from all the recent pressure, so she let her hair down and really enjoyed herself, as of course did the kids, who had no idea of the situation and were far too young to understand. Luke relaxed a bit and participated considering his very tense state, but he refrained from drinking more than two pints of beer. Eventually of course, the evening ended and by one thirty in the morning, Luke began to suggest making a move.

He did that knowing that within a few minutes he may well have been walking right into an ambush and possibly a fatal one at that. If he was correct in his assessment, this could have been his last few minutes alive. Luke felt stony faced realising that possible imminent death is a very lonely experience indeed. Luke managed to still appear cheery on the outside and thanked the hosts for their hospitality. Luke led the way, quietly monitoring his family members whereabouts, in case any strayed.

As soon as Luke reached the footpath, he moved to the middle of the road, to give him just that split second extra time, should anybody try to jump him. Within seconds of his appearance, a car parked thirty metres down the road flashed its headlights frantically three times. Luke took half a second to look and assess the two male occupants. He realised this must have been some sort of signal to another car parked higher up the street. "This is it" he thought to himself, and still walking forward he took out and opened the penknife blade, before hurriedly switching on the beam of the torch and focusing it to a tight spot. This would enable him to dazzle his assailants and the capability to inflict some damage that may require hospital work and deliver painful blows with the metal torch. All this took no more than a few seconds, but to him it seemed like everything went into slow motion, an eternity when he was vulnerable before being prepared for action.

Kim and the kids who were close behind him, were walking down the edge of the road and on the footpath. All were oblivious of what was happening. The two guys in the car opened their doors just slightly. Their car was parked on the left-hand side of the road facing up with the driver nearest the kerb. There were no other cars nearby. Luke took up a position a couple of metres from the offside front wheel. The distance was critical. In this position, he couldn't be caught by a door swinging open or knocked over by the car if it was started, even suddenly. Luke kept track of the movements of his family by listening to them walking and talking. They were slightly behind him, proceeding on without the slightest clue as to what had been planned by others to happen in the next few seconds.

Luke already had the torch beam on ready to swing straight into the eyes of either man had they jumped out, to dazzle their vision. As his family walked on, seemingly in slow motion and had their backs to him, Luke flashed a penknife blade at the two guys in the car defiantly. His stern gaze fixed on both alternatively. They stared back in a menacing silence. All three of them knew that the slightest move on the part of the two men would have meant Luke would react. Luke was on a hair trigger setting. His plan, if even one of the guys moved, was to initially smash the passenger door window. That would have made a very loud noise drawing witnesses to the event, whilst also effectively marking the car for the police. If the worst came to the worst, the torch would be used to dazzle one of the attackers and the penknife used to slightly wound him, enough so that he may have required hospital treatment. If anything was going to happen, it would be in the next few seconds.

At times like that, time seems to slow right down, seconds feel almost like a minute. The grim-faced men sat in the car holding their respective doors slightly open. Luke glared at them in defiance, telepathically daring them to make a move. In return they kept staring back angrily, frustrated by this unanticipated turnaround of a situation neutralizing their advantages when they had expected to be the people in control. The other car team had not responded to their flashing headlights signal. They had obviously fallen asleep whilst waiting for their victim to arrive. Second after protracted second ticked by with this stalemate scenario. Luke was hyped up ready for anything, but assessed his family movements, watching them out of the corner of his eye until they were nearly at the house, a mere thirty metres further down the road.

After what seemed like minutes period of stand-off, but was less than one minute, with the eyes from both sides burning into their respective opponents' eyes, Luke made a move by gently moving in an arc around the car, close enough to rush in should he need to, but not so close as to be caught out by a swinging door being flung open. The two guys did not move a muscle. Luke backed off heading home but keeping a close eye on what these potentially dangerous strangers were doing. Luke knew they would have been watching him in the mirrors. As he moved further away and close to his house, he folded down the penknife blade discreetly and saw that both car doors were being closed. He reached the front door as his wife and kids gathered around waiting for him to unlock and open the front door. They were all still oblivious as to what had just happened.

Once inside, Luke closed, locked, and secured the front door, closing the curtains behind the door. Since his suspicions had been raised, Luke had always kept all the curtains tightly shut to avoid giving any clues to outsiders as to where he may have been at any given time, in the house. Only then did he say to Kim what had just happened. Kim was quite drunk but not so much that she didn't realise what could have happened. She sat aghast at the fact that Luke could easily have been quickly stabbed to death or even knocked out and bundled away in a car to be tortured and killed at his aggressor's convenience.

Luke knew he couldn't call the police as it may well backfire on him. All his evidence was still circumstantial. No dead body had ever turned up. He was now tottering on the edge because of all the stress he was under. The police would have picked up on that and jumped to the wrong conclusion. All police believe they can spot someone exhibiting weird behaviour far quicker and better than any trained psychiatrists. Luke had no choice, he was very much on his own, with even his wife still slightly doubtful of the story on his situation.

One thing Luke did know though. Because the men in the car would have been fully aware of which house Luke had gone into, if he had got it wrong, then the police would be banging at his door within less than an hour. Normal innocent people would have just phoned the police immediately to explain they had just had a nutter wave a knife and a huge torch at them, in a very defiant and aggressive way, daring them to get out of the car.

The police never appeared, at all, reaffirming Luke's suspicions.

The frustration of repeated failures to follow or catch Luke out was leaving his adversaries unnerved. They clearly believed Luke represented a major threat to their freedom and security. In their minds, Luke must have known much more than he did. There had been no Police presence at Luke's house, so the conclusion was that he had effectively been silenced by their shadowy threats. But they knew that might only have been a temporary situation. A transient period of silence would need to be moved up a gear to ensure a permanent silencing state.

There were two ways that was going to be achieved. An accidental death would be the perfect answer or if that proved impossible, to lift and torture so badly that like all victims of this persuasion tactic, he would never talk to the Police ever again. Or an execution. In their panicked minds, Luke could be the catalyst for their imprisonment for many years ahead.

Luke saw the situation slightly differently. He knew that by their reactions that he had stumbled on something big but whilst he believed they must have been disposing of a body, he had only his gut instinct and a very limited amount of circumstantial eye-witness experience to back up his conclusions. Luke did not have the choice of back tracking on his report to the Police or approaching one of these guys to make peace and assure them that he would stay quiet for both of their sakes. To do so would only indicate that they had won, and that Luke was able to be intimidated.

Basically, if someone was a betting man, it looked like a certainty that Luke was a dead man, one way or another. The only way he could avoid that state would be to move to another country or stay hyper alert for many years to come, if indeed Luke was going to survive that long. It was High Noon for him with absolutely no one to call on for help, not even the Police.

When Luke reached the conclusion that his death may be imminent, it changed the base way he thought. Suddenly the little pleasures that made life become more sweetened and yet veiled with a tinge of sadness that he might never manage to do them again. To see his kids, grow up, enjoy rounds of golf with friends, savour drinks with the wife and their friends, achieve other ambitions in life and even have an unlimited supply of loving hugs from the wife. All of these would be gone soon because Luke was as good as a dead man.

But then, the realisation of what he had to lose, made his attitude harden. He would be the wariest target about. He would give them the hardest project they had ever undertaken. Somehow, he intended to survive, even though it was obvious there was only him to look after himself and Luke was up against a team, of what looked like utterly ruthless gangsters. Luke had no idea of who they were or even the slightest clues as to their identities. They on the other hand, knew exactly who Luke was. And of much more importance to them, they knew exactly where he lived. But if they made a mistake, Luke would make them pay the price.

The match was set, and Luke was most definitely the underdog.

Unfortunately, Luke's problems were slightly more complicated than that. Straight life threatening is one thing, satisfying the other people aware of his story, that it was true, was another new dimension to add to his problems. His doctor, who was a good GP and in whom Luke confided the exact facts of his situation, as his only means of therapy available to him, wanted to be sure there weren't any underlying psychiatric problems with his patient. The GP arranged for a psychiatrist to see him and assess him. To Luke, this seemed a major inconvenience but understandably necessary if he was to move his case forward. After all who knows if they are going off the rails, as mentally derailed people often believe they are chugging along ok. The problem was that when he started to see the psychiatrist, he only saw him for an hour, once a fortnight, and because of the convoluted nature of the story, it was going to take a while to explain the story, never mind the psychiatrist getting his head around the facts and assessing his mental health at the same time as well. After a few meetings, Luke was asked to bring in his wife as well to the appointments and after that, his judgement was straight and to the point. There was nothing wrong with Luke, outside of exceptional stress and in his opinion, Luke would be best to say nothing more to the Police about his situation. So, problem solved.

However, Luke's problems were just beginning. Luke decided to return to work from being off with stress as he knew that would help to cut off the oxygen supply to Luke's boss, Damian's ability to make insinuations of instability. With the re-commencement of work, there was a meeting to go to, down near Cambridge. On the morning of the flight down to Stansted, Luke got up early, leaving well before six o clock and after checking that no suspicious persons were about, hopped into his car. It was dark and over an hour before dawn.

As Luke drove through in the dark, there were only a few cars on the road initially, but as he approached the airport, the numbers of cars increased. Luke was not concerned in any way that he was being followed. Luke arrived at the airport car park, parked up and went to the queue for the flight. Standing there Luke suddenly realised that a man that looked distinctly like the man he had seen before at the swimming pool car park, was at the ticket desk for the company he was flying with, and it looked like he was buying a ticket. He joined the queue right behind Luke, so Luke kept a sideward body position to him, to ensure he could keep an eye on this guy who looked scarily like the man who had been monitoring him at the swimming pool.

Luke felt really freaked out at this, as he had not noticed any car obviously following him down to the airport. Was it the same man? Upstairs, once through the security check, Luke was in the area of the departure gate for his flight, when he noticed him coming past. However, he walked on and disappeared towards some other gates. Luke relaxed and thought to himself that it must have just been his overactive imagination and that his physical similarity must have purely been a coincidence. Ten minutes later though, Luke was on his mobile phone when he swung quickly around to find the very same guy right behind him, very obviously trying to listen in on his conversation and standing no more no more than four feet away. Upon eye contact with Luke, he quickly moved off. At Stansted, Luke went to pick up his luggage at the carousel when he saw his suspect walking past. He did not pick up any luggage and Luke watched him very carefully as he walked past, straight out of the exit, carrying no luggage at all. For his part, the stranger kept his stare straight ahead and walked past. Even Luke had to ask himself was he going a bit mad? This guy had a grizzled, evil look about him but then so do thousands of people. But he did have a very distinctive appearance and Luke wasn't going to forget his face in a hurry.

Luke went to work, agitated by this unexpected but unverifiable concern that he may have been followed by the same guy that he had seen before. What was going on? Luke just had an ominous feeling about the whole situation.

At work, Luke received congratulations from the overall boss that he had come into work, despite having been off work with stress. His body language suggested complete insincerity to Luke, but that was the lowest priority of his worries. Luke functioned capably if not as well as he would have liked to perform, considering his sleep deprivation. There was the usual politics. The company had a range of characters, male and females, but benign individuals were the exception. Most were happy to manoeuvre politically and if they gained any advantageous information, they would be happy to utilise that to their own advantage.

Luke's behaviour significantly changed at this time, and he started to gain a cautious reputation, socially and in business. Over time, all his compatriots thought Luke had some information on his Managing Director, enough to be damaging, but not enough to do him any long-term, lasting harm. They thought Luke's withdrawn quieter side coming to the fore meant he was being beaten down, soon to join the list of ex-employees. The truth was, Luke was hanging on as best as he could, and having to deal with work as well as his shattered mental state allowed. His weakened appearance meant people at work were more likely to take the chance to nip at his heels when they could. Luke had always been more than capable of generating respect in the past, but that was ebbing away, and it surprised him how many compatriots proved ready to have a go at undermining him when opportunities arose. He had always been friendly to work colleagues, but some could see the writing was on the wall, Luke was on his way out. That made him fair game as Damian wouldn't disapprove. The truth was none had even the remotest idea of what was really bothering him. Nor indeed, would many have cared anyway.

A few days later, on his way back to Edinburgh from the meeting, Luke read with interest that a man's body had been found lying in amongst some discarded rubbish wrapped in plastic, close to a main road in Central Scotland. It gave no further details other than the Police were investigating.

Luke wondered to himself, could there be any connection with what he saw up the glen. He wasn't sure but he felt there may have been. He thought "I'll read the papers in a few days, and they'll give more details on it". As the days passed, there was no further mention on the subject other than that the name of the dead man was Andrew Coyne and the usual plea by the Police for any witnesses that may have seen anything suspicious, to come forward.

## Chapter Six – Tightening the Screw

In his job, Luke spent most of his time in the field seeing customers. He covered the length and breadth of Scotland including the Isles. To see customers, he had to make appointments and he usually did that on Fridays for the week ahead.

Luke's boss had been piling on the pressure. Initially he wanted him and the rest of the team to see last customers around about 4.30pm. Usually the last call would take up an hour to two hours. Then he would have to go to the hotel or drive back home, which could take a couple of hours, so it was not uncommon to not get back until 7.30 or 8.00pm. Call rates were pumped up, but Luke had been doing all this anyway, even in an expansive territory, many times geographically bigger than other territories, within his team. However, whilst that had been done, another straw was added. Once back home, he was to go onto his computer, fill in his reports and download them to the office. The new software turned out to be a nightmare. It took ages to load up, was very fiddly to fill in and it often crashed, losing all the input data, meaning Luke had to re-do the details. All this could take over an hour and then he had to upload it to the Head Office. At that time, all the data had to go down the telephone line, so by the time all this was completed, it was often beyond 9.00pm.

Starting usually at 8.00am in the morning, this meant his family life suffered. He just didn't manage to find time for his young kids. Damian, his boss closely scrutinised his reports and timesheets, regularly asking for explanations. When it came to the other three team members, they did not receive the same scrutiny. In fact, they were invariably home by 4.00pm doing their reports and finished by 6.00pm. Luke's sales figures were miles ahead of his compatriots. He was achieving 35% of the total team turnover but his territory had only 22% of the potential of the rest of Britain. Luke and Damian, as two individuals just couldn't stand each other, but Damian held all the aces, wielding his power against Luke at every available opportunity. Annual appraisals for the other team members were always good but not for Luke. Luke held on as best he could, hoping that Damian would move on to pastures new, but he never did. Stressed to the eyeballs because of his work situation and his experiences since the glen, Luke was unsure about moving as he felt too beat up by his circumstances to be able to sell himself properly to a new employer. There was also a very stubborn side to Luke, meaning he just wasn't prepared to give Damian the pleasure of winning.

Damian decided to up the pressure even more. His next decision was to instruct that the Territory Managers were to do five days in the field or at the least minimise office time to almost zero. He sneeringly suggested that between appointments, they could take any spare time to make the next weeks call rota by phoning the clients and booking time slots. In the more compact territories, this may have been feasible to a degree, but when the area covered is expansive, such as in Luke's case, often it was difficult just managing to arrive five or ten minutes before the appointed time, giving just enough time to prepare for the call. On Fridays, Luke not only organised his appointments, but completed any promises made to the customers and ensured everything was all as it should have been. He found Fridays very busy days and often struggled to get all the work done within the time, so this new directive was really going to make everything even more stressful for him. How would he cope with this new instruction?

In the meantime, Luke had noticed new people moving up and down his street that he had never seen before. Was he becoming overly paranoid or was there justification to his suspicions? Amongst the new faces was a young man that Luke had noticed a few times and suddenly he was always around the school gates when Luke had the job of dropping his kids off at primary school. He was just sitting there, in amongst the parents, but not interacting with them or ever with kids of his own. Was his presence innocuous or did he have sinister reasons for being there? Luke couldn't be sure. He just had to bear the possibilities in mind.

Another person had started to appear regularly, the same guy who had been down on the flight to Stansted. Luke's office looked out onto his street and by the time Luke reacted to get down and try to catch him up or see where he was going, he had always disappeared. This was unsettling to Luke. Who was he and why was he constantly appearing? Luke was unsure, his reasoning was that there must have been a connection with the events up the glen many weeks before. Whoever he was, he was certainly interested in Luke's whereabouts and his routine. But why?

Luke's boss, Damian was completely unaware of these developments in Luke's personal life situation, but he had his own agenda against Luke. Luke sometimes noticed that if he was back home doing his essential office work on a Friday that there were people lingering about. The people he had been unsure of prior to this, quite often walked past his house, sometimes several times in a day. He had lived in that house for many years and yet had not noticed these people before. Was it his imagination or had he just not been alert? With most people, they simply wouldn't even have considered it, but with Luke his gut feel was that there was something wrong.

On the next Friday, he had made an appointment to see an important group administrator in the early afternoon. He set off about an hour before the agreed meeting time but on driving up his road to the road junction only 150 metres, noticed a man emerge from a gap in the roadside hedge watching him pass. This man then pulled his shirt up his arm and referenced his watch, quickly following that by seemingly being intent on looking at Luke's car number plate. Luke felt this guy had been monitoring his departure and not all that subtly in comparison to some of the other people he had noticed. Who was he and why was he doing it?

One more week passed on and Luke had decided that he wasn't going to do any Friday calls as his administration work had fallen back, and he needed to really catch up on it. Completing the promises, he had made to customers was in Luke's mind, far more important than doing a few extra calls on the Friday. He had developed a good reputation from customers for seeing promises made good and they felt they could trust his integrity. Once a request had been made and agreed, they felt happy that Luke would do it for them.

Luke made several trips out to his car to pick up items he required for his tasks. He noticed a lady just standing, seemingly on her phone about one hundred metres up the road. This just did not feel right to Luke as she had not moved in twenty minutes and yet was not in a garden or beside a car. After a further ten minutes in the house, Luke peered out to see if she had moved on. She hadn't. Luke decided to take a photograph or two of her, as her prolonged period of immobility had once again prompted Luke's suspicions.

Luke gathered a camera, fitted it with a medium range zoom and went out to his car, holding it close to his body, so that the lady would not see him carrying it out. Once in his car, he wound down the passenger window, prepared the camera and drove gently up the road towards the lady. On drawing level with her, Luke observed she was still standing with the phone to her ear but showed no sign of talking. He quickly fired off some photographs before she realised what he was doing. Even at that, she made no move either to turn away or to ask Luke what he was doing. Luke proceeded up the road and then came back around the loop to home again. She was still there when he went back into the house. She had been static on that one spot for well over an hour. When Luke looked out again, he saw her making off back up the hill. Luke felt these two people had been monitoring him, but they were nowhere near as discrete as others he had noticed. Who were they and why were they there?

Luke decided that he should check out the registered Private Detectives living within thirty miles of him to see if the lady he had photographed was one of them. There were only six Private Detectives listed in the Yellow Pages in the local towns and cities, all working from home. He didn't want to look in on the premise that he may have wanted to hire them for a job, as that may have blown his cover. He didn't feel his ability to lie would be adequate and anyway, he might have been recognised. During the daytime they would probably be out working, so Luke decided to do night-time surveillance. One by one he ticked them off, visiting and monitoring by walking past or with binoculars from the parked car. Only once did one of the Private Investigators look suspicious of Luke as he drove past and observed him in his driveway. The last one to be checked out made it easy for him as they had not drawn curtains, even though it was dark. Eventually after waiting for nearly an hour, she appeared larger than life in her living room and Luke was able to confirm she was indeed the very same person that he had photographed a week and a half prior on his street.

Luke believed that Damian was behind this lady being asked to do some surveillance as if these Private Investigators showed he was at home when his reports had shown he should have been somewhere else, seeing a customer, he would have had a strong case to enable disciplining of Luke. For his part, Luke had not falsified his reports, so he had no worries in that respect. These types that Luke suspected were linked to his work, stopped immediately after he had photographed the lady as she would almost certainly have informed Damian of Luke's actions. Luke now held photographic proof that at least one Private Investigator had been employed to carry out surveillance on him.

There still remained the question of the other people that Luke felt had been also carrying out surveillance. Was it just his paranoia? These others never referred to their watches for the time or remained blatantly obvious by being static for long periods. If they were carrying out surveillance, they were far more capable at it than the Private Investigators had been.

A couple of months passed by with a quietening of the presence of suspicious looking people outside of the guy that had been on the flight to Stansted. He still appeared regularly but each time he was observed by Luke, he disappeared just as quickly. Luke had his concerns about who this guy was and why he was there, but he had to admit he was as hard to catch as thinning fog. One minute he was there, the next - gone. Luke still had no idea who he was but at least Luke was able to recognise him very quickly by his build, walk and facial features. His features had become completely engraved in Luke's mind.

The tranquillity was to end very soon. Heading north on a dual carriageway, doing sixty miles an hour, Luke pulled in from the fast lane to find a rear tyre had just suddenly deflated, but he was lucky that a parking bay was only seventy metres ahead and he was able to pull in there. A drill bit had somehow been picked up by the tyre and Luke thanked his lucky stars he had not had a serious accident.

Two weeks later, Luke was coming around a tight bend in a country road when bang, he suffered another blow-out of a back tyre. It took all his strength to keep the car from heading into the fence and the river just a few metres beyond. He took the tyre to a Tyre Garage where the mechanic discovered another drill bit in situ in the tyre. It had entered the tyre blunt end first and the tyre had resealed around the drill end, until pressure of the turning tyre caused the sudden release of the air within the tyre. Moving at speed, the car had been very difficult to control in this sudden burst and a few miles per hour more would have left Luke through the ditch and with a potential bad accident. Luke was by now very suspicious and asked the mechanic if it would have been possible to pick up a six-inch drill bit like that from the road. "No way" answered the mechanic. "I think we should call the Police, right now" said the mechanic, emphasising the "right now". Luke managed to dissuade the mechanic from that line of action, as yet again he realised this still was not outright proof. The tyre had to be replaced with a new one. Luke took the tyre home to store with the drill bit still in place within the tyre. That had been two new tyres required, but Luke was unable to give the full details to his managers as he was having problems with Damian. It was just put down to bad luck - two tyre bursts in two weeks. Every day thereafter Luke checked the tyres on his car, as the drill bits must have been lodged perpendicularly to the tyre on the inside edge and only entered the tyre when Luke reversed his car before driving away from where he was parked in the mornings. The seal had been tight around the drill bit until the pressure from a sudden turn caused the explosive release of the tyre air. Luke was lucky he had not suffered a serious car crash or a fatal one for that matter.

## Chapter Seven – First Help

Henry, one of Luke's team members had received promotion of sorts into a Brand Manager position. At a meeting down in England, his replacement came along and was introduced to the rest of the team, whilst Henry who was moving to a different department was invited out for a meal with the team he was leaving. The evening was convivial with good fun had by all, but John admitted to Luke and the rest of the group that Damian had asked him to do one little bit of research on the internet on Luke. In his somewhat inebriated state, he volunteered a list of places where he had found Luke's name appearing, always for wildlife photography. Even Luke was pleasantly surprised by the comprehensive listings. Of course, nearly all were from the stock library sales with a few extras. Luke promptly offered that he had been unaware of some of the findings and joked "you must have been searching on a different internet from the one I use" to howls of laughter. However, the fun portion aside, Luke again found Damian researching Luke for any information he could, undoubtedly, to use against him at some time.

Damian had been unable to attend that meeting because of other commitments so within a month he decided to promote Kirsten, another one of the Team members to become the Field Manager of the small team. Kirsten was blatantly ambitious and had been suggesting she wanted a promotion for some time. She enjoyed being in the team and didn't particularly want to move to one of the other departments as she had precious little experience outside of her field. This move suited her purposes right down to the ground. Luke had mixed feelings about Kirsten. She was good fun as a compatriot, but Luke found it difficult to trust her, as she had a devious and manipulative side to her character. Although it hadn't materialised, Luke always felt that generally, she didn't have much malice about her, but she was an over-claimer. She certainly didn't work long days often unless it was to impress managers. Luke and Kirsten had teething problems, but they soon got back to what seemed a good working relationship. However, Damian had every intention of calling in some favours from Kirsten for promoting her.

A few months later, Luke was up north in the Inverness area and after a few days of work in the North of Scotland was returning to his home near Stirling using the A9. This road had many long sections over mountain moorland, and over 100 miles distance with only a few smaller towns between the two main county towns. It had sections that were dual carriageway, but most was just two-lane highway. Luke was well used to this road and generally travelled at close to the speed limit of 60 mph, when he could. He was crossing the moor north of Drumochter Pass, one of the most remote sections of the road, heading south when he suddenly noticed an arm swing from the rear nearside passenger window of an oncoming car and to his horror, a half brick sized rock was propelling in his direction right toward his face. Luke had no time to do anything other than to duck his head as quickly as he could. There was a huge bang as the sunroof of his estate car exploded. Luckily Luke had the plastic slide pulled over and this prevented most of the glass from falling around him. Whoever had thrown the rock had been only six inches too high but must have thought they had got a direct hit as they would have seen the explosion of glass from Luke's car as they watched in the mirrors. Luke's luck was in that day, as the rock been just six inches too high to deliver a potentially fatal strike. He had another sixty miles to drive before he could put the car into a suitable repair garage.

It also wasn't raining which would have made the journey very unpleasant with a smashed sunroof. He pulled into the first layby he came to and assessed the damage. The whole sunroof was smashed into thousands of little cubes of glass. Luke breathed a sigh of relief and realised how truly fortuitous he had been. He also began to conclude that the people who had tried to cause this potentially fatal accident must have been tracking his car somehow and the car had been awaiting his arrival at that part of the road as it was suitable for the launching of a projectile. He was up against a team of guys, and they certainly weren't messing about. By the looks of it, the preferred option, as far as they were concerned, was an unfortunate fatal accident.

As Luke drove down towards Perth, he had to decide was it time to go to the Police. Luke was becoming more stressed but also more enraged and determined to catch one of these guys - a citizen's arrest or at least some sort of irrefutable evidence. His theory was that these guys were assuming he knew more than he was letting on, but sooner or later they might slip up and then the law would have them. The danger was that Luke was becoming so angry about it all, that if he caught one of them, he may well have gone too far and killed him. By now, in Luke's mind, they would certainly deserve it.

As time had passed more information had been released on the body that had been found close to a road in Central Scotland. Andrew Coyne was a light league criminally leaning businessman. He had dabbled in dubious businesses but there wasn't much else on him. The pleas from the Police on information about his death had apparently gone unanswered. He had been killed in a frenzied stabbing attack, with over 28 distinct deep puncture wounds. There had been no mention of whether the body had been dumped whole or cut up and dumped as bits in bags. The Police were deliberately limiting the information about the case.

The bottling up of Luke's emotions was good for his assailants but not good for Luke. His stress levels were only being matched by his anger levels. He was beginning to crack, slowly but surely. If it got worse with no-one to turn to, he may even start to turn violent himself and then he really would be in trouble with the Police. Why didn't the Policeman give him a chance to give a fuller, more in-depth explanation, instead of just dismissing him as yet another nutter.

Luke was now proving to be a thorn in Damian's side too. Damian had always succeeded in removing people he didn't like from the company and to date, always very quickly too. Luke was hanging on like a limpet on a rock that had tightened up after receiving a warning tap. Like the limpet, it was beginning to seem to Damian that the only way to get him off his rock would be to destroy him. That thought didn't particularly upset Damian. In fact, he had just the very thing in mind.

Luke now decided that it was time to seek advice from a big gun. Not about Damian as that was the more minor matter. Luke's father had been a Policeman in Northern Ireland. In fact, his grandfather had been too. Policing seemed to run in the family blood. It was to his father that Luke turned for some advice. In the summer, Luke went over to see his parents who were based in Northern Ireland, travelling with his wife and kids. They always had a great holiday together there and everybody was looking forward to it.

Luke's father had seen it all during the troubles. He was regarded as a hard but fair man, agnostic and religiously unbiased with good friends on both sides of the religious divide. He had seen death on a scale that no-one should see. He had carried a head back from a field after a bombing blast had sent an unfortunate victim's head spinning off. He had asked a cameraman to film a torso he was holding to show the depravity and consequences of bombing. It hadn't been shown as it was too unsavoury for the general British public. He had seen many of his colleagues killed. He had seen unbelievable atrocities committed on both sides of the religious divide. He had experienced being chased by shooting gunmen whilst driving home from his work. They had machine gunned his car and he crashed, his car rolling over onto his roof. The gunmen assumed he was dead and moved on, but he emerged shaken and bruised but still alive. Critically, all the bullets had somehow missed him. On another occasion he had jumped into a car with a car bomb which had been abandoned outside his Police Station where he was the senior officer and drove it into a nearby cemetery before running away like the wind. Sometimes luck favours the brave. It did not explode, allowing army bomb disposal to send in a robot to neutralize it. Luke felt almost embarrassed to bother his father with his troubles. However, Luke's situation had become completely desperate, if not yet serious.

It was because Luke had grown up during the troubles as a Policeman's son that he had developed alertness matched by almost none. At that period, the slightest oversight could be fatal. Gut feelings could be solidly substantiated by checking out situations and in Luke's case he found he had developed that ability to a fine art. When other people exhibited similar suspicion, it was usually just classified as paranoia, but Luke had no mental condition, just very hard real-life justifiable experience as a training.

Luke chose his moment and explained how his initial experience had left him wondering and uncertain about what he had observed that night but had had confirmation with each coincidental clue coming his way. There were now plenty, and Luke was left to conclude it must be a gangland event, but how was it going to end? Could the Scottish Police do nothing? Luke's father was now retired. He said he would have a chat with some people he knew within the Police, but it would be difficult to do anything without knowing who the players were. That was the big problem. Luke just didn't know who these people were. In the meantime, he recommended that Luke just kept alert and re-assured him that sooner or later they would be liable to make a mistake that would put them away for whatever the initial crime was. This was only mild comfort for Luke.

Luke's father did recommend that he wrote it all down in the chronological order, almost like a dispassionate Police statement, when he got back to Scotland. So, when Luke and his family returned, Luke knuckled down and wrote the details on his computer. Even though he was trying to be frugal with the details, he still filled twelve pages to bring the account up to date. It was just as well he did.

## Chapter Eight – The Point of No Return

The situation at work had left Luke distrustful of many of his colleagues. As a teenager, he had seen how people could change and if the mob was alright with it, then a lot of them would follow and do things they wouldn't even consider under normal conditions.

During one period of serious unrest from the protestant unionist side in the 1970's, a mob of about sixty to eighty men gathered in his hometown. They headed to a small housing area, almost exclusively housing Catholics. The inevitable attack began with a petrol bomb but ironically, it happened to be the home of a Catholic police reservist. Facing the mob were just two policemen. The mob advanced menacingly with sticks, clubs and petrol bombs onto the policemen who fired warning shots in the air. Then hooded men appeared and started firing on the policemen and the Catholic community. By the time it was over, two Catholics had been shot and wounded and a protestant paramilitary was dead.

Tensions within the largely protestant town went through the roof. At that stage of the troubles, the public supported their own paramilitaries thinking they were glamorous virtuous soldiers for their side of the religious divide. That misplaced view would slowly change, but it certainly didn't happen overnight.

The next morning as Luke arrived for school, he found he was surrounded. "You're one of the police bastard's sons" said one. "All policemen should die" said another spotty faced kid stretching out to abruptly shove hard at his shoulder. "Your dad should die" added a third, all in their broad Northern Irish accent, as Luke was pushed and shoved around the school play yard within the confines of a moving circular ring of teenage boys. About fifteen lads, some from his year at school seemed to be taking the role of cajoling and pushing him about as an obligatory duty, to be performed as zealously as possible. And yet the day before, Luke would have described many of these boys as his mates. The bustling circle of pupils attracted a teacher. "What's going on?" he shouted, as the small mob wheeled round to face him. "Nothing Sir" was the disharmonious reply. The bell rang. "Right", said the teacher, "get to assembly and if there is any more of this nonsense, you'll have to deal with me."

That was the first of many insights Luke was to receive into the true nature of ordinary people, giving the merest hint of the shocking capabilities of a mob or the horrendous callousness of individuals, especially those motivated by the volatile, emotive, political factors prevalent within Northern Ireland at that time. Time and time again, within Northern Ireland, mobs were to display a complete disregard for the law or even the slightest hint of common sense. It was as if they lost touch with reality, that their conduct as one body meant they were no longer responsible for their own individual actions within the group.

Of course, there were always mob controllers, people who could stir up a crowd. In Luke's workplace, Damian, the boss, excelled at creating a negative atmosphere within his work staff. Divide and conquer was his motto. If he didn't like someone, he would happily condone others within his team for being unpleasant to them. Most people reacted compliantly to Damian's wishes and were happy enough to act in a malevolent way that Damian would want them to, against any people on his hit list. Damian was no different to tens of thousands of bullying bosses, but he was at the top end as a performer as he was smart, devious and devoid of a conscience to hold him back. He was the classic exhibitor of "small man syndrome - 100% pure bristling malice". Given a little more research to tick the boxes and he may have been referenced as having "psychopathic or sociopathic tendencies". Damian had given Kirstie promotion, so Luke wondered what the payback was going to be for her promotion.

Assessing Kirstie's strengths, Luke knew she could be great fun in company, quite capable in her work but she had a ruthless side to her as well. She was articulate, attractive and because of that, she was manipulative, especially with men, and very ambitious. Luke invested in two small Dictaphones, one for the car and one for carrying, preferably at all other times. With Kirstie, he anticipated any damage would come in the form of an accusation, so he would need to be able to record and prove himself free of guilt. Luke wasn't the only one who thought that, several of his work mates had voiced concerns that Kirstie would be capable of falsifying accusations, if she thought it would suit her purposes.

Because Luke was really getting stirred up by the "accidents" he had been having, he also had a stone chisel lined up at the side of his bed. It would be a truly brutal weapon if used against someone but in the event of somebody breaking into his house with a mission to kill him, the stone chisel would be a very effective weapon. Being hardened steel and heavy, if Luke had to throw it or swing it at an assailant, it would certainly deliver a very painful wound as a minimum. If thrown at an intruder, it might give him the vital few seconds to engage with his attacker. It may even have delivered a fatal wound, but Luke decided that was a risk worth taking. He was all for staying within the law, but the law seemed incapable of protecting him in his situation. Better to be safe than sorry. He also kept three huge metal Maglite torches, one in his car, one in the house and one by his bed which would also enable him to inflict damage if he had to defend himself. Luke was not fooling around anymore; he really was getting stirred up. He found sleep difficult, even though he used sleeping tablets and would still wake up with any unusual noise, inside or outside his house.

It was in this volcanic situation that unwittingly Kirstie decided to up the pressure. She phoned Luke when he was at a meeting along with four other compatriots. She was uncharacteristically aggressive to Luke, who just defended himself without any real problems, as her accusations were poorly thought through. The other four compatriots sat somewhat bemused at the meeting table but silently whilst this tirade was going on down the phone. They could all hear what was being said. Luke was angry but bit his lip and swallowed his desire to reciprocate against her belligerence. Eventually she hung up, but the other team members could see that Luke was fizzing with anger. Luke knew this had been the price for Kirstie's promotion.

The next day Luke got a phone call again from Kirstie. This time Kirstie was ice cold. In anticipation Luke had the Dictaphone recording the conversation. Her opening line bore no surprise for Luke. "I have lodged an official complaint with the company that you were obnoxious down the phone to me and several times, you told me to go and fuck myself."

"Ok" said Luke "when was this phone call supposed to have happened?"

"Yesterday, when I spoke to you about 11.00am," said Kirsten.

"Ah well" said Luke "you do realize that there were four other people all sitting within a metre or two of me and they all oversaw the whole thing, heard every word and certainly witnessed that I didn't tell you to go and fuck yourself, not once."

"They'll back me up," said Kirstie.

"If it goes to court then they'll have to commit perjury to back you up. I think in the long term, not all of them will back up your falsified accusations. Risk of jail to them and all that," said Luke.

Kirstie hung up. Right or not, Luke did feel that Kirstie's heart wasn't in this ill-advised move, but she had gone through with it anyway.

The writing was on the wall. Damian wanted Luke out regardless of the fact that he was always a top performer amongst the extended combined teams. For his part, Luke was now completely sickened of the bullying. He had always over the past seven years given within the top three greatest percentage increases in turnover in the whole of the three teams with a total of over thirty salespeople. Despite this he had only received grief since Damian had become the new boss. Luke knew it was time to consult a solicitor and start proceedings for unfair dismissal.

He was told the first stage was to contact the Human Resources Officer and inform them that he was so unhappy that he wished to sue for unfair dismissal. Luke felt that he was just going to be feeding all his grievances right into the lion's mouth. However, as that was what he had been told he had to do, he begrudgingly decided to go with it.

The Human Resources Officer was a lady called Ruth, small in stature, always had a very tidy office and dressed wrapped up in thick but tight-fitting tweed outfits. She struck Luke as though she would have been wrapped just as tightly within her own skin as well. They agreed to meet after she flew up to Glasgow to discuss the problems as Luke saw them. Luke picked her up at the terminal and they went to a local Hotel for the informal meeting. They started the meeting by just discussing life in general and it took on a warming atmosphere.

Ruth asked Luke about his interest in wildlife and photography. Luke told her about a recent trip to look for Scottish Wildcats at three thirty in the morning. He went up through several steep fields crossing over stone walls. He came to a gate and was in the process of crossing the gate and landing on the other side when he suddenly noticed a dark bulky shape only twenty feet away. It was a huge beef bull in the semi-gloom of the very first hints of dawn. In a situation like that a bull may turn on the person as he did not know the person, be spooked or just feel aggressive.

Luke knew he was standing on the wrong side of the gate and the whole situation could turn nasty very quickly indeed. Luke talked gently to the bull saying in a soothing voice "hello big fellow, how are you?" The bull just stood without any sudden movements or sound. Luke realised if he proceeded into the field further, he could have been vulnerable to attack by the animal which was considerably faster and weighed in at more than ten times his weight. Luke decided that discretion was the better part of valour and quickly hopped back over the gate, in a light-footed way despite the heavy photographic equipment on his back. He walked up to take a two hundred metre detour whilst the bull stuck its huge head over the stone wall to watch him go. A lucky escape indeed for Luke. But Ruth enjoyed the story and Luke's detailing of the situation.

Eventually Ruth moved on to discuss the problems. Luke explained the problems, as he saw it. There were phone calls which had been coming in regularly, with someone holding on the other side in an ominous silence, until eventually voiced messages were being left which had a very aggressive tone. He explained that they were probably an attempt to intimidate because the language sounded Arabic and may have had something to do with the bridge incident. He revealed that he had found out that the number came from the town where the head office was based but he did not reveal any more details or that he had proof that it was connected to Damian in some way.

He also outlined the fact that he was always being asked to do more calls, higher increases and experienced far more scrutiny and micro-management than his team-mates. He suggested he had evidence of Private Investigators being employed to assess his whereabouts. Again, he didn't give any details of how he had come to that conclusion or of any proof. Finally, he mentioned that his now immediate boss, Kirstie, had made an accusation against him saying that he had told her to fuck off.

"And did you?" asked Ruth.

"Certainly not" was Luke's reply.

However, what he didn't say was that he had recorded the conversation and had proof that it had been falsified. Nor did he reveal anything about the other factors affecting his life.

Ruth kept an upbeat and soothing presence during this discussion. She remained unruffled and Luke felt that just maybe she was genuinely unaware, indeed naïve, to all of these problems that had helped stress him highly whilst the other personal problems were pushing him into the red danger zone and were seemingly almost insurmountable. At the end of the meeting Ruth said that it had been an eyeopener to her and that she was going away with an awareness beyond anything she had expected. Luke felt warmed to Ruth. He offered to give her a lift back to the airport terminal and they chatted on in a relaxed atmosphere. Ruth said she would see if she could do anything to sort out the problems discussed. She thanked Luke as they arrived at the drop off point, adding that she had enjoyed the meeting and hoped it would all be sorted very soon. Her warmth disarmed Luke.

As he pulled away from dropping her at the drop off point, he turned to give one last wave goodbye to Ruth. Ruth was not looking though. Her face had changed completely. Distracted and deep in thought, she looked angry but worried at the same time, like she was contemplating a very difficult problem but at the same time, knowing that this could be a real nightmare for her and the company.

Immediately, Luke realised he had been taken in, been made a bit of a fool. Luckily though, Luke had not revealed key points of proof. He sensed that the problems were not going to be easily sorted, as he had begun to hope during the meeting.

## Chapter Nine – The Fight Back

Luke had other people now to see. A friend had recommended a solicitor and so he and Kim made an appointment to speak to him. He had a reputation for being the best solicitor in town. There were one or two that had climbed into the next level, the world of barristers, but they were way out of Luke's financial cost zone. Jason, as a solicitor still charged a hefty fee of £175.00 per hour for consultations and that wasn't before any other hidden extras.

Jason reminded Luke of an efficient poker player, he would reveal the cards but only a minimum at a time and each time costed another hour's consultation.

Apparently, the normal procedure was to lodge a grievance with his employers of bullying and unfair dismissal, which Jason helped with, for a small fee of course. The company would then organise up to two meetings with management members and if it still wasn't resolved to Luke's satisfaction, then he would be able to take it onwards to court.

But first, he was going to have to start the process. The letter was drawn up and despatched and in due course a meeting was organised. It meant that Luke had to fly down to London for the meeting. With a last consultation, Jason offered his advice, seeming to indicate that there would be excellent chances that it would all be sorted very quickly after this meeting.

A few days later, a letter came through the post. A meeting was organised down in the Head Office to discuss the complaints. The flight tickets were also in the letter with details of how to get there. Luke was allowed to bring one compatriot as a second witness and reference person to discuss and give an extra opinion, when Luke wanted it. A member of the sales force volunteered. John was ambitious but also a very capable person. He had a reasonably balanced outlook on life, so he seemed like a good choice for Luke. However, Luke fully sensed that John was also looking for promotion and he wondered if he volunteered to inform straight back to Damian. In the devious world of business, it is very hard to know who to trust. Nearly all could be smiling assassins if it suited their case.

Because Luke's complaints were against the boss, not many people were willing to take that risky stand, so Luke decided to accept John's offer. The others in the sales team were silently hoping that Luke's case might reel Damian in a bit, but they would never admit it. "Never stick your head above the parapet" would have been a suitable motto for most of them.

The appointed day arrived, and Luke and John duly flew down from Edinburgh Airport and got a taxi to the Head Office. The meeting seemed to go as smoothly as it could have. There were two managers conducting the meeting, both female in their late thirties and early forties. They came across as wanting to be helpful to Luke, keen to listen to his case and find out what he knew. They were mannerly and considerate. They asked probing questions but the whole meeting had an air of informality about it.

It was just as well, as Luke had not slept well the night before and had got up at silly hours to fly down from the airport. In fact, Luke had not slept well for weeks as he was stressed out with the two different situations in his life. He felt like a half-shut knife, more of a hazard to himself than the sharp man he could be. His responses were not as quick or as sleek as he would like, but it was what it was because of his long-term existence right on the edge.

The positive nature of the meeting meant Luke found himself quite liking the two managers. Never a good idea when they might be considered to be opponents. Luke didn't have a gripe with them though and by the time Luke and John were heading back to Scotland, he felt quite sure they had become sympathetic to his case and would be putting a favourable aspect to those higher up the ladder.

Bad news in a letter always arrived on a Saturday morning. This was because it gave the recipient time to cool down over the weekend and not just phone up the office in an impulsive rage about the contents. It was obvious from the contents of the letter that despite the friendly ambience at the meeting and the empathetic tone, the whole meeting had merely been to extract all the information they could on what Luke held against the managers.

Luke and Kim, who was equally disappointed with the letter, now had a decision to make. They could either take the easier road and stop the proceedings or go for the next step in the process, another formal meeting, in the hope that sense, from their perspective, would prevail. Luke discussed the options with Kim. To give up at that stage would leave Luke as a marked man, as well as somewhat humiliated. The company now knew just about all that Luke had against Damian's behaviour. To proceed onwards might mean failure and jeopardise his reputation, perhaps forever. However, both Luke and Kim felt their case was rock solid and the only real choice was to proceed to the next stage, to be brave and have self-belief.

Jason, the solicitor, expressed his disappointment that the meeting hadn't swung the case in their favour. In reality, that is almost certainly the tactic used by just about all bigger companies. Sicken the person with the complaint and they might just cease. Luke had been changed by the whole range of his experiences, he was now certainly no withering violet and becoming less so by the day. He and Kim decided to continue to the next stage. The solicitor's letter was sent notifying the company of the fact.

To add insult to injury, the company then decided to have their top medical doctor meet with Luke to do a psychiatric assessment. This meant yet another flight down to London. Luke went in to see the doctor and they had a fifteen-minute session. The doctor asked Luke about his situation, everything from what had prompted his complaint to what books was he reading now. Luke answered each question in turn. When asked about the current book, he said he was reading a book about Colonel Paddy Mayne.

"Are you aware of him?" asked Luke.

"No" said the doctor "who is he?"

"Paddy Mayne was probably the single most successful British soldier during the second world war. He played for Ireland in rugby before the war. He became second in command after David Stirling in the SAS and took over after David Stirling was imprisoned in Colditz. Paddy is believed to have destroyed more enemy aircraft and killed more soldiers than any other allied combatant in the war. He was so determined that once when all his fellow SAS soldiers were killed before an operation started, he still went on himself and completed the mission to destroy many enemy aircraft solely. He was exceptionally aggressive and tough but undoubtedly somewhat of a psychopath."

"Oh, I see," said the doctor.

Shortly after that, the session was over, and Luke had to fly back to Scotland.

A letter arrived at Luke's home a few days later. It was addressed to him, but copies had been sent to the Human Resources as well. It stated quite simply that there were signs of stress exhibited by Luke but no mental illness at all. Obviously that line of argument wasn't going to bring any dividends for the company.

The next meeting was organised. Again, the presence of a compatriot was offered to Luke. This time John was reluctant to go with Luke, which rang the warning bells belatedly for Luke. Sure enough, soon, John got promoted to becoming a manager. If you're prepared to sell your soul to the devil, you might just get what you want. Luke went this time with an older compatriot, a genuine character with no hidden agenda at all and nothing to gain from doing so.

Alan was an old hand, been in the team for what seemed like forever, straight as a dice but fully aware of the sort of tricks some of the more senior managers could pull. He had a knack of not getting on the wrong side of managers, a very rare skill indeed. Unpolitical but a people person, he was genuinely interested in his compatriots and never had a bad word to say about anyone. His only drawback was that he was somewhat deaf. Luke wondered if something important might get said but Alan wouldn't hear it. Regardless, Luke was glad to have him along, as he was a real gentleman.

Luke wondered, what was the point of this meeting? The company had stated its position that they did not find reasonable grounds for Luke's complaints. What could another meeting achieve if that was their attitude? Why not cut to the chase and just go to court and see what the court would think? Luke didn't realise it but there is a set procedure in these situations with companies. In the first meeting, the plan is to always listen sympathetically and perhaps even give the impression of being behind the complainant. The reality is they always have to do a u turn and say that they did not believe there were real grounds for a complaint. This would have the effect of weeding out a very high proportion of complaints, as many people would give up at this point. The solicitor had never told Luke this though. He had just advised on what to say and wished him luck.

So how could the second meeting sort it all out? Luke couldn't see the point of it but just had to go along with it anyway. He planned to defend his role and show that his work ethics and integrity were unmatched, apart from by Alan.

On the due day, both men arrived at the airport and flew down to London. They got a taxi to the Head Office and arrived in time for the meeting. They both waited in the canteen and had cups of coffee. Alan was his usual supportive self, a very genuine individual. Ironically, the lady who Luke had met in the first meeting came in, recognised Luke, made a cheerful nod and said hello. Within two seconds, she obviously remembered that the letter sent subsequently after the meeting had not been favourable to Luke and he noticed her body language change as she realised that he might not view her so auspiciously. Luke realised that she had just been ordered to do what she had done and at least the genuine initial response showed that she felt warmed to Luke.

Slightly later than the nominated time, Luke and Alan were called into the meeting. It was a new lady chairing the meeting, ironically called Alana with a man called George beside her to help. It didn't take long for Luke to warm to her, even though he knew effectively she was the opposition. She had obvious intelligence and seemed genuine, concerned, patient and level in her approach. All were attributes Luke appreciated. "Why did they always select people that seemed so personable and easy to like" Luke wondered to himself.

The meeting proceeded smoothly with Luke being asked about his role, work performance and attitude to his team and company, all of which he seemed to portray an honest but favourable response to, backed up by data he brought with him into the meeting. The question of terrorism came up in the meeting as well, as Luke had informed people within his company about the Forth Road Bridge incident. Luke was asked his opinion about Islamic extremism and more specifically the likelihood of terrorism developing and its direction. Luke sensed a trap here. Say the wrong thing here and it would be used to discredit him in the future or just be sufficient to tip the balance. Luke though felt sure about his opinions, he did have an insight into terrorism gained from a childhood in Northern Ireland as a policeman's son.

At the time, there had been no substantial terrorism outbreak and people still thought it would fizzle out. Luke said "I think that there are enough people out there that want a cause, justified or not. Muslims are no exception. Some will listen to negative preaching, misguided individuals who feel angry that others do not abide by their perceived religion and rules. This will represent only a tiny minority as the vast majority in any religion just want to live in peace and harmony amongst other religious or secular people. And that's the way it should be. But that small group of angry people will be disproportionate and cause huge harm. Yes, I do believe there will be Islamic terrorism events in the near future and London will be a targeted city. In fact, I will make the prediction that there will be bombings within London, and it will happen when the police are distracted by some other event. Crowded locations are liable to be targeted too, causing as much death and destruction as the terrorists can. Wait and see." His predictions were to prove to be spot on.

Luke was asked why would these people believe they were justified in committing atrocities? "Well," said Luke "there are people who have warped views on everything and all they need is a cause, with the emotions whipped up by irrational, hatred inciting orators who are basically bigots and then, there you have it, an explosive lethal concoction set to go, claiming many innocent lives with it, before it can be dealt with. I've seen it all happen before in Northern Ireland. Why we even allow these people to preach their obnoxious beliefs is beyond me." Luke continued "these types exist in every society, it's just when we let them thrive or pour fuel on their fire, they take off. It's not confined to Muslims, it can be protestant, catholics, jews, hindus, sikhs, blacks, whites, you name it. It's just that Osama Bin Laden has started something that a small proportion of Muslims will want to join in, because they feel they want a cause to fight for. Luckily, it's only a small proportion of any group, but they can be a disproportional problem. A real thorn in societies side."

Alana looked at Luke, her body language suggesting she didn't believe that there would be much more Muslim terrorist events. "I can see you don't believe me" said Luke, "but give it time and you'll see. It probably won't even take all that much time before it starts to happen."

"Have you seen many examples of terrorism, Luke?" asked Alana.

"Yes, some," said Luke. "Many were conveyed by my father who has had numerous experiences as a Policeman in Northern Ireland. But some I experienced first-hand. I've had a bomb go off in the next street from where I was sitting waiting at traffic lights on my motorbike. The blast knocked me off my bike, but the buildings to my side prevented shrapnel damage to me. Obviously, once I recovered, I got out of there as quickly as I could."

Luke continued "we've had protestant paramilitaries create a roadblock outside our house - twice - once when my father was in the house, once when he wasn't there, as he was away on duty. My brother and I were only about 14 or 15 but we would have done what we could if they had attacked the house. To be honest, at that age, we would have been easy to kill. But not so easy now" Luke at this stage was thinking about his recent experiences but didn't say anything about that.

"Why were they there?" asked Alana who was keen to get a little more insight into this situation.

"They were merely proving they could do it and that they could threaten the Police, if they wanted. They even petrol bombed two Police houses on the second night, but luckily not our house" said Luke. "I could go on about many experiences, but I don't think we'd have the time to cover them here, today!"

"Quite" said Alana. "Let's ask you why you believe you had some Private Investigators being commissioned to check you during work time?"

"I had noticed unusual behaviour by a man up the street from me," said Luke. "I was suspicious as he had been there for some time, but I had an appointment to go to, so when I jumped into my car and drove past him, I saw him pull his sleeve back as he noted the time I had departed. A coincidence? Maybe, but when on the next Friday a lady was 100 metres up the road on one of only two possible places where someone could monitor my house and she was still in the exact spot twenty minutes later, I thought this is too much of a coincidence."

"I sneaked out later with my camera, drove up slowly and then quickly took some photos of her with her phone to her ear, as she had been there for over an hour. I drove back to my house. After another ten minutes, she left the spot she was at. I'm sorry, but nobody does that sort of thing for that length of time. But just to check it out, I got the addresses of all the local Private Investigators and checked them out one by one by viewing them from a distance in the evenings. Sure enough, eventually through my binoculars, she came into view in her living room - the exact same person that I had photographed"

"We don't use Private Investigators in this company," said George. "Anyway, they're very expensive to hire, you know" continued George.

Luke snorted a laugh, pulled a smile, and shook his downturned head a few times. When he looked up again at Alana and George, he could see Alana's eyes burning into George with a frowned face that had "you idiot" written all over it.

"I used to work with a company that did employ the services of Private Investigators" said George who looked embarrassed because of his previous announcement. He may have been telling the truth, but Luke thought the body language suggested he was trying to cover his mistake, as quickly as possible.

Alana wanted to assure Luke that he would not be targeted anymore, that for everyone's sake it would be better if we just calmed the whole situation down.

Luke asked, "what if the managers just carry-on making things unreasonable for me?"

George intervened "If they do, they will regret it. Yes, they'll definitely regret it!"

"How do you mean?" asked Luke "because I think they're a bit out of control and they seem to believe they'll be able to get away with anything they want."

"No" said Alana "they'll be told that they've to stop targeting you, so you don't need to worry about that."

Luke thought to himself "I wish I was working for you rather than Damian and his cronies. You seem a very reasonable boss."

The meeting came to an end, and they all said goodbye to each other. On the way back to the airport, Alan chipped in and said "I think the meeting went well. In fact, it had gone as well as we both could have hoped for."

"Yes, your probably right, but I don't believe they realise that Damian won't listen to a word they say. I doubt if he'll change anything about his behaviour, at all," said Luke.

When they got back to the return airport, Luke thanked Alan "Thanks for all your help today. It's been a long day and you've really gone out of your way to help. I can't thank you enough."

"That's no bother Luke. I enjoyed it. Quite an experience and quite an insight into what Damian has been up to. However, I think he's met his Colombo in you. Hopefully he'll start to behave himself from now on if the spotlight is on him now," said Alan.

Luke grunted a half laugh, half snort "Well maybe, but I doubt it. Anyway, thanks again Alan. Good trip home. We'll speak sometime soon." With that they went their separate ways. Luke knew Alan was a genuine guy with no hidden agenda.

The meeting letter arrived with Luke a few days later. It said that they didn't believe there was any connection between the events Luke had outlined and any company managers, but that they were happy to ensure that there were no retributions against Luke from the managers. Luke was less disappointed in the findings this time, he had worked out that that was how they would present it, even though the evidence was completely irrefutable as Luke saw it. He now had the decision to make, should he progress the complaint to court or just swallow his anger and pride and see how it went from there. After all, he had been assured that he would not be targeted for reprisals. He decided to see how it went at work.

In less than a week, Luke was heading down to another meeting. This time it was a half year conference, and all the team was going to be there.

There was an obvious air of tension within the managers at the meeting, but Luke brass-necked his way about. There was a lot of speculation within his team-mates as to what had been going on with Luke, but none asked any questions. Alan was his usual cheerful self, but the rest were befuddled as to what the situation was. Was Luke on his way out or had he shaken

Damian to the core? Either way, they didn't want to be involved. If Luke was about to be crushed like a worm, then that was his problem. If he managed to constrain Damian, then they were behind him all the way, from the side-lines, of course. Nobody though, truly believed that Damian would be on his way out.

The conference lasted three days, so the air between Damian and Luke was taut. Just before departure time, Damian made an unsavoury comment to Luke which just triggered an inevitable angry response "now you'll be getting back to work Luke, as you've wasted far too much management time."

Luke had had it with Damian. The red mist descended, and he replied "so are you going to stop paying guys to try to intimidate me on the phone or have falsified accusations made against me. I know you're behind those and many other things. I know with absolute certainty."

It was obvious that Damian was flustered at this. He lifted his arm, pointing to the door and said, "out of this room now."

Luke was boiling with rage but managed to hold back saying anything else. He turned and left the room, but he knew it was never going to work from that moment. All the team was having lunch and then all were to depart homewards to all around the country. Luke set off home knowing the decision had been made for him. It would be court next.

**Chapter Ten - Enlightenment**

The next morning Luke phoned Ruth and declared that staying within the company obviously wasn't going to work. "I'm afraid it is a case of see you in court" said Luke to Ruth. "I'm sorry it has come to this" said Ruth "but if that's how it is, then that's how it is. I'll see if I can pull any strings this side. I'll be in touch, Luke."

Later that day Ruth phoned Luke back. "We're thinking of offering you six months of salary as against signing a compromise agreement, but it's an awful lot of money."

"Is it?" said Luke who by now was thoroughly angry with the whole situation.

Normally a very tolerant and polite man, he just clicked his finish call button on his mobile phone.

The phone rang back. "If you'd let me finish" Ruth said "I was going to tell you that we'll give you a year's salary instead. If you go to court, you might get nothing at all or you might be awarded less than that. So, what do you think?"

Luke was keen to leave as soon as possible, as he was thoroughly fed up with the whole situation. "Alright that sounds acceptable" said Luke "but I want a good reference from you guys. It's no more than I deserve."

"Well, we don't normally do references until somebody asks for one" said Ruth.

"I just want a written copy before this is all signed up. Is that, ok?" asked Luke.

"Yes OK" said Ruth, "I'll get it organised for you and the copy of the compromise agreement for you to sign."

"Alright that'll do," said Luke.

A few days later the compromise agreement arrived. Luke had a solicitor read it over in case there were any hidden sinister clauses, but the solicitor reported that there were none. The reference hadn't arrived, but Ruth assured Luke it was merely because of the workload she was under. So, Luke, being trusting against his instincts, signed the compromise agreement without this request having been fulfilled. Luke hoped it was going to be a new start in his life. He needed far less stress in his life as he knew he was still a target from the report he had made to the Police several years before. His health was beginning to suffer with heart problems and insomnia.

Two weeks after leaving the company a report came on the news about a James Shistire-Aylott being exposed for fraudulently promoting his ex-wife's harp recordings as genuine. He was semi-retired, worked as a freelance recording engineer and lived at the exact address that had been reported to Luke as the address source of the phone calls. His photos were all over the papers, so Luke was able to see who this rogue was, the very man who had been phoning him and leaving aggressive sounding foreign language phone calls. "Bastard" thought Luke, "now that I've signed this compromise agreement, I can't expose you for the creep you are."

Within another two weeks, Luke was contacted by a compatriot in his field of expertise. "I've started in a new job and I'm needing a Salesman to cover Scotland for me. Would you be interested?" he asked Luke. Brian had known Luke for years and knew that he was a safe pair of hands. An interview was arranged and within a month Luke had started with Brian as his boss.

A few months later, Luke was over in Northern Ireland with his family to see his parents. He popped down to the local shop to pick up some odds and sods, including the morning papers. On the front pages of the Scottish newspapers was a photograph that caught his eye. Luke gasped. There was a photograph of the very man he had seen checking him out around his house, the man who had travelled down on the same flight to London, who had followed him up to the primary school when his son had been unwell with another man along with numerous other encounters. Luke bought two of the papers and headed home to find out who this mysterious guy was. His name was Callum Mallachy and he was a very notorious Glasgow based gangster. He had died of a heart attack. He had a very interesting background and a successful career smuggling and selling drugs. He was ruthless and had been up on an attempted murder charge but had been acquitted. It seemed no charges ever stuck to him, and he'd run rings around the law.

Luke showed the photographs to his father and said, "this is the very man that I have seen dozens of times monitoring me since that incident up the glen, all those years ago."

"Well, now you can maybe piece all this together and work out what has been going on. This is a good thing because before you were just stabbing in the dark" said Luke's father. "Just be careful though because it may bring more trouble in your direction. Do you really want to find out?" Luke's father asked.

"Absolutely" said Luke. "With all the stress this has brought, the ostracism from work mates, the disbelief from the cops and the thought that they may even suspect me of all people of either being a nutcase or involved in some way. Too bloody right I want to work it out" said Luke.

"And proof" said Luke's father, "if you were a policeman, you'd need proof!" "I don't need that; I just want to know what was really happening because it caused me so much stress" said Luke.

In some ways it was good news for Luke. Now he had a chance to find out what the hell had been going on and get closure. But it also brought enhanced danger with increased risks of future attacks. Luke wanted closure and he wanted to know what really, was the truth.

Luke started researching Callum who had entered the world of crime as a teenager selling small amounts of softer drugs. He had moved on to break ins and burglary. But Callum was nothing if not smart, in fact exceptionally so by criminal standards. He wanted to become a main player in the city and in Scotland. To do that you had to think outside the box, do things in a new way to avoid the law and keep one step ahead of other city godfathers. He needed a way to import drugs direct into Glasgow to make the maximum profits.

Surstromming is a Swedish fermented fish invariably presented in a can which when opened squirts out juices for a foot or two along with an instantly gut wrenching, horrendous putrid smell. It is so bad; it makes skunk spray smell like a desirable Eau de Cologne in comparison. The person that opens it, if not battle hardened to the smell, will find themselves instantly gagging, usually just seconds before actual vomiting because of the smell. Callum had seen the results of this played out on some friends of his after one of them dared his compatriots to prove their manhood by eating a tin of fermented fish, which, after all is eaten regularly by Swedes. Of course, no self-respecting Glasgow hard man gangster with a couple of drinks down his neck is going to refuse a so-called fun challenge like that. The results were spectacular. Hard men that he respected and had known for years were on their knees gagging and throwing up all over the place. Only one challenger managed to put a single piece in his mouth and that instantly re-appeared pushed out by a pressurised projectile vomit column of liquid shooting it several feet away from the green faced spluttering man who looked like he would never ever recover from the experience. Callum had never seen such a strong reaction before.

It instantly got Callum thinking. Before you knew it, he had invested in a tiny unit in an Amsterdam industrial Park. The fermented fish was brought in as large cans and repackaged into smaller cans, with every number 18 and 19 can on the production line receiving a little sealed package of drugs. Any custom officer that wanted to check out the tins would invariably pick one can from the top layer. They were packed in boxes of 36 cans, a layer of 12 with three layers in each. When the outer box was opened from the top or the bottom, the cans holding the drugs were in the middle of the middle row, the least likely to be examined. Once a can had been opened, the customs officer would be so taken aback, indeed shocked by the smell, that would end the inspection. Usually, the customs officer involved had to take a fifteen-minute break in fresh air until there was no further involuntary responsive reactions from his gagging belly and the last molecules were dispersed completely away from the victim. One or two had begged to be released from their work commitment that day so they could go home, lie down, and die. No dogs were of any use for this work either, for obvious reasons. It certainly worked for Callum.

The drug mule cans were collected and picked out in Glasgow, the remaining cans were labelled and repackaged into outer boxes of 36 again and sent over for a highly discounted price to Iceland, Greenland, the Faeroes, and Sweden where such food is regarded as a peculiar delicacy. Where they didn't sell, they were simply dumped without the labels, effectively untraceable. The scheme made Callum a very rich man indeed.

As he became more powerful, Callum took on enforcers to look after his business interests. He was certainly smarter than nearly all his competing gangsters in Glasgow. He took on one or two young lieutenants to entrust in his drug running business and developed close relationships with them. In some ways he was a bizarre enigma of a man who could have a close friendship but was utterly ruthless and ambitious as well as very dangerous.

The violent side developed as he became more dominant in the Glasgow gangster scene. There were always troublemakers trying to gain an illegal edge. There were less details on the internet on these aspects about Callum, but Luke did gleam that he had been up on an attempted murder charge and got off with it. Others though hadn't and had gone to jail for long spells as a result. Luke realised that he must have been seen as one of those hurdles to Callum but a particularly difficult one as he couldn't be bought or accessed easily for intimidation, because Luke had an almost blind faithful belief in upkeeping the law, especially against serious crime. Luke also was easily the most alert of potential victims that Callum had experienced.

This made the task of eliminating the perceived threat from Luke, for Callum very difficult indeed. Even though the police had never approached Callum, it was perhaps obvious that Luke hadn't seen enough to bring any charges against Callum, but

Luke hadn't made this fact public to calm Callum and his cronies. Little wonder that Luke had been a major thorn in Callum's side.

There were other details on the enforcers that Callum had employed. One that popped up on the internet with a photo caught Luke's attention. He recognised him as the man that had been with Callum at the school gates when Luke had gone up to see his boy in the primary school as he was reportedly somewhat ill. At that stage Callum was still an unknown, indeed unrecognised person to Luke who was only suspicious about him being one of the men he had watched at the top of the glen. When Luke came out of the school that day, he saw a man (Callum) instantly try to engage with a young boy to distract from the fact that he was standing at the gates. The other man was a man called Mike Duncan. When Luke had suddenly arrived unexpectedly after coming out of the school gate, Callum spoke to a nearby boy to distract from suspicion. Mike Duncan didn't seem to know what to do and so he just stared into space as Luke passed the two men. It had registered with Luke that it did in fact seem very suspicious and that's why he took as good a look at the two men as the few seconds allowed.

Intrigued, Luke carried on researching on Mike Duncan. He had been murdered shortly after being up at the school gates, only about a month or so after. There had obviously been a lot of history involving Mike's name with plenty of gangland people in Glasgow. He had gone to a pub and met a friend who persuaded him to stay, sit down, relax and catch a bit of craic. A big mistake. Shortly afterwards a man walked in and right up to where Mike was seated. He proceeded to stab him multiple times in front of a shocked crowd before running out and calmly wiping the knife over with tissue and then dumping it. It was all over so quick. The Police were looking into the case but at that time nobody had been arrested or charged.

Luke then researched the nature of the man who had been reported found dumped close to a main road not far from Edinburgh and discovered by a dog walker, not long after Luke had his experience up the glen. His name was Andrew Coyne. He had owned a taxi business in Edinburgh but had been pestered by a Terence Argyle who had been demanding protection money.

Terence Argyle was a particularly unsavoury character. He hailed from Drumchapel in Glasgow and had been nicknamed the Chapel Bastard. A small man, he was a truly malevolent psychopath. He'd resorted to pouring boiling water over victims whilst torturing people without any concern or restraint. There were reports that he had tormented Andrew Coyne's life by demanding a tidy sum of money from his taxis business. Luke also read that Andrew Coyne had approached Callum Mallachy to have Terence Argyle executed. Allegedly Callum had promised to do the job, taken the money offered up front and then done nothing in the classic con. Andrew Coyne had disappeared a couple of months before his body was found. He'd received a phone call early one evening and said to his wife that he had to go out for an impromptu business meeting. His wife saw him get into a car with about three men and drive off. He was never seen again until his body was found. He had over twenty-eight stab wounds in his body.

From what Luke could ascertain from the jumble of internet notes on Andrew Coyne, it seemed he had been a low-key rascal rather than a hard-core rogue. It was little wonder he'd been susceptible to intimidation from the likes of Terence Argyle.

The fact that there was a connection between Andrew Coyne and Callum Mallachy, with the date of his body being discovered just after Luke's experience suggested to Luke that there must be some link between them. This needed more examination. Could the meeting that Andrew Coyne had gone to, have been with Callum Mallachy and a couple of his men? Maybe he demanded his money back and it had gone badly with Andrew being stabbed to death? It was a distinct possibility. This was not a world that Luke had any knowledge of, he had merely delved into it because of his unfortunate circumstances. Nor did he know the characters. The only real strength Luke had was an awareness of the criminal world from the police side and his suspicious nature which had kept him safe, if somewhat mainly by luck, to date.

Luke's concern that all this was going on and the Police still weren't sure whether he was right, wrong, or unstable. He also knew he was up against some serious players, even though Callum was now dead. Maybe the Police still doubted about Callum, but Luke had seen Callum so often, both near and far now that his facial features and looks were completely ingrained in Luke's mind. But trying to be rational, Luke thought maybe it was all just paranoia on his part that the Police didn't believe him. Yes, maybe that was it. Luke didn't have to wait long to find out.

Luke was still very stressed out and was considering going to the Police with his suggestion that Andrew Coyne was connected to Callum Mallachy and maybe, just maybe, there was a connection between the two which had caused the death of Andrew Coyne. Before that he wanted to see his doctor about his heart, as he was beginning to be experiencing irregular heart rhythms. When you only have five to ten minutes with a doctor, and you talk about heart arrhythmia as a new problem but also that you believe you may have found a connection with a dead guy who had been stalking around your house to a person who had been murdered and his body had been found sixty miles away. Luke was so engrossed in what was going on, that he never really considered the way that other people may see his suggestions.

The letter from his medical practice came through within a week. Luke was to see a Forensic Psychiatrist and give him a fuller picture of his situation than the five or ten minutes allocated with the GP allowed. They were also going to see that he got an appointment with a heart specialist and that would come through very soon.

The due date arrived, and Luke went to see the Psychiatrist. He introduced himself as Dr. Brennan. This meeting was mildly worrying for Luke as the good doctor did have the power to section Luke. It could potentially have led to a "One flies over the Cuckoo nest" scenario, but Luke tried not to think like that. He was allocated one-hour sessions, usually two weeks apart. To help the doctor remember the information, Luke supplied an eleven-page summary of what had happened to him. After the third session, the good doctor announced that he had heard enough and that he would be able to decide when Luke came back for the next session. This was either very good or very bad, middle ground didn't seem to be an option in this assessment. When Luke returned for the fourth and final session, he was completely aware that if the doctor decided there was something wrong, he could be sectioned and locked up in a psychiatric ward. The additional bad news on that was that whilst it only took one doctor to lock you up, it took two doctors to sign your release.

Luke went in to find a young doctor sitting with Dr. Brennan, the psychiatrist. "Take a seat Luke" said Dr. Brennan. "This is Adam, he's training to become a registered psychiatrist. Adam has been looking at your case, alongside me. We have both come to the same conclusion."

"Oh shit, what's coming next" thought Luke.

"Do you mind if Adam sits in with us, Luke" asked Dr. Brennan.

"No, not at all" answered Luke.

"We're very happy to inform you that we both believe that you are telling the absolute truth. Your story is probably the single most unbelievable account we have ever heard and yet we know you are not mentally ill - stressed, yes - but not mentally ill. We also know that you are not lying."

"How did you work that out" asked Luke. "Because when someone is lying, there are professional ways of checking it out. You have consistently told your version and even though so many people both professionally and in your private circles have told you, you must be wrong, you have never once changed or modified your account. Although it has been rough on you, this experience has strengthened you, making you a much stronger character. All we can say to you is good luck, but I don't think that people will ever believe your story. As I have said, it is, well, unbelievable, even though it is true."

"Well, I'm very glad to hear that is the outcome" said Luke "so is that it?"

"That's it, Mr. Walker. You're free to go" said Dr. Brennan. With that Luke rose to his feet, shook hands with Dr. Brennan and Adam, said thanks and left.

Dr Brennan's words about Luke's story being unbelievable was going to come back to haunt him very soon.

## Chapter Eleven – First Feedback

Brian as a boss was a talented individual and within a year, he had moved on to a new job and a step or two up the ladder. Luke had enjoyed working with Brian but fancied going into self-employment as he had a business idea rumbling at the back of his brain that he thought would surely prove popular.

He knew that when people or pets died, they mainly just received a commemorative headstone, often with only a name or very basic details. If cremated, they maybe got nothing at all. This had always been the way for hundreds of years, so Luke thought it might be time for a change. His idea was to produce photo-tributes on metal which would be lightfast and endure for a hundred plus years. These could allow the most basic of options such as a small circular photograph to be mounted on a headstone showing the person or pet, right up to a larger print with text and several photographs showing the subject and giving an insight into the life or shared experiences of the deceased. Luke had discovered a suitable product to use, which if the manufacturers claims were to be believed, would be lightfast for over one hundred years.

Luke left the company only a couple of months after Brian had departed and started out on his own. He had some money from the payment made to him, so he decided to use that to cover the costs of starting his business. He started to call on Funeral Parlours, Crematoriums and Veterinary Surgeries but with almost no return for his time and effort. Funeral Directors actually came across as resistant to the idea, as they felt the way they organised the business had not really changed substantially for hundreds of years and why should they buck the trend. Vets on the other hand were more concerned with life rather than after life. There was some interest but not enough business to cover the costs involved. It was also Scotland, where the people seemed to be less emotive about their pets than in the more affluent parts of England.

Luke wondered how he had got it wrong, but when a friends' son died young and Luke offered to do a Photo-tribute free, he still didn't get his offer taken up. Luke had failed to appreciate that the subject was too sensitive for many people to write a loving or even objective summary on their departed family member or friend. This little attempt at being an entrepreneur had left him depleted in finances after all the investments for the business and time spent on it. They say entrepreneurs often have to fail before they will succeed and enjoy the benefits of a successful business. Luke just wanted to by-pass this learning curve but found it was like one man trying to get past fifteen rugby players who were all excellent tacklers on hard ground. Every crunching tackle hurt.

Luke decided it might be easier to go back to his original line of work with a new company, as that way the income was safe. And this was where he discovered slowly but surely, he had obviously been black balled. Prior to leaving his company after the settlement, he had always been headhunted for nearly every post. Now though, he found that he was either ignored or just received a no thanks letter to an interview. He did get one interview and was told they were keen to go ahead with a second interview as soon as possible, but the invitation never arrived. It was slowly becoming obvious that Luke was actively being blacklisted within his previous employment arena. Proving the fact was going to be virtually impossible. Luke needed to do something as he was beginning to fall into an ever deepening, financial hole. But what or more importantly who should he speak to.

Luke had a female acquaintance who worked as a Human Resources Officer for a big company in the local area. He asked if he could meet with her for lunch to ask her about what is legal in company procedures and see if he could get any advice on how to deal with this ex-work problem. Luke had become inure to the threats to his life and thought nothing of being honest within the boundaries of not releasing names. It just didn't faze him in the way it might have disturbed others. This cool delivery about a disturbing story was going to create problems. Luke expressly did not give any names, but he did mention to her that he was having problems with people trying to intimidate or kill him after he had witnessed suspicious activity up a glen. Luke was obviously wound tight by his situation, but he described his story without getting over emotional. However, this had the effect of freaking his friend out. After lunch she left and on leaving, she said she would see what she could do for Luke.

The email later that afternoon was clear and concise. He was not to contact her again. Luke realised she may have found what he told her as very concerning, but she had obviously thought she was dealing with a complete nut case. His main concern had been his work problems, but because he had divulged a little insight into his other problems, it was far too much for her. There could only be one possible conclusion. Too late in the day, Luke grasped that he had said too much and the fact that he wouldn't give any names suggested he was just making it up to her. Luke tried to phone and explain. She flatly refused to speak to him. Luke had dug an even bigger hole for himself.

A couple of hours later, the phone rang. It was the Police. It was PC Robertson who said he needed to come around and speak to Luke and would he be available in an hour. Luke had been planning to go to the gym but said he would be available. Luke knew exactly why the Police were coming around. He promptly printed off two copies of his summary on his experiences, so he could have one copy for reference and allow the PC to read the other.

Right on time. Knock, knock. Luke opened the door to find PC Robertson greeting him but introducing PC Allan who was with him. "We need to have a word with you Sir. Can we come in?" Luke brought them in and pointed them to the main settee. "What can I do for you gentlemen" said Luke, knowing full well what the answer would be.

"Yes, do you know a Maxine Payne sir?"

"Ah yes," said Luke.

"Well, we have had a complaint that you have phoned her today at her work when she had instructed you by email not to contact her again. Is that correct, Sir?"

"Yes, but I was only trying to explain something to her. However, before you go any further, I have something for you to read. It'll give you a little bit more of an insight into my situation." With that Luke handed over the two copies of the summary his father had suggested writing.

"There's twelve full pages of information there, so it will take you a while to read through it. I am happy to sign them as a statement if you require it. In the meantime, I'll go and get you a tea or coffee each. Which do you prefer?" Both PC's asked for coffee with milk, no sugar.

Luke went through, spoke to Kim and explained "they're here because of all the things that have happened recently" said Luke, slightly tongue in cheek, worried that she might go a little ballistic.

"About time," said Kim.

"Can you make them two coffees with milk, no sugars? I need to go and get something," said Luke.

After a few minutes, Luke re-appeared with a tyre and sat in a chair close to the two PC's.

When it looked like both men had read the paper Luke had presented them, Luke said "As you can see, I have now identified the main guy involved but he has died of a heart attack. Believe it or not, I'm still getting suspicious people around me, watching my every move at times, mainly at night and in the mornings. If I go out of the house towards them, they invariably jump in the car and drive away."

PC Robertson said "I see you say that you pulled a knife on these two guys, just up the street here. We'll have to arrest you for that. You can't just do that sort of thing with the general public."

"You're right" said Luke "except for one fundamental flaw in your case."

"Oh, what's that then?" asked PC Robertson.

"Well," said Luke, "if those really were just genuinely innocent members of the public, what would they have done?" The two PC's looked blankly at Luke, then PC Allan shook his head and lifted his shoulders as if prompting Luke to give the answer as quickly as possible.

Luke continued "If they really were just innocent members of the public, the first thing they would have done after I left, would have been to phone the Police and say "we've just had a "nutter" pull a knife on us and dare us by his body language to step out of the car. Furthermore, we know which house he went into, so you can go and arrest him." "But that didn't happen though, did it?" continued Luke.

The two PC's shook their heads in unison. "No, it didn't" said PC Robertson. Luke continued "I've got this tyre here to show you one of the drill bits still in it. Look, that drill bit is about six inches or more long. That was a rear tyre, and the bit was placed well in towards the inner edge as you can see. That was so I couldn't see it."

"Yes, you're lucky it wasn't a front tyre, you would almost certainly have crashed then," said PC Allan.

"I believe the farm shed I saw these guys in, burned down a couple of days after I was there. Suspicious, eh?" said Luke.

"Absolutely" said PC Robertson.

"If things are becoming that bad" said PC Robertson, "we could take you in under protective custody."

"Well, the thing is, although I know some of whom these guys are, we have no proof that they were disposing of a body," said Luke. "Or indeed what they were doing that night" continued Luke. "Yes, we could surmise, but that's all. You couldn't look after me for years to come and that wouldn't be much of an existence. Luckily, I have been well trained by being the son of a

Policeman in Northern Ireland. Objective suspicion is completely ground into me now, it's an integral part of my character. If there's something going on, it would be truly rare for me to miss it. I'm quite capable of going into immediate fight mode if I need to. I can handle myself quite well. If they make a single half second mistake, they will pay for it."

"How regularly do these guys appear?" asked PC Robertson.

"Well, they seem to be quiet for a month or two and then new suspicious guys appear, and it starts over, until it's obvious I have noticed their activity. Then they disappear for another month or two."

"I didn't know your father had been in the Police," said PC Allan.

"Yes, he rose to Chief Superintendent. Anyway, if there is any more trouble, hopefully they'll make a mistake. We only need the one mistake and justice will be served on them, like a tonne of bricks from a great height, don't you think," said Luke.

"Agreed" said PC Robertson. "We'll take this statement with us, if that's alright."

"That's ok by me," said Luke. "I can sign it for you" said Luke, before doing so.

The Policemen stood up. "Oh, by the way, don't contact Maxine Payne again or we'll have to come around to see you. None of us want that."

"Alright, that's not a problem," said Luke. At that, the two Policemen left and jumped into their squad car, driving away into the darkness. "What a bitch that Maxine is" thought Luke.

---

There were no subsequent visits from the Police, no requests for further information, nothing at all. Luke began to wonder if they had done nothing about his information or decided to merely put it to bed. Perhaps they were going to wait and see what develops.

A week or two later, Luke got a phone call from a detective who said he wanted to ask some further questions. An appointment was made for two murder squad officers to come around two days later.

The officers duly arrived, and they went over the details once again. Luke suggested that there may have been some link to the body that had been found in Central Scotland. Luke asked, "was that body cut up and placed in several bags or complete".

"We can't discuss the details of ongoing cases, Sir. Sorry." At the end of the meeting, one of the officers announced "If we don't know who the people were, up in the Glen that night, it's going to be difficult to progress this inquiry. But thank you for your help in the meantime."

"Yes, well I'm at a loss to know who the men were as well" said Luke "But if they make a mistake monitoring me, then we'll maybe find out."

"Just be careful, Sir. If they are gangland types, they could well be very dangerous," said the officer.

"Oh, I'm fully aware of that," said Luke. With that they jumped into their car and were gone.

---

A few days later, the phone rang. It was a detective from the murder squad. He said "thanks for your help the other day. We just need to ask you one key question."

"Okay" said Luke "ask away."

"Right Luke, when you were watching these guys putting the heavy bags in the car, did you actually see them putting them into the car boot?" he asked.

Luke winced heavily and knew that the truth wasn't going to be of help to the case.

"Oh, of all the things you could have asked me. In all honesty the car boot was open away from me and it was also dark. I watched them carrying the bags directly to the boot, but once they reached it, they were hidden by the body of the car and the boot door. I heard the bags being dropped into the boot, but I cannot honestly say that I actually witnessed them placing them in, because they were in the dark and the open boot blocked me anyway, even if the light had been perfect. There was though only a second or two between me seeing them and the noise of the bags being dropped in the boot."

"But you definitely didn't observe them dropping the bags in the boot?"

"Well, no" replied Luke "but I don't think them being in a blind spot makes much difference, as that's obviously what you're thinking, isn't it?" asked Luke.

"A good Barrister would get them off because of that little gap in your observation" replied the detective.

“He’d need to be a fantastic Barrister to do that” replied Luke. “I’m quite sure I could give a reasonable case against any Barrister” continued Luke.

“Maybe” said the detective “but efficient Barristers are out there and so we won’t be able to take your observations any further for now. Thanks for letting us know about it anyway.” With that the detective said goodbye and hung up.

“Shit” said Luke “it might not be able to help you murder squad guys anymore, but these guys are still trying to top me. If they knew about this, they’d be in the pub all night celebrating. In the meantime, I’m still going to be their number one target. Fucking great! Fuuuuuck! I wish now I’d just kept my big mouth shut.” Luke was in no doubt that it wasn’t over for him yet, not by a long way. That realisation showed in his face. However, he wouldn’t be putting it out to anyone.

## Chapter Twelve – The Realisation

By now, finances were becoming hard, and Luke was no longer making a reliable income. Luke found this even more stressful than the threat of violence or attempted intimidation, but in combination, the two acted like catalysts, hyping up the stress levels more than the sum of both added together. The first signs of marital problems began to show and Luke was short and cantankerous with his kids.

After many job applications, Luke finally secured a minimum wage job which at least helped to pay off the bills. The job was reliable if somewhat low income but after a couple of months Luke took a phone call from an ex-competitor in his old employment field who knew Luke very well. He had been promoted to a manager and had a member of staff off on long term sick, but it was an important area, so he needed it covered by a locum. The job was only for three months but the rate of pay was four times his current salary, so the three months work would bring in as much money as working for one year in his current job. Luke contemplated this offer, but within ten seconds he informed Graeme that he would be happy to take up his offer of employment. Graeme had been on a level footing with Luke when he was out in his Area Managers job, but with a competitor company. Graeme knew Luke was a safe pair of hands and that is why he approached him. At the time, Luke thought "I'm back. I'll be able to get back in with the crowd again and earn real money again."

Luke completed the three months commission and was given an excellent reference. This again made Luke think he would be back to his old line of work, and it would be happy days. But in fact, all that happened was that despite applying for numerous jobs in his old field, he still didn't get anywhere. He was blacklisted and he was 100% certain of the fact, but with zero percentage tangible proof, other than historical assessment. He also wasn't quite sure why either, as all he had done was defend himself when he had been bullied all those years ago.

After this time interval, Luke noticed yet more activity with people watching him. He saw a guy taking up position in a car a hundred yards up the road from him. He noticed he was still there some twenty minutes later. Luke didn't care about being cautious and proceeded to march straight up to the car to find out who this man was, but the man jumped out of the car and simply started to walk away. Luke thought he had maybe made a wrong assessment and stopped. However, two days later, the same car was parked with the boot towards Luke's house and the same man was out of the car, standing sideways on to Luke, just to the front of the car. The boot was raised so the number plate couldn't be seen. Again, Luke's suspicions were raised, and he started to walk towards the man. This unknown man, who was standing at ninety degrees to Luke about eighty yards uphill, just closed the boot, jumped into the car, and quickly drove away, before Luke could reach him. Luke was becoming very agitated with this repeating situation.

Luke wanted to know why his information had been blatantly disregarded by the Police, so he asked to see the local senior detective, DCI John Wishaw. Before he did that, he supplied details of the bridge incident and the recapturing of the escaped prisoner in written form to the officer by email. This was so that the officer would realise he wasn't dealing with a punter suffering from an over-active imagination or paranoia. When he went in to see the detective, he raised the subject of the bridge incident and asked, "I presume they were able to confirm that was a terrorist team on the bridge?"

"Yes, they did" but quickly realising he shouldn't have said that he added "but if you tell anyone I said it, I will deny it."

DCI Wishaw then continued "I believe you believe you have some information which might help in a murder case. Which one do you mean, as there are 14 men in the local area that have just gone missing, there one day and gone the next, with no obvious reason for disappearing." That number seemed large to Luke as it was only a moderate sized town.

Luke then told him about his history and experiences with Callum Mallachy and how Callum had followed him around locally, even on a flight down to Stansted. Luke told the detective that he believed there may be a connection between Callum Mallachy and the death of Andrew Coyne. It was possible that Andrew Coyne had approached Callum Mallachy to have the endearing Terence Argyle killed. This was because Terence Argyle had been parasitizing Andrew Coyne for protection money, which was crippling his financial position. Terence Argyle was a very nasty piece of work indeed and had poured boiling water over victims as well as tried to scoop out an eyeball with a spoon. Even hardened gangsters disliked Terence and would not trust him to any extent at all. Callum had taken the money for doing the assassination but in the classic con, had simply not bothered and kept the money.

Luke suggested that Andrew Coyne may have tried to demand his money back, that it may not have gone well and Callum with his cronies had stabbed him to death. The detective took notes about Luke's suggestion of a possible murder motive.

"First though, I need to be sure about your ability to identify Callum," said the DCI. He called in a woman constable and asked her to produce a photo line-up. Ten minutes later she came back in and handed the print sheet to DCI Wishaw. He in turn presented it to Luke and said, "now point out Callum Malachy please".

Luke looked at the 16 men in the photographs, but without even noticing the other fifteen men, Luke was drawn in like a powerful magnet to the picture of Callum with a cold shiver. He pointed to Callum within two seconds of being asked.

"Well," said DCI Wishaw "you certainly nailed that without any hesitation at all." He continued "Ok, I will ask some further questions and come back to you very soon."

With the meeting over, Luke was seen out of the Police Station by DCI Wishaw who shook his hand, thanked him, and said goodbye.

A few days later a letter arrived for Luke. It was from the Police, and it basically said thanks for speaking to letting us know your thoughts, but we can confirm that we know that Andrew Coyne was not killed by Callum Mallachy. It went on to say that they could not discuss how they knew this but that was the situation. This left Luke thinking "I wonder if they don't even believe me? There were all the factors involved to make a perfect motive for a murder." However, after a period of contemplation, Luke decided that surely the Police wouldn't lie.

So as far as Luke was concerned, then either he had got it completely wrong with the person or there was something very weird going on and what he had witnessed up the glen was a totally innocent situation.

But what about the drill bits in the car tyres, the rock that had smashed his sunroof to smithereens, not to mention the guys that appeared to be wanting to get out of their car at him? Had he completely misread that? How could he have been so wrong when he had been so right about so many other crimes that he had reported before to the Police?

Luke was suffering serious stress levels from all of this, his inability to get a long term or permanent decent paying job whilst his own little business was barely bringing any income, the fact that the police seemed to be pooh-poohing his suggestions, the fact that his marriage was now under serious strain and that nothing seemed to be going right and that there were no answers forthcoming or even ideas as to how to proceed to wriggle out of his hell hole scenario. His head felt like it might explode. What was he to do?

Luke still felt that the fact that he had received an excellent reference from the locum job meant surely that his blacklisting would be over. Sense told him, it would be just a matter of the next suitable job role and things would return to normal. But it was not to be. Luke completed application after application over the following weeks but all in vain. Luke became more and more depressed and was beginning to see how people could completely lose hope and commit to the final act - suicide. But he wasn't quite at that point yet.

After all, enemies wanted him dead anyway and suicide would be just helping that person's cause. Anger is a great motivator to bring back determination, the grit one needs to get through uncharted waters, regardless of the obstacles, the adversity or angst.

Luke decided the only way to sort this was to grab the bull by the horns. He phoned the Human Resources officers in his original company that he had had the problem with years before. When they answered, he explained who he was and that he needed to ask them why they were making life so difficult for him by keeping him out of a job. Luke was taken aback that at least two of them cheered loudly when he said that. "Yes" Luke said "we had fallen out and I had moved on to pastures new, but I had largely forgotten about the treachery and the underhand tactics employed by your company. I feel that I had been wronged severely by you as a company and that I could have had some people, both within the company and outside of it, up on police charges. Indeed, even more evidence came to the fore after I had departed from you. So why are you being so vindictive?" This query produced a wheeze of derision and Luke became fully aware that his effort had cut no ice at all. Luke thought their persistent hatred for him was strange if not bordering on beyond obsessive. Were they uncontrollably lusting to successfully crush him like a worm under an oversized boot. This meant he would have to explain more about what had really happened to him, than he wished to!

The thought of trying to explain a sufficient outline of his story to civilian office workers, who were guaranteed to be almost completely naïve about serious organised crime, made Luke wince. He had tried it before with a street wise, battle-hardened Police Sergeant and he had seen the results of that.

Luke took a deep breath and said "Look, you guys have no idea of what was really happening to me at the time I left the company".

"Oh yeah, what was that" came the sneering reply from the HR officer, which was ended with a snort so forceful, Luke almost expected phlegm to come flying out of his phone and land with a splat on the side of his face. Luke held his phone a few inches further from his face and frowned in a bemused way at the phone, disbelieving the vitriol he was receiving from the other end.

"Right, I'll tell you then what really was happening. I had witnessed what I believed to have been two guys cutting up and disposing of a body" said Luke.

"Oh really" said the HR Officer with a slightly confused tone mixed with disbelief.

"And like you" Luke continued "the Police didn't believe me. In fact, the imbecilic Policeman inferred he would have me sectioned if I made anymore claims like that. I then went on to receive attempted intimidation, ambushes, drill bits in my tyres and even a half brick sized rock chucked at my car which smashed the sunroof whilst travelling down the A9.  I was on my own until several years later when the facts became irrefutable. So, you can understand I was set to high alert, under exceptional stress and in true battle mode. Meantime you guys were giving me a hard time during this period. And you didn't seem to like the fact that I defended myself fairly well."

The HR Officer seemed dumb struck. Eventually after a few seconds of befuddled thought, he spluttered out "I find what you're saying a bit hard to believe."

"Alright" said Luke, "but if you want to check my car reports which you should still have, you'll see that I had several punctures all within a short time period and suffered a smashed sunroof which required replacing."

"Oh, I see" came the concerned reply, as this mental picture had been totally outside of his expectations, and he wasn't quite sure how to handle this situation.

Luke butted in "In fact I still have a good mind to sue the Police for blatant incompetence. This whole situation would not look good for them, at all."

"Well, true" said the HR Officer "if indeed, what you're saying is the truth."

"So, what do you want us to do?" said the HR Officer.

"Well, for one thing you can stop blocking me from getting a job, I want to be able to discuss what happened in the past whilst in your employment and I want you to confirm that that is ok by a legal letter," said Luke. "That's not unreasonable, is it?" asked Luke.

The HR Officer hesitated for a few seconds and said, "You can do whatever you want!" He sounded a lot meeker now, without the prickly, condescending and somewhat belligerent tone that he had previously adopted.

"Can I get that in writing," said Luke.

"You can do what you want, Luke" repeated the HR Officer.

"Well good" said Luke "but I will expect a confirmation of that in writing in the next week or so."

Luke knew that the information had been entirely unexpected by the HR Officer, but he doubted if the HR Officer would honour the written confirmation to him.

As the weeks past, no confirmation letter came through and Luke realised they had either decided they had too much to lose by sanctioning the request or that they had been presented with a very good con.

For his part, Luke still couldn't understand why there had been so much vitriol directed at him. Surely, people would leave companies under a bit of a cloud all the time, but they wouldn't receive the level of acrimony that Luke had experienced.

To keep his spirits up, Luke had been going to the Gym for regular circuits and other training classes. These classes were busy, challenging, and good fun, even though they were exhausting at the time of exercising. There was also a chance to meet new people and form friendships. This made the classes quite social events as well. There were people of all ages, shapes, sizes and fitness levels. One young lady in her twenties sometimes joined the classes and became chatty with Luke. Luke just thought she probably had a fairly friendly nature and didn't think much else about it. She was always curious as to what Luke had been up to and she took an interest in his activities. Luke was outgoing in nature anyway and liked to chat and joke with people, so he responded quite positively to her friendly banter. She called herself Charlene and Luke never suspected anything suspicious at all, even after she requested to become a friend of his on Facebook.

Luke was unaware of it but one of the gang members had asked her to form a friendship with him and keep them up to date on anything of interest that Luke might divulge. This would ensure that if he was starting to divulge any details about his experience, they would hear about it quickly.

## Chapter Thirteen – The Low Point

Luke did have a useful friend though. He was a Chief Inspector in a specialized Police force but not based locally. Fergus McIntyre had gone for promotion in another division of Police work but had chosen to continue living where he had been before, as his kids were still at school. It just meant he sometimes had to stay away from home for a few days at a time. Because all their kids had been at the same school and formed friendships, Luke and his wife had become friendly with Fergus and his wife. Fergus proved to be a useful contact. Luke had explained his situation one night and the inevitable happened. Fergus found it hard to believe. This was frustrating enough for Luke but when Fergus told him a couple of weeks later that the local Police were still not entirely sure whether Luke had an overactive imagination or not, Luke just found the whole situation very deflating. What would Luke have to do to make them realise he was being entirely honest, that he had had several very close calls. Perhaps they were waiting until he had either died or disappeared, so that they could then be absolutely certain. This left Luke feeling enraged by the seeming incompetence of the Police.

However, Fergus did keep an open mind about the subject. He did admit that there were a lot of signs that Luke may have been justified with his suspicions. Fergus did say that the latest trend is for people to just disappear. This was less messy for gangsters as there were no forensic clues left as in a shooting or stabbing. Often, no dead body would even be found. They would observe the targets movements for months sometimes to find out where they could overcome an unlucky victim and bundle him away to deal with as they wished. Fergus knew also that Luke had picked up on a lot of circumstantial evidence that he had been monitored in the past few months, so he warned him to be very vigilant.

Because of this, Luke had even considered suing the Police, but Luke's father was strongly against it, saying the Police would only discredit him in court, leaving Luke even more disillusioned and angrier than before. Reluctantly, Luke agreed to not go down that road. His father was convinced that a mistake would be made by the gangsters, vindicating him.

Luke thought to himself "what if I make the first mistake, I could end up dead?" He knew that he would just have to become used to having to be very aware all the time and to keep a lookout for the slightest clues. The stress from this was extraordinary but the biggest stress factor on Luke was his lack of money caused by his previous employers blocking him from making a proper living. The jobs Luke was able to acquire were usually minimum wage and only a limited number of hours per week.

Despite having virtually no money, like everyone else, regardless of their financial situation, Luke got his fair share of scam phone calls. Luke enjoyed playing these highly immoral criminals, who invariably were controlled by organised criminal gangs, misleading them into thinking they had an easy target on the other end of the phone.

"Is that Mr. Walk, eh Mr Walker?" would invariably be the opening line with uncertainty about the exact name. "Speaking" would be Luke's response. "My name is Fassin and I work with Microsoft" was the reply."

"Oh, you know that's brilliant, can you believe I was just wanting to phone your company because I'm having a problem with my computer. Now isn't this just so fortuitous that you phoned," said Luke.

"Oh really" came the delighted answer "well that is good news, because I will be able to fix it for you. What is the problem with your computer, Mr Walk?"

"Oh, you are so kind to help me out" said Luke pulling a mock but unobserved, delighted face "my computer seems to be running so slow at the moment. I'm absolutely sure there is some setting wrong with it."

"Well let's see if we can fix it for you. Are you beside your computer now?" asked Fassin.

"Yes" said Luke.

"Well, can you go to the start button and click it. You should see a settings symbol appear."

Luke interjected "If I just allow you to take over the computer from your side, would that help you sort out the problem more easily?"

"Why yes, it would. That would be perfect. We'll just do that Mr Walk."

"So where are you right now" asked Luke throwing in a seemingly disarming question. Silence.

Luke's tone changed "well no, we definitely won't be doing that. You must think I have just arrived from the planet Zarkon. I have better things to do than help you scam merchants. Goodbye. Oh and don't call again."

As Luke was in the process of ending the call all he could hear was a very loud "Fuck you." just as he clicked off.

"Oooooh, manners indeed" said Luke, pulling a face of mock shock. But he was maybe just a little too cocky for his own good.

On one occasion that normally impenetrable, suspicious barrier did get infiltrated.

"Hello, is that Mr. Walker" asked a female Glaswegian voice.

"Yes, indeed," said Luke.

"Mr. Walker, my name is Sharon and I've been asked to do some research on local health issues. Would you mind answering some health questions, Mr. Walker?"

Luke thought for a moment and couldn't see any potential scam here, so he answered "Yes, that should be ok."

"And do you mind doing that just now? It would be very helpful if you could" said Sharon politely, who wisely didn't present the option of some other time, which would probably have resulted in a polite permanent postponement.

"Yes, well ok, I can spare a few minutes" said Luke.

"Thank you," said Sharon. "In that case, can I ask if you use any painkillers or drugs for pain relief?"

"No, not normally" said Luke "unless I have a bad headache or some other problem, but that's quite rare as I am relatively healthy normally."

"Do you have any joint pains at all" asked Sharon.

"No, except for my shoulder bone which became detached when four huge heffalumps jumped on me during a rugby match on hard ground. It pops out sometimes and can be very painful then," said Luke.

"Oh, that's interesting" said Sharon "and do you need painkillers for that?"

"Well, it does hurt a lot but no, I never use any painkillers for it" said Luke.

"And do you think you ever will" asked Sharon.

"Well, no, never, at least as long as I can" said Luke.

"Thank you for your help," said Sharon.

Suddenly a thought came to her "Oh, before you go, I did mean to ask, do you ever suffer from blood clots?" asked Sharon.

"No, not to date," said Luke. Then suspicion rushed into Luke's head. "Why did you just suddenly change direction and ask me that?"

Click. Sharon had hung up straight away. Luke, who was still on the phone shouted at himself "Oh, you complete dickhead. You're a fucking, brainless idiot."

Luke knew that they must have worked out a time and place that they could grab him. He knew that they were liable to abduct him and give him a heavy beating to ensure he would be too shocked to dare give evidence to the Police. The reason the question was asked about blood clots was to work out the likelihood of him having a stroke or dying either during or soon after the beating. They had phoned to find out as it looked like the beating may be imminent. Luke though had lost faith in the

Police and didn't say anything to them about the phone call. He knew he would have to stay ultra-alert for the next month or two or more.

The next day, Luke noticed the Police travelling up and down his street at least six times in cars and vans. Before that, it would be exceptional to see one Police car in a month. Luke realised the Police had obviously been listening in on the conversation but were now effectively telling the gangsters, by going up and down the street, they were aware and ready to intervene at any time. Despite the fact, that the Police had been listening in on the phone call, Luke was glad, as it confirmed to the Police that he really wasn't just making it up. All those unfortunate accidents were planned. Luke really had been spot on, about his claims of attempted ambushes and near accidents as attempts to silence him.

The fact remained that Luke was still a target for these gangsters, and he knew it. This did cause Luke a great deal of stress, but the lack of money caused him even more stress. Luke had tried dabbling in various photographic services, but the onset of digital technology was making professional photographers effectively redundant. Crunch time came a week or two later when he totalled up his accounts and realised, he had no more than five pounds in his bank accounts. He would either have to declare bankruptcy or make some dramatic changes very soon. He didn't have even enough money for one fish supper and with barely any money expected in from his business, that situation was hardly going to change, except for the worse. It was time for a re-think of his situation.

Within a few days he had been to see the Bank Manager and re-mortgaged his house to the tune of £40,000. This really set Luke back as he thought he had cleared the mortgage and could take a more relaxed view of his finances, but that was not to be. Unfortunately for Luke, the poor monetary situation meant even more stresses on his marriage. The cracks had been expanding for a while but now they were opening faster than a Mexican Daisy in bright sunlight.

Put all these stresses together - having to be ultra-alert all the time to avoid being badly beaten up or murdered, having no worthy income stream and no prospect of help, having to take on a loan just to keep his head above water and then to top it all, his marriage breaking down, meant Luke was close to surrendering to the pressure. He would feel like bursting into tears at the slightest, normal life obstacle being thrown in his way. He began to consider suicide as an option, one possible answer to his situation. But something twigged in Luke that that was not going to be the answer. He needed to fight back, stay absolutely determined to overcome the odds against him and to fight with guile. If he hadn't taken that attitude, then his world would have just completely crumbled to dust. It was going to be a long hard road to recovery, but he had no choice. It was do or die.

A week later, Luke's wife declared she was leaving him and she took the kids with her as well. She left him to look after his own finances as best he could. When life finds you vulnerable and down, it always takes as many extra kicks at you as it can, whilst you are on the ground.

## Chapter Fourteen – Between the Rock and a Hard Place.

Luke had many things to unravel in his life, but one of the first was going to be why all this had happened in the first place. Luke felt that Callum Mallachy had to be the main player in the events to date, but if the Police had said Luke's suggestion of the murder victim was wrong, then who had been disposed of that night, if indeed Luke was even right about there being a victim in the first place. Did he believe the Police knew the answer? No, was the only conclusion Luke could come to! Would there be any convictions involved? Unlikely, as good barristers would swing the jury's thoughts towards doubt. The only way a conviction may have been likely was if some attempt was made to abduct or kill Luke and he managed to come out best in the outcome. Luke had to remain alert to that possibility, but he needed to avoid that at all costs. If they just gave up trying to get at Luke, then the certainty was nothing would happen. From his point of view though, Luke wanted closure. That somewhat irrational desire might still see Luke in very deep water yet.

Callum Mallachy was dead but the fact that there was continued activity against Luke, meant the other members of the gangland still felt threatened, so what could have been the actual situation. Luke just didn't know. He started to research Callum using books and the internet. He discovered that Callum had a considerable web of intrigue and of deceit. He had had plenty of allies but even more enemies. One of his greatest allies was a young man called Frank McIntosh who had been entrusted with sourcing drugs from North Africa, picking them up in Spain and delivering them to Amsterdam, where the goods were canned before being transported over to Scotland.

Frank was a ruthless, yet affable young man but totally devoid of morality and indeed conscience. He was very much a ladies' man with a very high success rate due to his good looks. But he was somewhat over-confident of his abilities to think on his feet and extricate himself out of a tight situation. One night he escorted a young lady home to her flat in a part of Glasgow he would normally avoid. After seeing her home and enjoying her company for an hour and a half, he started walking home but was recognised by two rival gangster members standing outside a bar. One guy grabbed him from behind, whilst his accomplice stabbed Frank multiple times in the chest. It was typical of so many street murders, cowardly and poorly thought out regarding the consequences. Frank had very little chance, as he didn't recognise them as a serious threat until too late. The murdering pair ran away from Franks' bleeding corpse but with zero plan as to how to minimise the risk of gangland retribution or how to evade the grip of the law. It would have been better for them if the law had caught up with them. As it was, there had been two unobserved witnesses close by who had recognised the men.

Callum Mallachy had both trusted and personally liked Frank. He had taken Frank under his wing as a dependable guy to work with. When told the news about Frank, he became incandescent with rage and vowed gangland justice against the two perpetrators.

Callum's henchmen went a hunting and made a few enquiries. It wasn't long before the two men were being asked about Frank and after some very rough treatment, were executed. The bodies were put into a massive bag each and placed in a huge freezer to await the next stage in the gruesome process.

All this though was not how it was being reported in the news. There was virtually no news on the circumstances, except that the two men involved in the murder had disappeared and were still on the run. The Police though had their informants and had been told by two sources, the details of what they had heard in the grapevine.

It was Fergus who had discretely told Luke as he was concerned about Luke's mental health and he felt it was better if he knew. The Police hadn't accepted it as 100% certain, because you can never put complete trust in men who made a living from dishonesty and crime.

A few days later, Luke put it to the Police that he believed the two runaway men, may have been in the huge bags he witnessed being carried into the farm shed. Unlike after the previous suggestion, this time he got nothing back from the Police at all, neither a confirmation nor a denial. Luke could only take this as a confirmation, or as close as he was going to get from the Police. It looked like that was as far as it was going to go. Indeed, now that Luke had accepted in his own mind what was almost certain to have happened that night, he proved to be content to leave it at that.

There was just one problem, he found that it looked like he was being monitored again. A car was parking close to his house with a man inside it at night and he would still be there in the morning when Luke got up. After seeing this several times in a row, he tried to go out of his house, but as soon as the curtains opened, the man took off in his car. Then another person took up a position up the road. This time it was a woman, which Luke didn't really expect but when Luke went to check her out, she jumped out of the car and walked away. Luke was still nursing a leg wound from tripping on tree roots and was in no state to pursue at speed, so he put it down to an overactive imagination. The next day though, there she was again. Realising she had been spotted, she quickly reversed her car and drove off. Another man was turning up regularly by walking past the house. Luke tried calling at him and asked him to stop but he just kept going. Again and again, he would turn up and always walked on, when requested to stop. Luke's leg injury meant he was not able to pursue him on foot.

It was time to speak with Fergus again. On being told the details, Fergus opened up a bit more with Luke. "This is not good news, Luke", said Fergus, "in the recent years, as I've told you before, the gangland strategy has been to monitor people often for months to pinpoint a weak point in the victim's timetable. Then pounce, a bang over the head, a quick bundling into a van or car and away they go. You really don't want to know the consequences from there."

"Oh, I am only too aware" said Luke sighing long and deep.

"Luke, I will make a phone call or two for you. In the meantime, stay as alert as you've been. Luckily, you are probably the most aware person I have ever known. Your schooling by the Northern Ireland troubles has put you in good stead for this situation," said Fergus.

"It was that that got me in this mess in the first place" replied Luke.

"Well true" said Fergus "just bear with me a few days and I'll get something organised. I better go now; my wife will be thinking I'm seeing some fancy woman."

"Quite Fergus, thanks for coming around. See you soon." Luke saw Fergus out, locked all the doors and went to his icy bed.

Luke felt so alone, now that his wife had moved out with his kids. Before turning over to go to sleep, he checked his long torch was right beside him and his rock chisel was positioned right where he could find it immediately, even in complete darkness. A gruesome tool but Luke felt he would rather use it than be killed because of being inadequately armed.

A few days later, Luke received a phone call. "Hello" said Luke. "Mr Walker" asked a man. "Speaking" replied Luke. "This is Detective Inspector Andy Brough. I wonder if I could ask you to meet me at the local Police Station. Nothing to worry about, just we've been speaking with Fergus McIntyre and he asked us to have a word with you. I would come to your house, but I think it may be better if you came to the station."

"No problem" said Luke "when would you want me to come around?"

"How about this afternoon, if that suits you about 3.30pm?" said DI Brough.

"Yeah ok" said Luke "I'll see you then."

Just five minutes before the appointed time, Luke turned up at the Police Station reception desk. An overweight middle-aged Sergeant greeted him "How can I help you sir?"

"I'm here to see Detective Inspector Andy Brough."

"Is he expecting you, Sir?" asked the Sarge. There was only one other person in the waiting room, a rosy cheeked thirty plus aged woman, wearing tight jeans and with a snotty nosed toddler. She looked as hard as nails with a somewhat vitriolic look about her. Luke quickly glanced at her to check whether she could be a risk. As Luke was about to answer the Sergeant, she glanced up at him and studied him for a second or two. Looking back at the Sarge he answered “Yes, absolutely.”

“I’ll just let him know you’re here” said the Sarge “take a seat” indicating the plastic seats which were beside the woman with the child.

Luke sat down two seats away from the woman. The toddler gazed up at Luke and then pressed his face into his mothers’ leg jeans, rubbing his snotty nose against three inches of her leg.

Luke nodded at her and said “the wee man got a cold, has he?” She grabbed a handkerchief and wiped his nose and her leg, then turned and said “Yes, he’s my sister’s son. I looked after him today, but I need to go to work myself now.”

“So, you’re handing him over to the Police” said Luke with a puzzled look.

“No, no, my sister is a policewoman. She’s coming off duty now and I’m just going to hand him over, so I can get to work quicker.”

“Oh, I see” said Luke, rolling his eyes at his own stupidity.

Just then, DI Brough came through the security door. “Luke Walker?” asked DI Brough.

“Yes” said Luke. “DI Brough” introduced himself to Luke and pointed his hand towards Luke. They shook hands. DI Brough indicated to him to go to the security door, he re-opened the door and they both went up two floors to his office. “Take a seat” said DI Brough, indicating the spare seat opposite his desk.

"Right, I'll come straight to the point, Mr Walker, we're aware that you may be being subjected to surveillance, is that correct?"

"Well, I strongly believe so, but I can, on very rare occasions get it wrong," said Luke.

"Well, we don't want to get it wrong as that could have very serious consequences," said DI Brough. "I'm informed you're from a Police family in Northern Ireland" asked DI Brough.

"That's right," said Luke. "Well, you'll be aware that sometimes people receive 24 hour protection but that's very unusual" said DI Brough.

"Yes" agreed Luke, nodding his head, but with a furrowed brow, wondered to himself where the conversation was going.

"In other situations, potential victims can agree to become "bait" to bring out the bad boys, but that is a dangerous game," said DI Brough.

"Yes" said Luke, this time without nodding his head, because by now, he really was wondering what was going to be suggested after the last statement.

"Look, I don't know any easy way to put this to you, but do you mind if we monitor where you are by putting a tracker device inside your car?" asked DI Brough. "That will help us quickly locate you if you're away from home," said DI Brough.

"Obviously you're expecting me to get into some sort of difficulty?" asked Luke.

"Well hopefully not, Mr Walker" said DI Brough, "but just in case."

"Well, I suppose it does make sense" said Luke, who suddenly felt even more insecure, even though he was fully aware of the precariousness of his situation.

"Yes, I think your right there, Mr Walker" replied DI Brough, "I'll give you my card and feel free to get in touch if you have any concerns."

"What, even about my mortgage payments" joked Luke who raised a half-hearted smile.

"Well, no, you might be best to seek advice from your Mortgage Supplier on that subject. But anything relating to Police matters, please don't hesitate to phone me." "Alright, fair enough" said Luke. DI Brough took him downstairs to the reception room and they said goodbye.

The next evening, a landline phone rang loudly in a house living room. "Hello" said Luke. "Hi Luke, this is Paul from the Bat Surveying Group. How are you doing, Luke? We haven't spoken for a while." Paul had been a long-standing friend of Luke's, as they had played rugby together, but they also shared a deep interest in wildlife.

"I'm fine, how are you?"

"I'm good" said Paul "I wonder if I could ask you for a little favour? You know that old disused railway tunnel about eight miles south of you, the one you surveyed for us a few years ago?"

"Yes, indeed I do. It's very long, creepy with a long bend in it, and its completely dark away from the entrances. It gives me the jitters a bit, that tunnel."

"How long is it?" asked Paul. "It must be about a mile long, at the very least I would say, Paul."

"So how long did it take you to survey it the last time?"

"It takes about two hours minimum to do it properly. There's never been bats found in it though. Do you really think it's worth monitoring, Paul?" asked Luke with the slightest hint that he really thought it would be a waste of time.

Ignoring Luke's unreciprocated enthusiasm, Paul continued "well yes, there's an old disused railway tunnel in Fife which was never used. Then suddenly a roost moved in with nearly 300 bats only two years ago."

"Were they just one species?" asked Luke.

"Yes, just Pipistrelles. But in your case you never know. There could be Long eared bats, Natterers or Daubentons" said Paul.

"I've never found a Daubentons roost, so that would be nice" said Luke, slowly beginning to warm to the idea of doing the survey.

"So would you be ok to go through the tunnel in the next two weeks sometime?" asked Paul "it might be third time lucky for all of us. And if you do find Daubentons, I'll want to hear about it the same night. There's suitable river habitat close to the tunnel."

"Yes, ok Paul" said Luke still less than enthusiastically. "What about the other tunnel a mile further down the line" Luke asked, rolling his eyes, unseen on the phone and grimacing as he realised, he might have just foolishly volunteered to do more than he wanted to do, but in a tone suggesting he should ask, if only out of courtesy.

"I've asked George to do it, so you don't need to do that one," said Paul.

"Oh, and make sure you tell the wife where you're going that night, just in case you run into difficulty," said Paul.

"My wife and I separated about nine months ago," said Luke.

"Oh, I'm sorry to hear that, Luke," said Paul.

After a few seconds of embarrassed silence, Luke lightened the conversation. "Why, .....do you think I will need to take out bogeyman insurance before I go?" said Luke jokingly.

"No, but there have been reports of a big black cat that's been seen in that area."

"Really?" asked Luke

"How long have there been reports like that?"

"Five years or so."

"And you're only telling me this now!" said Luke.

"Well, even if it is real, it doesn't mean it's going to be a man-eating black leopard" said Paul jokingly, laughing at the other end of the phone "and anyway, why do you think I never do that tunnel?"

"Aye, very funny," said Luke.

"Oh, and just before I go" said Paul "is your life insurance sum adequate and fully up to date?"

"Thanks for your concerns, Paul". "Mmmm, it's always lovely talking with you, Paul" said Luke, now expressing his opinion in a slightly bemused tone.

Paul continued "Oh, and by the way, if that Leopard does bite or rip off one of your legs, you'll still be able to finish the survey, won't you. I mean you can hop, can't you?"

"Yes of course. I'll take a couple of litres of blood just in case I need a quick on the spot, self-administered, transfusion. But I'll let you know if I think I have found any Daubentons, Paul, even if I have given myself a blood transfusion."

"Aye, you should be okay" said Paul, "and as far as I am aware vampire bats haven't reached this part of the world either, at least probably not, despite climate change, as far as I'm aware. Mind you, if you do hear something land beside you in the dark and it runs up your remaining leg, I would swat it pretty quick. You will want to see a certain amount of benefit from your blood transfusion."

Both guys laughed at Luke's sarcastically toned response "Mmmm, Yes........I will. Thanks."

They knew each other well and understood the limits. There simply weren't any, as long as it was funny.

A few days later, Luke went to a gym circuits class. Whilst waiting for the class to start, Charlene, a young lady that Luke sometimes chatted to, came over to speak to Luke. "Hi Luke, how's things with you?" she said.

"All good" said Luke though in reality, it was far from how he was feeling.

"Have you been out to see any interesting wildlife recently" asked Charlene.

Luke always was pleasantly surprised that Charlene showed an interest in wildlife, as she never struck him as that type at all. X Factor or Love Island or similar programmes, but not wildlife. "No, not really" said Luke "but tomorrow evening, I'm going to an old disused railway tunnel about eight miles south of here to check if there are any bats living in it."

Charlene looked intrigued "how long a tunnel is it?"

"It's almost a mile long, Charlene" replied Luke.

"And you're going alone, through that" asked Charlene.

"Yes indeed. I've done it before, several times" said Luke "other than the odd bogeyman, man-eating leopards, claustrophobia, anxiety attacks, collapsing roofs, unseen piles of rocks or ill-timed heart attacks, there's nothing for me to be worried about," said Luke.

"Rather you, than me," said Charlene.

The class instructor intervened before anymore could be said "Right let's get everyone warmed up." The class all moved into position as the instructor started up the music and off they went for what proved to be an exhausting hours workout.

Later that evening, Charlene contacted her male friend who had asked her to report back on any interesting developments regarding Luke.

"Luke is apparently going to an old railway track tunnel tomorrow evening to check it out for bats," said Charlene.

"Is he indeed?" came the reply, "Did he say who he was going with?"

"Just himself" replied Charlene.

"Is he indeed" came the answer.

"Why do you want to know so much about Luke? He seems like a really nice guy, but at times he has a quiet sadness about him" asked Charlene.

Blanking the question, the caller asked, "why do you say he is sometimes sad?"

"Oh just, that's the way he comes across but usually when I talk to him, he seems to shake out of it" said Charlene.

Changing the subject again, "whereabouts is this tunnel, he was talking about?" asked her friend.

"He says it's about eight miles south of here" said Charlene.

"Alright, don't say anything to anybody else, do you understand?" said her friend.

"Like to who? Who else wants to know this sort of stuff?" said Charlene.

"Say nothing to no one" said her invisible friend in a mildly irritated way, oblivious of his grammatical error.

"Oh, alright. There's no need to get tetchy," said Charlene.

"Right, I'll speak to you sometime" said Charlene's friend.

At that, he hung up. Charlene, still holding onto the phone said "It's no bother. Thanks for your help, Charlene. It's no bother at all. Anytime." Her tone had more than a suggestion of sarcasm combined with annoyance. Suddenly a belated thought came to her, "I hope they're not going to do anything bad to Luke. I think he's quite a nice guy." Then her phone rang. It was a girlfriend, so all thoughts about Luke and the previous conversation just went straight out of her mind.

Early evening on the next day and Luke prepared himself for his little scheduled recce. He momentarily thought about the joking regarding the potential leopard which was etched into his brain but dismissed it as so unlikely that he didn't decide to take anything other than a huge Maglite metal torch. He put on his hill boots which had seen him through all sorts of terrain from wet boggy ground to slippery rock surfaces. Good strong boots are essential for country use, but the most important outstanding attribute of boots is their grip in slippery conditions. There are some well-known brands of boots which act like they have bars of soap on their soles. Luke had found this out to his cost in the past. The wrong boots, a slope and wetness underfoot and his feet disappeared into the air. That would be just embarrassing if on soft grass but on a hard, irregular, rocky seaweed and barnacle encrusted foreshore, it could be very damaging to a person and equipment.

It was a twenty-minute journey to the old railway line. Luke parked up off the road and walked up to the old track line. He followed the line until it went over a bridge above a river. Immediately after the bridge was a bare rock surface within which the line continued into the tunnel. The tunnel was at least ten metres high and the same wide. The first ten metres had dripping water falling from the roof, but after that it dried. The floor of the tunnel had grey gritty dust or bare rock. Whilst in the first lit part of the tunnel, Luke couldn't help himself but check for tracks in the dust. There was a line of fox prints but also two sets of human shoe prints which had crushed out over some of the fox prints. These looked quite fresh but didn't go very far in, before whoever it had been, both decided to turn back.

"No torch with them" thought Luke to himself, "they would have been unwilling to move into the blackening gloom." Luke had had no such reservations and had previously walked in without even using the torch, except to check sections of the roof for signs of bats. On this occasion, Luke had brought his binoculars, so he could look for bat shapes and check them with the main torch beam.

The tunnel followed a shallow arc which meant that the tunnel mouth became no longer visible after about three hundred metres and remained in total darkness for another five hundred metres until the other tunnel mouth came into view about four hundred metres away again. This lack of use of a torch had landed Luke in trouble previously as he had come across a heap of the floor dust and grit piled up to about waist height. He had tripped and fallen onto the heap, getting covered in the dust, but otherwise was none the worse for his minor accident, as he had only been walking at a slow but steady pace. However, Luke had taken a mental note as to the locations of these heaped dust, grit and rock debris piles to avoid making the same mistake again. There were also arc shaped inlaid cuttings, about eight foot high, four feet wide and four foot deep. These were to protect workmen on the lines when a train came along. During the days when the railway was operational, the workmen would necessarily quickly make their way to these shelters and stand in until the train had passed by.

Once Luke had gone ten metres into the tunnel, beyond the dripping roof part, he shook his head to get rid of two big cold globules of water that had annoyingly fallen from the roof onto his head with the second one rolling down the back of his neck. Luke uttered a "yuk" in disgust as the cold wet water drops rolled down the side of his face and down his neck. It was a warm and clear summer's evening outside the tunnel and the roof was visible for the first fifty metres from the entrance, so Luke began the inspection of the roof. On his previous visit last year, he had forgotten his binoculars, which meant, even with a good torch, it was sometimes possible to imagine a little odd-shaped extrusion to have possibly been a bat. This required extra viewing until Luke could be sure, one way or the other, as to whether it really was a bat or indeed a group of bats. Luke wanted to be less bothered by nagging doubt and by holding the binoculars with one hand and the torch with the other, he could obtain a clear if somewhat shaky view. However, it could be tiresome looking vertically up and he had three quarters of a mile or more of tunnel roof to check.

So onwards and upwards looking he progressed, stopping every five metres to make sure he didn't miss anything. As he reached about the three hundred metres mark, the light from the tunnel mouth disappeared altogether. He was now in complete darkness apart from his torch. Being summer, he had not really needed to use the torch for months and Luke had assumed that because the beam seemed ok on testing, that there would be no problem on the night. Luke carried on as quickly as he could.

Outside the tunnel, a mere five hundred metres away from Luke inside the tunnel, two dark Mercedes cars pulled up close to his parked car. There were three men in one car and two in the other. All the men got out and met between the two cars.

"It looks like we've got him" said one man in a broad Glaswegian accent as he glanced at Luke's car, which was parked beside their car, "he must be in the tunnel!" He continued "You two come down with me to the far end of the tunnel and go inside there for him."

Pointing at the other two he ordered "You two go in this end of the tunnel and start to walk through to catch him."

Referring back to the two travelling with him, he said "After you get to the other end of the tunnel, then start to go in and you'll catch him between you" said the man. "What do we do if he comes out the far tunnel end or when we catch him" asked one of the men. "Then give him a bit of a duffing to subdue him and bring him into the tunnel a couple of hundred metres and wait for the others to arrive. It's very quiet here but we just don't want any noise attracting any passer-by. You can do the job fairly far into the tunnel and just leave him there. It'll probably be weeks before anybody finds him. Understood?" said the man.

"Understood" came the mumbled replies. At that, the three men jumped into the car they arrived in, turned it around and headed down the road about a mile. Once there, they parked up and two of the men made their way up to the old railway line, where they walked along to the tunnel entrance. The Boss stayed in the car, as look out. When they reached the tunnel, one guy went to one side of the outside wall of the tunnel and the other guy went over to the opposite side wall. They entered the tunnel and started to make their way into the gloom.

Meantime, the other two guys had started to make their way up to the line and crossed the bridge to the tunnel mouth. As they approached the tunnel mouth, one cautiously leaned out from the edge wall of the tunnel and peered into the darkness. He could see and hear nothing except distant birds outside the tunnel calling behind him in the surrounding wooded area and the cascading water of the river below. He indicated to enter the tunnel with him.

The two men progressed up the tunnel, one on each side of the tunnel, all adhering closely to the sidewall. The boss had told them all to bring torches, but they were only to use them reluctantly as they may have given a clue to their presence. None of the men were even sure if Luke was in the tunnel. If they'd looked on the floor, they would have noticed Luke's large boot prints overlying their own prints from their visit earlier that day.

As they approached the three hundred metre mark and the curve took them into absolute darkness, one of the men piped up "I can't see a fucking thing". "Shush" said the other in as hushed a voice as he could. They shuffled on as best they could and then one man tripped on a big coarse rock and landing on some other rocks shouted out "Oh fuck, that hurt!" In between hushed but angry outbursts, he carried on, "I've cut my fucking hand."

"Shush, keep the noise down" said his mate in a hushed voice, making a frustrated attempt to get him to quieten down.

At that precise moment, back in the town Police Station, DI Brough received a phone call from Sgt. Anne Smith. "Sir, I think we may have a situation developing here with regards to Luke Walker."

"How do you mean" asked DI Brough.

"Well, the tracker device on his car shows there is an Organised Crime vehicle in close proximity to his car," said Sgt Smith.

"Right, I'll come right down to have a look," said DI Brough.

Two minutes later he approached Sgt Smith who then showed him the satellite view on the computer, indicating the position of Luke's car, right beside the tracked gangland car. "What's in that area" asked DI Brough.

"There is an old railway tunnel just above those cars" piped up a WPC.

"Shit" said DI Brough "they might have him in that tunnel. Somebody phone him right now, to see if he answers. Sgt Smith, round up at least four Policemen right now. We need them to go to that tunnel straight away."

"Right away, Sir" replied Sgt Smith.

"There's no reply on his phone. It's just going to answerphone," said the WPC.

"Phone it again and leave a message telling him he might be in great danger and that we're on our way," said DI Brough. "Grab two Policemen to go with me," said DI Brough.

At that DI Brough headed straight out to a Police car in the yard, where he was joined by two PC's, one jumped in the front driving seat and one in the back. Lighting the blue lights, they headed out the yard as quickly as they could.

Back in the tunnel, Luke had become aware of the noise back down the tunnel from the guy's clumsy fall and the angry expletives he had uttered. He suddenly realised the developing situation that he was in and the danger to him. He immediately started heading towards the far tunnel exit as quickly as he could. He hugged close to the tunnel wall to be less visible, even in the blackness. He was wearing muted brown coloured coat and green trousers, his usual attire for wildlife watching. These colours were the best for being less visible as they merged into the greens of the country and even in the greyness of a tunnel. On reaching the straight for the tunnel, he noticed the other two guys silhouettes against the light of the tunnel exit. He was trapped between these guys and the other guys back in the tunnel. What was he to do? The guys progressing towards him from the far end were unaware of his presence as they were looking into the absolute darkness. Luke decided his best option was to go back to the area of total darkness, where he might go undetected or somehow escape past them in the cover of the darkness.

Back outside the boss heard the Police siren at least thirty seconds before a Police car with two Policemen whizzed past where he was parked. This unsettled him a lot, but he was aware that such things do happen. Probably a pure coincidence. At least that's what he told himself. The Police car had gone past without even noticing him, zooming on to some unknown destination.

DI Brough meantime was in a Police car with three miles still to go to the destination. Sgt Anne Smith came on the radio "Sir, the tunnel exits about a mile before where the cars are parked. There is a lane up to it just about fifty metres before the hotel on the left side as you go up the glen. Over."

"Right get the Policemen up at the cars to go into the tunnel as quickly as they can. Tell them to leave one man at the cars until back up appears. We'll turn into the track and go into the tunnel at the bottom. Tell the other Policemen to be aware that we'll be coming in from both directions, in the tunnel. Understood. Over" said DI Brough.

"Understood, Sir. Over" said Sgt Anne Smith.

Another Police siren was heard coming up the glen. This put the boss really on edge. Again, it was a Police car with two Policemen which whizzed past oblivious to his presence. "Shit" he thought "is this connected with us?" The boss rolled the options over in his mind. He tried to phone one of the guys, to tell them they may need to abort, but he couldn't get through. It was a quiet road and he wouldn't normally expect much traffic, so to get two Police cars whizzing past within two minutes, that was worrying.

Inside the tunnel, Luke knew there was a heaped pile of grit and dust close to his position. He found it in the dark and dusted his face, hands and hair to dull his skin reflections as quietly as he could. He moved into a track shelter in the walls of the tunnel, squeezed into the back as far as he could and waited. A weak torchlight was now visible shining in the area Luke was hiding. He knew someone was approaching, and there were at least two men coming from the top exit with another two men coming from the lower exit. He wondered could it just be an innocent situation, but he discounted that idea as extremely unlikely, and it might prove a fatal mistake to assume that. He might have slipped up this time anyway and it still looked likely it might cost his life. How was he going to get out of this one? Adrenaline surged through his body as he awaited developments.

Outside the tunnel, a third siren was heard by the boss coming up the road. This was just too much for him. He started his car and made his way down the thirty metres of track turning down onto the road, just as DI Brough came around the corner in the Police car.

"John" said DI Brough to the Policeman in the rear seat "get that car number."

"Yes sir" said PC John Moncrieffe.

Getting on the radio, he spoke "DI Brough here, there's a car heading down this road we've been on, a Mercedes, registration number Sierra, Tango, zero, nine, Oscar, Tango, Zulu. I need a car to stop it and hold the driver for questioning. Understood. Over"

"Understood, Sir" replied Sgt Anne Smith.

They turned into the track, headed up the track where the three men got out and headed up to the tunnel entrance. They noted the tracks of two men in a muddy bit beside the old track, fresh and heading towards the tunnel.

Inside the tunnel one man approached waving his torch from side to side looking for Luke. The shadows showed the heap of debris lying on the floor of the tunnel. The man avoided it and carried on. He passed by Luke without realising it. Luke knew though he had heard two men up the tunnel. Fifty metres further on the two men joined the single man. "Where's Jimmy?" asked one man.

"He's tending to a cut in his hand. He'll be along in a minute," said the other man.

"Did you guys see anything" continued the guy.

"Nothing at all. I really thought we would have had him. I wonder where he is" said another of the guys.

"Right, let's go back to Jimmy and then we can all go back to the cars."

Luke could see Jimmy's torch shine coming towards him. He was fifty metres to his right. To his left the other three were approaching steadily. Luke knew, the chances of being unobserved by four men was slim. What was he to do? Stay where he was, and risk being found or try to get past the one man either unobserved or by surprising him. Luke had to make a decision quickly, as all the men were closing fast.

Keeping a low profile and sticking close to the wall, Luke advanced in the direction of the man called Jimmy.

Jimmy was still waving his torch from side to side when his mate shouted "Hey Jimmy, I've just seen a man's silhouette in your torchlight. He's right there beside you."

"Where" said Jimmy just as he collected Luke's long metal torch just above his midriff full whack. Jimmy let out a raucous painful grunt as he fell to the ground. "Oooh, you bastard" he yelled as his three mates were running at full tilt to support him.

Luke had taken off the second he hit Jimmy. Luke was still suffering from a leg injury but nevertheless, the adrenaline allowed him to run reasonably fast. But Luke had forgotten one detail. He had put his torch on but he had glanced behind him to see how far away his pursuers were. He forgot about the pile of rocks that had claimed Jimmy on the way up the tunnel.

Down he went like an express train falling off a high bridge. He banged his head hard and felt woozy, knowing he had to get up, but he couldn't.

Within a few seconds the three men had him by the scruff and were lifting him upwards.

"Right, you bastard, hit our mate would you. You're going to pay for that" said one of the guys as he took a swing at Luke with Luke's own metal torch. Luke didn't know it in the darkness, but his right eye had just been detached with the force of the blow.

"Kill the bastard" shouted Jimmy "he's broken some of my ribs. And hurry up, I need to get out of here. I'm in fucking agony."

"It'll be my pleasure" said one of the men "nobody will ever even find your body in this tunnel, you fucker." Approaching Luke again, brandishing a long thick knife straight out, whilst another man held onto Luke from behind and the other man shone a torch on the scene, Luke knew the only way he might avoid imminent death would be by getting the blade out of his hand. With refocused awareness, Luke energetically kicked at the blade, knocking it out of the man's hand and then he kicked back hard and downwards with his boots on the shins of the man holding him.

Death had been postponed for another few seconds. The man let go of Luke as he reeled back in agony. These moments took up only seconds and yet felt in slow motion to Luke. Death still looked like the inevitable result.

## Chapter Fifteen – Salvation of a Sort

"POLICE. Stop right there! Nobody moves!" came the shout. A groggy Luke thanked his lucky stars, which were still visibly spinning around inside his head. A few more seconds and he would have been dead. Saved by the cavalry or in this case the Police, just in the nick of time.

Three Policemen advanced out of the gloom from the top end of the tunnel. The four men beside Luke all considered a gloomy future ahead. Each had their own thoughts. Jimmy with his cracked ribs and sore hand just wanted this hell to come to an end. He wasn't going to do anything rash.

But that wasn't the case with the man who had been about to stab Luke. He didn't fancy ten plus years in jail. He quickly pulled out a stubby pistol and pointed it at Luke who was only six feet away from him. "Don't move Coppers or this fucking shit gets it," said the man. Luke couldn't believe his luck or rather the lack of it. Just when he thought he was saved, this happens.

None of the Policemen in the tunnel were armed, except with tazers. They stopped. They were still twenty-five metres away, so what could they do.

The man with the gun wheeled round facing Luke but putting Luke between him and the Policemen. Luke raised his arms with his hands about face height. The man with the gun indicated to Luke to start walking forward, whilst he walked slowly backwards, keeping an eye on the Policemen. He wanted to put as much distance between himself and the Policemen. The other three men didn't move. "Are you guys coming" he said to them in a frustrated, angry tone. Silence apart from a groan of pain from Jimmy. "You guys are gutless" said the man wielding the gun, again in an angry and frustrated tone. He started to back up, indicating to Luke to follow.

After one hundred and fifty metres, the call came from the semi-gloom "STOP. POLICE. Hands up."

The man with the gun quickly grabbed Luke by the coat and swung the both of them around so that Luke's back was towards the officers. Two of these Police were armed but there was no viable cover for them. DI Brough was behind his two officers, almost in the middle of the tunnel, whilst the two officers were at each side of the tunnel. "Put down your guns or this guy gets it" shouted the man with the gun. The Policemen didn't move. The man with the gun let a shot off down the tunnel. Luke knew this was the time he would have to react, or somebody would be killed.

Within half a second, he had grabbed the pistol pushing it to the side of the man, bending his fingers, hand and wrist backwards, which was a very weak position for the shooter. A shot rang off and ricocheted off the tunnel wall up towards the other men further up into the gloom of the tunnel.

Somehow, nobody in the tunnel further up was hit. Without hesitation, Luke hooked his leg behind the man with the gun and pushed him backwards, whereupon he fell backwards. He still had the gun in his hand. Luke reacted instantly, aiming, and kicking his heel into the man's stomach but instead hitting the solar plexus of the man's chest, ripping his diaphragm. Unable to breathe, the man was as good as dead, but even so, being completely wound up by the urgency, Luke kicked the gun away from the man's hand, just in case.

The armed Policemen had dropped to their knees with their guns out pointing forward, but as all this activity happened, they quickly ran up beside Luke, pointing their guns at the dying man. When they realised, he was dying, they quickly tried to resuscitate the man, but to no avail. He was dying and there was no reversing it. His burst diaphragm was a death sentence.

By this time, the three other officers further up the tunnel had arrested the three other men, including Jimmy who was breathing very painfully because of his broken ribs.

"If your ribs are broken, it'll be a while before you'll be able to breathe without pain, but we'll get you off to hospital and they'll be able to give you a painkiller," said his arresting officer. The other two prisoners were relatively subdued, although one wanted to know, slightly vociferously, what had happened to AB (his name was Dean, but he had been nicknamed the archbishop, ironically because he was a nasty piece of work, which then became shortened to AB). The arresting officer said nothing to him except that they would find out in due time.

To DI Brough, the operation had been mostly successful, but they had one dead gangster as a result and for Luke, there would be the consequences of the inquest. This was the first operation for DI Brough which had resulted in a fatality and despite his bluster and hardened exterior, it brought real sadness to him.

DI Brough had to go to the tunnel mouth to call in forensics and a team to examine the crime scene, plus an ambulance for Jimmy. Jimmy was taken to hospital, where they found he had three cracked ribs, but luckily, they had not punctured his lungs.

Luke also required an ambulance. He was taken to a much larger hospital where the eye specialist took a look at his eye. He had a retinal detachment in his right eye and the next day they scheduled the time for an attempted saving of the eye. When it came to the local anaesthetic being administered into the eye, Luke found it very painful indeed. Luke had had a few operations in his time and had become somewhat blasé about the pain with these procedures, but he found the eye operation to be quite painful. The eye operation went ahead but was only partially successful.

Meantime, the processing of the incident scene went ahead. Photographs, measurements and statements were all taken and collated. DI Brough had asked about the car seen leaving the scene. It had disappeared.

The gangland boss, who was unknown to the Police, was too street wise to have taken the obvious routes, leaving himself vulnerable to stopping and arrest. He had quickly turned onto small country roads and made his way slowly back towards Glasgow over the narrow hill roads. He had contacted some of his men for help and they left his burnt-out car in the hills not far from Glasgow. It was reported the day after the incident. The plates proved to be ghost plates, false, untraceable.

Shaun, the gangland boss, had got away because of his suspicion but he had happily abandoned his compatriots. Ironically, despite his lack of loyalty to them, his men never flinched once and hinted about his involvement in the crime. They all said AB was the boss and it was him that had instigated the action. They said they thought they were only going to give Luke a beating and didn't realise that AB intended to kill him. That claim was countered by the Policemen who had approached them first and said they heard Jimmy telling AB to kill Luke and hurry up about it. Jimmy claimed that he only said that because he was angry at Luke for hurting him and he hadn't really meant it.

Luke was a worried man, not because of hurting Jimmy, but because he had accidentally killed AB. It was all going to be going through an inquest and Luke didn't know how it would all shake out. A few days after the eye operation, Luke was sent home. He had a difficult two weeks ahead of him.

To try to repair the eye, he had to lie face down in bed. The doctor recommended lying during the day, across the bed with his head unsupported over the edge of the bed. He was told he was not to move away from the bed for any more time than ten minutes in any hour. For stimulation, the doctor recommended Radio 4 as it had a wide range of topics. Luke was now alone, and he refused to ask for help from his ex-wife. She had given their kids new phones and new numbers, so he had no way of contacting them. He also didn't know where they were. Obviously, this inactivity was very boring, and it felt like the longest two weeks of his life. Frenetic activity of any sort was not allowed. He was to be as still as possible for the two weeks. More than ninety percent of his time was lying motionless facing downward in bed. He had to dissuade his few good friends from coming to see him as he wasn't able to speak to them in the conventional sense.

Despite his best efforts, the eye repair was only partially successful as he was down to about 20% vision field in his right eye and even that was only the bottom right area. In effect he was as good as blind in his right eye.

With 24 hours a day to endure face down for two weeks, Luke did have a little time to think about the stresses of the recent events. In the privacy of his own bedroom, in the early hours of one morning, he spontaneously burst into tears and cried like he wouldn't stop, ever. It had all got to him, but Luke did feel better for the crying. The stress of it all was overwhelming, the attempts on his life, the loss of his eye, his low income, no prospects of a well-paid job, marriage failure, loss of contact with his kids, and now a court case hanging over his head because of the death of a man who had been sent out to kill him. He didn't dare think if anything further bad could happen.

Once he was well enough, Luke was asked to come into the Police station and write and sign a statement about what had happened in the tunnel. This took up ten pages of A4 paper to complete. The statement was taken and filed ready for the forthcoming court case.

Luke did ask slightly anxious questions about what was liable to happen in the court case, but all he got back from the officers was to try not to worry unduly.

"Try not to worry unduly" thought Luke, "you're not the guys having to justify your actions. If this goes wrong, I could be in prison." DI Brough was also getting it a little rough. He had been suspended on full pay until an investigation into his actions that day were completed by other officers.

Luke was contacted by Paul who quickly heard on the grapevine about the fact that there had been four men arrested in the very railway tunnel that Luke was to cover. When he heard that Luke was in hospital for treatment on his eye, his curiosity was insatiable. He tried to contact Luke by phone, but Luke just sent him a text reply saying he'd had an accident, that he couldn't speak for a while but would be in touch in a week or two's time. Several weeks after the incident, Luke got in touch with Paul.

"Hello Paul. It's Luke here. How are you doing" asked Luke.

"I'm fine, but more to the point, how are you, Luke? I'd heard you had your eye damaged somehow?"

"Well yes. In fact, I have pretty much lost the vision in my right eye." said Luke.

"Why what happened exactly?"

"Well, I'm not allowed to say as there is a court inquest coming up very soon. I can say though that I was involved in a fracas and didn't come out altogether unscathed," said Luke.

"Where was this fracas you mentioned?" asked Paul.

"It was in that railway tunnel I went to do the bat survey," said Luke.

"No, you're winding me up" said Paul gasping with surprise.

"No honestly," said Luke.

Paul's tone indicated he was genuinely taken aback. "And can you tell me anything about what happened" asked Paul whose inflated interest showed up in the urgency of his voice.

"I'm sorry but I'm not really allowed to. Sorry" said Luke.

"I wouldn't tell anyone," said Paul.

"Yes, sure you wouldn't" thought Luke. Paul wasn't really a gossip, but juicy news like that was like the next breath - you could only hold onto it for a while. "Sorry Paul, but I've probably said too much already," said Luke.

“Well George did the lower stretch of tunnel just down the track from you and he had no problems” said Paul “Completely unscathed he was. You weren’t jumped on by a Black Leopard were you” asked Paul, still digging for more information.

“No, nothing like that,” said Luke.

“Do you want to meet for a pint sometime soon” asked Paul. “Well, that would be nice as long as you try not to ask about what happened to me,” said Luke. Luke could hear Paul groaning softly, as he didn’t want to hear that on the other end of the phone.

“I’ll not do that, you know me, Luke,” said Paul.

“Yes, I do” said Luke, “but I think you would” thought Luke. “Anyway, we’ll make it a definite to go for a drink sometime soon, Paul,” said Luke.

“That sounds good” said Paul “speak to you soon”.

“Will do, bye for now,” said Luke.

“Bye” said Paul as he hung off.

Shaun hadn’t disappeared off the earth never to be seen again though. He sent a lady friend to see Jimmy in his prison a couple of weeks later. Her main mission was to find out exactly what had happened in the tunnel. Mary had come from one of the toughest estates in East Glasgow. Mary was attractive, curvy, short in stature, in her thirties but she looked older and mentally she was a fairly hard case. Shaun had given her the occasional package of cocaine for some sexual favours, which Mary was happy to oblige him with. He asked to meet her in a local bar. “So, you want tae go back to my place after this drink” she said to Shaun.

“Aye maybe, but there’s something I want to ask you to do for me before that,” said Shaun.

“Are you wanting Ella to be with us as well. I don’t know where she is though, this afternoon, Shaun,” said Mary.

“No, no, I want to find out what happened to some mates of mine. They’ve been arrested and are in Boulderfield Prison, awaiting their trial. I have a friend called Jimmy, Jimmy Watson. He was arrested, but apparently, I’ve heard that Dean McKenzie died at the scene when the Police were there arresting them” said Shaun.

“What - AB McKenzie” asked Mary.

“Yes, the very man” said Shaun “do you know him”?

“That bastard nearly choked me to death one night, cos I refused to go back to his place with him. He was a bad one alright. If some guys hadn’t stepped in to stop him, I would’nae be here. I can’t say I’m sorry to hear he’s dead,” said Mary.

“Yes, he was definitely a bit o’ a Psycho. But anyway, I need you to go and see Jimmy and find out what happened that evening for me. Is that ok, Mary?”

“How do I get there? I don’t drive?” asked Mary.

“I’ll get one of my men to drive you. They have prison visitors at 2.30pm on a Tuesday or Thursday. Can you go on one of those days, Mary? Just say you’re Jimmy’s girlfriend and you want to see him. Is that ok? When you see him, ask him all the details of what happened,” said Shaun.

"Aye, no problem. I presume you'll see me reimbursed for my troubles, Shaun?" said Mary.

"Of course," said Shaun "right I'll go and get it organised."

Three days later and Mary rolled up to the prison reception and went in.

"I'm here to see Jimmy, my boyfriend" she said to the prison guard.

"We've quite a few Jimmies in here. What's his surname?" asked the guard.

For a moment, Mary went blank. "Ah, ah, Jimmy from Glasgow" blurted out Mary.

"Well, that's narrowed it down to about fifteen guys" said the prison guard "Any other clues to which Jimmy we're talking about "he continued with a somewhat sarcastic look on his face.

Suddenly Mary remembered "Jimmy Watson, I ahh, just always call him by his first name".

"Do you indeed, been seeing him a while" said the prison guard with a suspicious glance at Mary "right go through there and they'll get you in to see Jimmy whatshisname."

"Watson" said Mary, giving the guard a vitriolic glance, which would have turned Medusa to stone, before moving on.

After the normal processing, she was presented to Jimmy Watson to speak to him. Jimmy groaned in pain as he moved into the chair.

"What's happened to you?" Mary asked.

"I've still got broken sore ribs, but they're getting better every day now."

"Shaun sent me in to see you" said Mary "he wants to know what happened that night."

"Does he? I thought it was too good to be true to have a girlfriend coming in to see me" said Jimmy with a deluded look of disappointment "What does he want to know?"

"Well, how did you get hurt?" said Mary.

"We were in an old railway tunnel looking for a guy, when he came out of nowhere and hit me with a whacking great metal torch, breaking some of my ribs," said Jimmy. "Then he ran away but he fell over on some rocks and the other guys managed to grab him. We were just going to give the fucker a duffing when the Police shouted us to stop. AB grabbed the guy and with his pistol started walking him away from the cops, but other cops appeared at the other end of the tunnel and told him to stop. He fired a shot at them, but the guy he was holding wrestled with him. Another shot rang out and then AB lay dying. The Police tried to resuscitate him, but he just died" said Jimmy solemnly.

"What, did he shoot himself?" asked Mary.

"No apparently, he had been kicked some way by the other guy and he'd just died. But the rumours are that he might be charged with manslaughter" continued Jimmy. "Poor AB, it was most unlike him to get caught out like that" continued Jimmy. Unknown to them a prison guard had moved within earshot of the two of them.

“Poor AB” said Mary in utter surprise “we’re talking about Dean McKenzie, he was a total bastard. I’m glad he’s dead and not a day too soon.”

Jimmy looked at Mary “Oh, so you had a bad experience with him, did you?”

“I most certainly did” said Mary “I’d happily dance on his grave.”

“Oh, I see” said Jimmy “anyway does Shaun need anything more from me?”

“No, I think you’ve told me enough to answer Shaun’s query,” said Mary.

“Well, I’d invite you back to my cell for a coffee, seeing you’re my girlfriend, but I’m in the middle of decorating the cell and it’s just a mess at the moment” said Jimmy with a sardonic but hopeful grin, implying maybe for the future.

“I’ll just wait until you’ve finished the decorating” replied Mary, rolling her eyes at Jimmy’s unrealistic but optimistic suggestion.

“Well, come again, girlfriend” said Jimmy quite loudly.

“Maybe I will” said Mary loudly to Jimmy as she rose out of the chair but continued in a quieter volume “but then, maybe I won’t” as she walked out of the room.

The next day, Mary met Shaun and explained all that had been told to her by Jimmy.

“So, this guy in the tunnel hit Jimmy and broke some of his ribs” asked Shaun.

"The Police arrived and called out before "he was given a lesson" by AB, you say" continued Shaun.

"That's what he said" said Mary "then AB forced him out towards the bottom tunnel exit, but more Police arrived. There were a couple of shots fired and AB was lying there dying."

"He definitely didn't shoot himself, did he?" asked Shaun.

"Jimmy didn't reckon so; he says he has heard that the man he was holding at gunpoint might be getting a manslaughter charge" said Mary. "They reckon there was some kind of tussle and somehow AB ended up mortally wounded" she continued. "Jesus, AB was quite a hard nut, I wouldn't have thought that would have happened to him. Him doing it to someone else, yes, but not to him," said Shaun.

"You've done well, Mary, here's some cash in that envelope for you" said Shaun. "I may need to ask you to sit in on the court case, to find out more, when that comes up in a couple of weeks. You won't mind doing that for me, will you Mary" asked Shaun.

"I'm more than happy to do it for you, if you keep supplying me with these envelopes" said Mary as she fingered through the notes in the envelope.

"You can claim to be AB's girlfriend in case that helps us get more out of the court case" said Shaun.

"Do I have to really be AB's ex-girlfriend?" asked Mary "I think I'd rather stick forks in my eyes."

"He's dead now" said Shaun "I know he didn't have any girlfriends in the last six months or so."

"I'm not surprised" said Mary "I've met some nasty and strange one's in my time, but he took the ticket. He also stunk; did he ever wash?"

"Yeah, I had to admit he was hard to sit in a vehicle with for any time" said Shaun "but eventually if you were in his company long enough, you couldn't smell him anymore."

"I tell you, Shaun, he won't be pushing up any daisies, that's for sure. They'll all be dead before they get above the soil" said Mary with true venom.

Shaun snorted a little laugh from Mary's remark. "Right, I'll be in touch about when I need you to go sit in on the court and listen in, on what gets said, Mary"

"Yes, no bother," said Mary.

**Chapter Sixteen – The Court Inquest**

In judicial terms, the inquest date arrived fairly quickly. The two-armed Policemen and DI Brough were to give evidence as well as Luke. The judge started with DI Brough.

"DI Brough, you were the commanding officer in this operation, is that correct?" asked the Judge.

"That's correct" replied Detective Inspector Brough.

"Describe the build-up of the scenario and go on to outline the subsequent events as you saw it" asked the judge.

"Certainly, Your Honour. We knew that Luke Walker may have been targeted by Gangland members as he had reported suspicious events some years ago that we now believe was gangland members disposing of a body or two," said DI Brough.

"You say one or two bodies" asked the judge, "are you not aware of whether there were two or just one as yet?"

"That hasn't been fully established to date, Your Honour, but we believe it probably was two" replied DI Brough "But we do know the likely candidates as they had committed a gangland murder but haven't been seen since."

"I see" said the judge, "continue DI Brough."

"Thank You, Your Honour," said DI Brough. "We had noticed a gangland vehicle going to the same destination as Luke Walkers vehicle and we decided it may have been a potential ambush being implemented, so I organised four Policemen to be sent to the location of Luke Walkers car and the gangland vehicle to check it out. I was informed it was beside an old disused railway tunnel, so I arrived at one end of the tunnel with two armed officers, and we proceeded into the tunnel from the lower end, whilst the other officers left one officer at the cars, just in case we had got it wrong or the gangsters turned up. Meantime, the other three officers entered the tunnel at the top end and moved into the tunnel to find where all these people had gone. They encountered the gangland members first, just as Luke Walker was about to be either badly beaten or executed. There was evidence to the latter being the intended objective. One gangland member, a Mr Dean McKenzie, pulled out a gun threatening to kill Luke Walker if the Police advanced. He then grabbed Luke Walker and proceeded away from the policemen further down the tunnel. However, at this stage me and my team arrived whereupon Dean McKenzie pulled Luke Walker around facing the armed officers. Then Dean McKenzie again threatened to shoot Luke Walker if the police didn't stand down. There was a standoff and Dean McKenzie fired a shot down the tunnel in the direction of the police officers. At this moment Luke Walker grabbed the gun and wrestled with Dean McKenzie. A shot was fired which ricocheted off the walls up the tunnel. Luke Walker kicked the feet from under Dean McKenzie who landed on the ground and Luke Walker followed up by kicking Dean McKenzie in the stomach and then kicking the gun from his hand. The two-armed officers and I moved forward to cover Dean McKenzie and ensure there were no more shots fired. However, on arrival we found that Dean McKenzie had sustained an injury to his solar plexus diaphragm, and he was unable to breathe. We tried resuscitation but it was unsuccessful. It would seem in the gloom and urgency of the action Luke Walker accidentally delivered a fatal blow to Dean McKenzie."

"Do you consider that the delivered fatal blow was definitely unintentional, DI Brough?" asked the judge.

"Yes, your honour, I do. It all happened in a very dark scenario and with the threat of further shots, it was understandable how it could happen in the heightened confusion of the moment," said DI Brough.

The other two-Armed Response Officers were then questioned, and their accounts matched that of DI Brough.

Luke Walker was then brought forward for questioning.

"First of all, Mr Walker, I want to ask how you came to be in that tunnel in the first place?" asked the judge.

"I am interested in wildlife, and I was asked to do a survey of the tunnel by a member of the local bat group to determine whether any bats had decided to use it as a roost. For whatever reason, none had, but my mission was to determine the true situation" replied Luke.

"I see," said the judge. "Were you aware of the potential danger you may have been in when you went into the tunnel' continued the judge.

"Yes, Your Honour, I was aware that I had been targeted in the past, but I didn't expect anything to happen on that particular evening. I had no reason to suspect anyone else knew I was going there," replied Luke.

"Can you outline the events that happened in the tunnel from your perspective" asked the judge.

"When I first became aware of the men in the tunnel" said Luke, "I tried to hide and almost escaped. I only had one man to get past and in the darkness of the tunnel I hit him forcibly with my metal torch and then ran to make my escape.

Unfortunately, I tripped on some rocks, and they caught me up. There were angry exchanges and it looked to me like I might be killed, probably by stabbing initially but the arrival of the unarmed policemen stopped them from proceeding in this action. Dean McKenzie grabbed me and using a gun and me as cover, threatened the policemen with his pistol. He dragged me towards the lower tunnel exit but very soon the armed policemen arrived. There was a stand-off, and a shot was fired in the direction of the Armed Response Officers, so I realised that I had to do my best to disarm Dean McKenzie. In the following few seconds, there was a struggle which unfortunately resulted in the accidental death of Dean McKenzie. I deeply regret his death, but it all happened so quickly, and I was so focused in disabling him to prevent him from causing any further harm, or indeed a death, that it all seemed like a blur."

"Thank you, Mr. Walker" said the judge "do you have anything further you wish to add to your statement?"

"No, your Honour' replied Luke. "In that case, you may stand down Mr. Walker," said the judge.

A few days later a statement was released to the media which said that no charges would be made against Luke Walker.

Shaun in Glasgow had been expecting this outcome. He asked to see Mary again. "Look Mary, they have declared that the guy who killed AB in the tunnel will face no charges."

"I'd give him a knighthood" replied Mary "filthy, sick psycho that he was."

"Yeah, well I need you to put your feelings aside for now. I want you to submit a complaint that AB was your boyfriend, that he was your life and soulmate, that you don't believe the findings of the inquest and that you want a Public Inquiry and compensation for his death," said Shaun.

"I won't have to act the part as well" asked Mary pulling a face that looked like she had just found something very unpleasant under her shoe.

"Yes', said Shaun, "you may have to. But if there is any compensation paid, you can keep the lot." This seemingly generous move was more considered than big hearted by Shaun, as he didn't want his name to be anywhere near this claim. One of Shaun's men organised an interview with a news team for Mary.

The next day the TV journalist duly turned up with his camera team to interview Mary. "Mary, you wish to make the point that Dean would never act in the way detailed by the findings, is that correct?" asked the journalist.

"That's right" said Mary "AB, oh, I mean Dean, just wouldn't be capable of such a thing. I think he must have been killed by the Police for no good reason other than he has got on the wrong side of the law a couple of times and now they're trying their best to cover it all up by saying he was killed accidentally in a tussle. Dean meant the whole world to me, he was a lovely, gentle man and I miss him so much. I'm going to find it difficult as I cannot see how life can be liveable without him in the future. That's why I want a full public inquiry to be carried out, to prove that the Police have corrupted the evidence to make AB, eh, oh I mean Dean, the fall guy in this fiasco."

"And do you have any evidence that backs up your claims, Mary?" asked the journalist.

“No, it’s just I know the type of man Dean was, and he would do anything to avoid conflict. He was one of the nicest men I have ever known” replied Mary.

“How long have known Dean, Mary?’ asked the journalist.

“Many years” said Mary “and we’ve been together for more than six months.”

The interview went out that night.

Shaun was always a smart cookie; he knew how to turn a seeming setback into a potential gain. He got some people with the necessary social media skills to go to work on trying to achieve a demand for a public enquiry on the tunnel incident. Many people quickly jumped on board the campaign, telling all their social media friends that the Police had made up the story to make Dean’s death appear as an accident during a tussle. A lot of people swallowed the story, hook, line, and sinker and genuinely believed there must have been a cover up by the Police. By the following weekend, there was a sizeable placard wielding crowd of about thirty people assembled outside the Police station closest to the original incident. They chanted and vocalised their grievances all day “what do we want”, “Justice”, “How do we want it”, “A public enquiry”. It didn’t exactly rhyme very well, but the crowd got it down to a fine art within about four repeat performances, much to the ire of the local residents. One or two local people took exception to the baying crowd, one shouting “why don’t you fucking clot heads fuck off somewhere else. Go and practice your chanting somewhere useful, like at the bottom of an ocean.” His views made no impression on the mob other than resulting in a few stuck up, strategically positioned fingers waved in his direction.

By early afternoon, another TV crew appeared on the scene. They asked to interview one or two members of the mob.

"Why are you here" asked the reporter.

"We're here to see that justice gets done for the death of Dean McKenzie, who was murdered by the Police under the cover of a railway tunnel, simply because he was in the wrong place at the wrong time" said one embittered lady who genuinely believed all she had stated.

"Did you know Dean McKenzie at all" continued the reporter.

"No, I never met him, but I have been told he was an extremely nice man. The Police shouldn't be allowed to get away with this crime."

"I believe his death was after a tussle with a civilian, not a Policeman" continued the reporter.

"That's according to the Police report, but we want to have it proven that the Police executed him for no good reason, using the tunnel as a cover where there would be no witnesses. Blaming it on a civilian is just typical cynical Police tactics."

"I see," said the reporter.

The reporter then spoke to a passing member of the public about the protest.

"Do you know why these people are protesting outside this Police station, sir?" he asked.

"Yes, they're protesting about the death of a guy killed in a railway tunnel about eight miles away," said the guy.

“And do you have any views on the subject, yourself” asked the reporter?

“Not really” replied the man “except to say that if people like these turn up waving their placards, then they’re leading a pretty sad existence, they should get a life.”

“Thank you, very much Sir” said the reporter, who then walked away and whispered to his crew “we’ll not be using that one, then.”

Next the reporter sought out Mary to get her views.

“Mary”, he said “I see you've got a little crowd going here”.

“Yes”, she said, “we're here to ensure justice gets done for Dean. The police murdered Dean in that railway tunnel and have now covered it up with their lies. A public inquiry is the only way that justice can be served for Dean. I miss him so much, but as you can see there are plenty of people who want to help” she said to the reporter.

“Thank you, Mary,” said the reporter who then departed with the crew.

The TV crew then went on to speak to the local MSP to ask his views.

“Yes, there are increasing public concerns that this incident may not have been represented properly by the Police and that there may be some issues incorrectly reported” said the MSP Frank Robbins. “I will be putting my backing into a Public Inquiry into the sequence of events on that day, as these doubts are damaging the reputation of the integrity of the Scottish Police force.”

The report went out that night much to the amazement and then amusement of the Prison warden watching the news that night who had overheard Mary's discussion with Jimmy whilst she was on a prisoner visit.

"So, Jimmy Whatshisname was being two timed by Dean with Mary who just loved everything about Dean" he thought to himself "you couldn't make it up!" He laughed heartily as he watched, but then reality hit in. "If she does get a public inquiry, I should really let them know what I know. Or should I just keep it quiet and keep my nose clean?" he thought to himself.

The next day, he requested to speak to the Prison Governor. Whilst there he explained in detail about what he heard Mary say to Jimmy whilst visiting him in prison. "I think she is completely off her head when she says she is so sorry about Dean's death" he ended to the Prison Governor.

"Well, thanks for letting me know about this. Well done," said the Governor.

The Governor then wrote a letter, outlining the details of the overheard conversation, to MSP Frank Robbins. Frank then took the decision to not pursue the public enquiry, citing information had come to him making it impossible to pursue that option. Of course, to the conspiratorial types in the general public, this just made the whole thing even more suspicious.

To Mary and Shaun, it meant they had wasted a lot of effort for nothing, Mary, because she was hoping for a big pay-out from the inquiry and Shaun was hoping to get Luke in jail where he could organise retribution very much more easily.

Meantime, Luke was feeling the pressure. Now he had accidentally killed a gangster and there was a baying mob believing the Police had colluded to cover up the death. The fact that the MSP Frank Robbins had withdrawn his pledge for a public inquiry sent the conspiratorialists into overdrive. The common belief was that the Police had threatened Frank Robbins in some way to ensure he didn't progress his promise. There were people asking for more details on the civilian involved and there were others that went further, much further, making deeply offensive comments. These troll types relished the opportunity to relentlessly pick on a person and do their worst to bully and hurt, using the cover of the internet to protect their anonymity.

Luke found all these factors increasing the stress on him. He began to wonder would his problems ever end. Whilst feeling very lucky to be alive, he wondered how long that would continue to be the situation. Another factor was to add to his stress even more.

Luke was trying to sell his house after his wife had left him. One of his radiators in his bedroom had gone cold. It had an airlock, so Luke got the key to open the end and allow the air out of the radiator. Whilst doing this he noticed a handkerchief jammed in behind the radiator. He got a wire clothes hanger and carefully pulled it out using the metal hook to do so. Some coins fell out to the floor as he pulled it out. It had the appearance of dried blood on the handkerchiefs surface. Immediately Luke was brought back to the night he had returned from up the glen. He remembered having placed the scrunched-up handkerchief and money on the edge of the shelf above the radiator after his return, too tired to care about its contents. It had fallen with the weight of the coins behind the radiator and remained there ever since, dried out by the heat of the radiator. The blood must have come from the tacky stuff on the door handle on the farm shed that night.

Luke got onto the phone with CI John Wishaw at the local Police station. He quickly explained the situation and the officer said" right, we'll come around to pick it up. Keep the handling to a minimum to avoid contaminating it, and we'll send it to get a DNA profile. It will probably reveal nothing but it's worth a try. I'll send a couple of officers round in the next half hour. Thank you for letting us know". At that Chief Inspector John Wishaw hung up.

Half an hour later, two officers arrived with plastic bags and gloves. Luke raised the handkerchief using the hook of the metal clothes hanger and lowered into the opened plastic bag. The officers thanked him, labelled the sample and headed back to the station.

Nearly a week later, the results came back from the lab. They showed the DNA profile which was matched to one of the guys who had committed the murder outside of the pub in Glasgow many years prior from saved DNA profiles. The results were shared with CI John Wishaw but also sent for the attention of the murder squad Chief Inspector Phillip Sutherland. The results we're not shown to Luke. Luke did phone to ask about the results, but he was told they couldn't say anything about the results outside of the investigation team. Luke always found this aspect of Police work very frustrating. They took every bit of help going but gave nothing back in return. However, Luke did understand why this was necessarily the case. Effectively though Luke was left in the dark about the fact that the DNA showed one of the guys at least involved in the murder had been disposed of that evening.

Luke had also been wondering why he had never been able to get back into his previous line of work, as it was relatively well paid. John, who had gone down to the first meeting with Luke provided him with the answer. Luke phoned John to catch up and see what had been going on in his old company. John told him that Luke had been described as the most hated man in the world by the CEO.

"How could that be" asked Luke "all I did was defend myself after I was being targeted by Damian and his cronies?"

"Well," said John "the office was moved to a bigger office near London with other departments from the company and a lot of people wouldn't move and they lost their jobs. The top bosses blame you for this".

"That's a bit rich as they were the ones that had gone outside of the law. I merely caught on to them and exposed them to the higher echelons for what they had done. Indeed, if I had stayed on a bit longer, I would have had even more irrefutable evidence against them" replied Luke.

"That's why they hate you, because you fought back and were a threat to exposing them, instead of running away or rolling over and submitting to their bullying," said John.

"Well, they've certainly stopped me from earning a proper living and by doing so, they broke their own conditions that they set. They were complete bastards, and I should have taken them through the courts" added Luke. "Anyway, thanks for at least letting me know, John," said Luke.

When contemplating his situation with the gangland people one day, Luke thought to himself, how did those guys find out who he was and where he lived. When he travelled back from the glen that night, he knew nobody had followed his car. But then, he realised he had been followed, but only for a while and close enough to have had his vehicle registration read and car make noted. There must have been a corrupt cop involved who helped bring all these troubles in his direction.

And now that he was thinking on that line, how did the gangsters know he was going into that railway tunnel on that particular summer evening date? No one knew except Paul, whom he had known for years and trusted implicitly. Then it came to him, Charlene knew, she must have been the one who told them.

As far as Luke was concerned, all the involved parties had been captured that night. What about the dirty cop? How was he going to get him exposed and punished? Luke's mind started to churn it over, sluggishly at first because he couldn't think what to do, but as the options started coming to him, he then had to decide on the best action plan to use.

Luke decided to ask to see DI Brough at the Police Station. "Well sir" said the duty Sergeant "DI Brough is now back and available. When would you like to come in to see him?"

"As soon as possible" said Luke "tomorrow if that suits?"

"OK sir would 2.30pm tomorrow suit?" asked the duty Sergeant.

"Perfect" said Luke, "I'll look in then."

Next day, Luke was met by DI Brough and taken up to his office. "Are you over your little tunnel incident? I must say you're looking well considering all that happened to you that evening."

"Well, sometimes the scars are much more internal than on the surface, but yes I'm getting there," said Luke.

"What about the vision in your eye' asked DI Brough.

"No good, I've got less than 20% vision in that," said Luke.

"Ah, not good at all. Sorry to hear that. Anyway, how can I help you today?" asked DI Brough.

Luke gave a light cough and started "I was thinking about my situation, about how the gangsters got my address and then how they found out about me going into the tunnel!"

"Right" said DI Brough, who with a sweep of his arm, picked up his pen and open his notebook.

"Nobody followed me from the glen that night back home and yet they found me" said Luke "except that someone did follow me for a mile or so along the glen road, close enough behind me to get my car make and registration. I believe that somebody within the Police must have informed them of my details" stated Luke, looking DI Brough straight in the eye.

"Corrupt cops do exist and from what you say it is a distinct possibility that must have happened, sorry, I mean could have happened" said DI Brough who inside his head was inclined to believe it looked very feasible.

"I know that later on, on the A9 I had a rock thrown at my windscreen from a car travelling in the opposite direction, which luckily just hit my sunroof and to do that they must have had a tracker device in my car. But on that first night, they were unaware I was there, so there is no way that they had a tracker device in my car. Therefore, I can only surmise that they must have had a cop check out my details for them," said Luke.

"I think it is worth checking it out" said DI Brough who was writing in his book and deep in contemplation, showing only a furrowed brow to Luke as his face looked down into the pages of his book.

Before DI Brough could look up again, Luke continued "Also, how did those gangsters know I was going into that tunnel that night?" DI Brough looked up at Luke and was about to utter something "You're going to say they may have had a tracker planted in your car somewhere. But they were there in numbers very soon after I entered the tunnel. They went to both ends of the tunnel as well. They must have had prior notice from someone," said Luke.

"Who did you tell about it?" asked DI Brough.

"Only two people, my friend Paul who asked me to do it for the bat group and even he wasn't told the specific night I was going. I did tell a girl in the gym called Charlene though and I mistook her curious questions for just an endearing friendliness," said Luke.

"I can organise to bring her in for questioning to find out. What's her surname" asked DI Brough.

"I don't know, I just know her as Charlene," said Luke.

"That's not a problem, we can get her details at the gym," said DI Brough.

"Well, hold your horses just for a moment. If you were to do that and there are any gangsters still uncollected by you guys as yet, they would know to go to ground. And then we'd never catch them," said Luke.

There were a few seconds hesitation from DI Brough who then grunted along with a nod in agreement. "Alright, what do you think we should do?" asked DI Brough.

"I think we should play this one close to our chest. I think I should act exactly as I have before. We don't know how innocent or otherwise she is. We can sort that out later. I think I should re-acquaint myself with her, playing down the rumours but give her just a little manicured information so that she can set off hopefully some sort of chain reaction that will give you guys the extra leads you may need," said Luke. "Manicured information, I like it" said DI Brough scratching his head, "normally I wouldn't take suggestions from a civvy terribly seriously, but I realise you have brought in more than any paid copper I know, so for you, I'm willing to listen. What did you have in mind?"

"I think I should just say to her in a naive way, that I know the Police are about to bust a whole load of gangsters here and in Glasgow. Then you guys can monitor for activity and see who starts to get a bit jumpy. If they're all in jail, she's the only one who may get a little on edge," said Luke. "At the same time, find and put pressure on this cop. With both ends, see where they match up like a DNA fingerprint and if there are any more, you might spot them, hopefully," said Luke.

"To do that properly, may take us into borderline illegal area," said DI Brough.

"Well, you have done it before when you listened into my phone calls," said Luke.

“Well, if that had happened and I’m not saying it did happen, it would have been before we fully realised what was going on with you,” said DI Brough.

“Another possibility” continued DI Brough “is that we set up another potential ambush location and feed it to Charlene. Then we could pounce on them more prepared than the last time.” “That definitely sounds like a plan, but you will need to rescue me earlier than the last time” added Luke.

“Right, there might be some possibilities with your suggestion, but it needs a bit of detail thought through. First though, re-acquaint with Charlene, but don’t give her any information until I say so. If you give her information on the first time, the whole chain will be suspicious. Talk to her at the gym at least two or three times first and then I’ll tell you what to say to her if we decide to go that way. I’ll check out the corrupt Police officer theory, in the meantime,” said DI Brough.

“OK, if you say so,” said Luke.

“I do say so” said DI Brough getting in his point assertively as though all the discussion had been fully planned by him and he was directing one of his own Policemen.

With that DI Brough took Luke down to the reception in the police station. “I'll be in touch,” said DI Brough.

“Well, you know where to find me” retorted Luke.

Luke went back to the gym a few days later. Because of his eye injury, Luke opted for a less boisterous training session. He sat on a training cycle to do a gentle workout. This was positioned close by the people coming into the gym. Eventually Charlene came walking in. She looked slightly aghast as she saw Luke wearing an eye bandage. “What happened to you” she asked.

“Oh nothing” said Luke “just a little minor accident. It's on the mend now.” “How are you anyway, I haven’t been in for a while,” said Luke.

“I had heard that you haven’t been in recently,” said Charlene.

“Oh, have you not been in either” asked Luke.

“No, I’ve been busy. Couldn’t make it in for various reasons,” said Charlene.

Luke feigned a surprised look. “Well in that case, you’ll probably find the first session back, quite tough,” said Luke.

“Yes probably” said Charlene “nice to see you again.”

“Hopefully I’ll be back to normal training classes, fairly soon Charlene. I’ll see you sometime in the future. I’ll keep an eye out for you” said Luke “if you’ll excuse the pun.”

Charlene looked mildly befuddled by Luke’s last statement. Charlene wondered was there more meaning to be taken from what he had said and moved on. Luke knew it was going to take a few encounters before Charlene would lose her suspicions about what Luke knew. In his own mind Luke knew it had been unwise of him to have said about “keeping his eye out”, but at the time, he couldn’t stop himself because of a streak of hidden bitterness. Unless he could control that, his plans for Charlene would fall to dust and Luke knew that.

Meantime, DI Brough had asked for any Police computer searches made on Luke’s vehicle number right back to about the date of the original incident, to be highlighted. Only two turned up. One was an incorrect input, with a correction made a half hour later. The other was by a WPC in Glasgow. She was approached and asked why she had input the five numbers into the search computer. She quickly pointed the finger at Chief Inspector Michael McGregor.

McGregor was not terribly surprised to receive a visit from the Anti-Corruption cops. He didn't know they had nothing substantial on him. They went to a quiet office and asked him "why did you ask the WPC to check out these five car numbers?" showing him a sheet of paper with the numbers listed. The AC cops eyes bore into McGregor as he thought for a few seconds, whilst they were looking for the slightest hint of a lie.

"I had been in Calder Street parked up for a few minutes, when I saw seven gang members walking past. Two of them had car keys in their hands and looked like they had just got out of some cars. When they went past, I took notes on the likely car numbers they may have come from and asked the WPC to check the owner's details to see if there was any possible connection. I didn't run a normal filed report as I was just doing a check, just in case" said McGregor.

"You do know that's not how it should be done, sir" said one of the AC cops.

"Yes, I know that" said McGregor "but if it had turned up something useful, I would have filed it properly. There was nothing showed up, so nothing gained, nothing lost. That's all it was."

"One of the numbers was a car from Orkney and it's never been off the islands. Did that not strike you as suspicious, sir" said one of the AC cops.

"Ghost plates - must have been ghost plates or misread" said McGregor who for the first time looked shifty to the AC cops.

"Why did you request the car's registered owner's addresses" asked the other AC cop "and then not follow up with any further research?"

"I just thought I had made a mistake on taking a note of the cars numbers" said McGregor who was now looking decidedly uncomfortable.

"You went to all that bother but didn't check them out any further at all. Why did you bother in the first place?" asked one of the AC cops.

"I admit I should have just done it properly on the day" said McGregor, realising that taking this argument further was going to be self-defeating and who was trying damage limitation.

The two AC cops looked at each other for a second, each thinking the same thing, "this guy is lying."

"Right sir, we'll come back to you soon," said DI Stuart McColl.

They went away and consulted each other. "He's lying. He could be up on a disciplinarian charge on not following correct procedures" said Det Sgt Bill McLarnon to the other.

"Agreed, but we're not here on a minor procedural charge. We need to prove he was supplying information. How are we going to do that?" said DI McColl.

"Phone records, that could well prove it. The man that Luke identified as the ringleader was Callum Mallachy. It would have been him that requested McGregor to supply Luke's name and address" said Det Sgt McLarnon. "He may have done it via one of his men. So, what we do is check the numbers that were texted or phoned by Callum and see if any of those showed up on McGregor's numbers of incoming calls or texts that day. If so, we've got him, don't you think?" said D Sgt McLarnon.

"Sounds like a plan. It might just work. Let's check those numbers out" DI McColl.

The officers then went to work over the next few days, first checking out the numbers that Callum had either texted or phoned just after the date that Luke had seen the guys up the glen. They then checked the incoming list of texted and phoned numbers on McGregor's personal phone. Sure, enough there had been one, registered to a Shaun with a false surname, now out of use and untraceable, but he had sent a text to Callum first, received a text back from Callum, and then the trail ended. It was time to drag McGregor in for a more in-depth interview.

McGregor didn't sleep well the night after he was first questioned by the AC cops, or indeed for the following few weeks. He knew they would be like bloodhounds, once they were on the scent, they would be virtually unstoppable. He wondered if he had been convincing enough when they had approached him. He was not going to feel relaxed for quite some time, as it was a few weeks down the line before they came back to question him further.

The next time it was in the interview room, not a quiet office. He was given the usual "anything you say may be taken down and used in evidence against you" and asked if he wanted a solicitor present. McGregor said "Of course not, I've done nothing wrong except a minor procedural mistake. This is all a bit over the top for that. Oh, and I did once double park for about fifteen seconds when I posted some letters into a post box, if you want to do me for that" he added sarcastically. Inside though, the butterflies in his tummy were doing somersaults.

Things were a lot more formal this time. One of the original AC officers was present. He introduced himself again as Detective Inspector Stuart McColl and his boss Detective Chief Superintendent Alex Lawson.

"I will make a start to proceedings" said DCS Lawson. "DI McColl is here to conduct the interview; I am here in an advisory role. Over to you DI McColl". DI McColl sat up straight, looked at DI McGregor and said "we spoke to you a month ago about a procedural misdemeanour you made. However, since then, we have looked at the details of the incoming and outgoing phone numbers on your mobile phone about the date there had been reports of possible gangland activity up a glen in the Highlands. The day after that you requested some car numbers to be researched by a WPC."

"That must just be pure coincidence, nothing more," said McGregor.

"Indeed" said DI McColl "but there were two gangland telephone numbers involved in the chain of calls made that day, both directly and indirectly to you. Would you care to comment on why these numbers were in a communication chain with you?"

McGregor looked shocked and after a few seconds said "No comment. Maybe, I will have a solicitor present before there are any more questions." The AC cops knew this was just a delaying tactic.

DCS Lawson rolled his eyes in frustration and burst out "you were asked if you wanted a solicitor present, you said no, just answer the question."

"I don't know why there were two gangland numbers in the chain. I do sometimes talk to these sorts of guys; you know in my job" said McGregor.

"On your personal mobile number" asked DI McColl.

"Look, let's cut to the chase" said DCS Lawson "what did these guys want. And no lies. We'll know your lying before you even open your mouth."

"No comment," said McGregor.

"Chief Inspector McGregor, you're suspended from duty, pending further investigation, until we can establish your integrity on this matter. Please hand over all your warranty cards and police equipment. After that you can phone your solicitor. This is very far from the end of this matter for you" said DCS Lawson.

## Chapter Seventeen – The Net Begins to Close

"DI Brough" said the voice.

"Speaking" said DI Brough.

"This is DCS Lawson, AC department in Glasgow," said the voice.

"How can I help" asked DI Brough who momentarily but illogically felt slightly nervous.

"Well, it's more of a case of how I can help you" said DCS Lawson "it looks like your theory about a possible corrupt cop supplying information to Callum Mallachy was right. Well done for suspecting that. We have a man under investigation as we speak. It will hopefully, just be a matter of time before he is charged and convicted. You can carry on your investigation knowing that is how they got the address of the witness. Do you need any other information from me whilst I am on the phone to you" asked DCS Lawson.

"No sir, thank you for letting me know. Good luck at your end," said DI Brough.

"Thank you for putting us onto this, otherwise he might just have carried on supplying information for years to come" said DCS Lawson.

"Callum Mallachy is dead now, sir" replied DI Brough.

"Ah yes, but once dirty, forever dirty" said DCS Lawson.

"Indeed" replied DI Brough "thank you Sir. Goodbye."

Once the phone call had ended, DI Brough sighed, tutted and looking annoyed with himself, thought "damn, I meant to ask who the likely new boss of that gang is, to find out if he's one of the men we have in custody from the tunnel." After a minute or two, he thought "I'll have to phone him back on that point." He got onto the control room and asked them to get DCS Lawson back on the phone.

A couple of minutes later, his phone rung. "DCS Lawson on the phone for you sir."

"Thank you" said DI Brough "Sorry about phoning back, but there is one question I could do with finding out. As you know we have men in custody after the tunnel incident. Do you know who the current leader of that gang is? We need to know if there are any loose ends out there."

"Sorry, can't help you there, we're Anti-Corruption department. Unfortunately, the guy we are holding is in the CID for East Glasgow, but we don't know if he was working alone or if there are any other rotten eggs in his department. That means it's difficult to know who we can trust in that section" said DCS Lawson.

"You know years ago when I first started out as a Detective Constable, one of the senior officers was exposed in the same way and it left our department almost ostracised for a year or two. I know just how the other guys in that team must feel," said DI Brough.

"I'll tell you what I'll do" said DCS Lawson "I'll make some discrete enquiries from some of the older hands who know that area and see if they know anything."

"I would very much appreciate that, Sir" replied DI Brough "Thank you again for your help."

Meantime, Luke was building himself back up, steadily, before going back into full circuits for training. He had seen Charlene and approached her with a friendly air, but she was still not as forthcoming as she had been before the tunnel incident. Eventually, she just came out and asked Luke direct "what happened to your eye, Luke?"

"Oh, I just tripped in that tunnel. You remember I told you I was going to a tunnel to survey for bats. Well, I had only just reached the darkest part when I stumbled on some rocks and banged my head. My own fault, I should have been more careful."

"So, what did you do" asked Charlene.

"I just had to go back and then drove myself to hospital," said Luke.

"And was there nobody else involved" asked Charlene.

Luke, checking her body language, realised she was genuinely unaware of what had gone on in the tunnel.

"No, just me," said Luke.

"Oh, I see" said Charlene "I thought something sinister might have happened".

"Why do you say that" asked Luke trying to look surprised.

"Oh, nothing, I just assumed that. That's all" said Charlene rolling her eyes round to meet Luke's gaze.

“Anyway, by next week, I’m hoping to start the circuits again and be back in the classes,” said Luke.

“Good” said Charlene “I’ll maybe see you then” who then turned to go into the class.

Luke carried on cycling on the training bike and thought to himself “as long as nobody informs you of what really happened.” If her contact was still about and didn’t want her to know about the violence that had been intended to be used that night, Luke should be able to play her to bait any remaining gangland members out there.

DI Brough came on the phone to Luke a couple of days later. “Good morning, Luke. This is DI Brough. Are you alone and able to speak for a minute or two?”

“Yes, I’m alone and ok to speak. How can I help you?” said Luke.

“I thought I would let you know that you proved to be right, in that we have found out how Callum Mallachy found out your details,” said DI Brough.

“Oh, was it a cop?” asked Luke.

“Well, I cannot give you any information on the exact details but suffice to say that there was a leak in the system, which has now been found and sorted. A bit late for you, but a good result for us both,” said DI Brough.

“And are there any more gangsters in the pipeline” asked Luke.

“We’re working on that. If there are, there will only be a few, at the most. Between the deaths that have happened in that gangland group and the arrests made that night, we’ve almost certainly broken the back of that gang. The trials will be coming up very soon and I'm as certain as I can be, they'll all be going, or rather should I say, they'll be staying in jail for many years to come," said DI Brough.

"Good" said Luke "I'm glad to hear it. It's all cost me a few grey hairs, to say the very least."

"Indeed" said DI Brough "we'll speak again soon before the trial starts. Bye for now." And with that DI Brough hung up.

"A few grey hairs" thought Luke "all this has nearly cost my life several times over, my job, my family, my income, my eyesight in one eye, I've had to live a life wondering what next and looking over my shoulder, and many friends think I'm not the same person I was years ago, but they have no idea why. The only real positives out of it are I'm still alive and wiser now for all this."

Paul phoned Luke a few days later "Hey Luke, do you fancy going for that pint we talked about a few weeks ago?"

"Yeah, ok Paul" said Luke "sounds like a good idea. There is that trial coming up of the people caught in the tunnel that I mentioned about, so I still cannot say too much about that."

"And are you included in that" asked Paul, tongue in cheek.

"Ah, very funny Paul. When do you fancy going? Do you fancy Thursday, what about down at The Broadsword and Feather Duster Inn?" asked Luke.

"Sounds good, about 8.00pm," said Paul.

"Perfect" said Luke "see you then."

Come Thursday and Luke arrived at The Broadsword and Feather Duster Inn, Paul was at the bar already.

"What do you fancy, Luke," said Paul.

"A pint of cider thanks, Paul".

After taking the pint of cider, Luke moved to a corner table, and they sat down together.

"So how have you been" said Luke "have you been keeping out of mischief."

"Yes, yes, no problem that way. I have been checking quite a lot of Bat sites this year and one or two of the Bat sites have disappeared for unknown reasons, although in one old church hall, they did some roof repairs and that must have disturbed them away," said Paul.

Luke let out a mumbled "Mmmmm" in a way suggesting he'd seen it happen many times before.

"I also went through that tunnel you had surveyed, because you didn't manage to finish it. Guess what. I found a roost of over a thousand Daubenton bats in the first four hundred metres. How could you have missed them, Luke" said Paul.

"No, really, you're winding me up, aren't you" said Luke.

"Correct" said Paul. "Nice to have one in the bag though" said Paul, gloating about having got the first wind up over Luke.

"Very good, Paul. You had me there for a second or two" responded Luke.

The ice broken, Paul obviously had waited long enough, in fact, Luke was surprised he hadn't been asked as he entered the pub.

"So, what's happening in this trial, Luke" asked Paul.

Luke thought he would just wind Paul up a little. "Well, the Police said that if I tell anyone, they will have to lock that person up for the duration of the trial, until it was over" said Luke.

Paul stared blankly at Luke for a few seconds whilst he contemplated if this could be even remotely true. Having decided Luke was winding him up, he continued "Oh come on. What happened in that tunnel" asked Paul.

"If I told you the truth, you just wouldn't believe me," said Luke. Luke could see Paul might burst in anticipation if he didn't find out in the next minute or so. "Alright" said Luke "I was witness to some gangland activity on a trip of mine up in the hills quite a few years ago. Ironically, I didn't see enough to convict any of these guys, but they kept trying to kill me, because they didn't know that."

Paul's jaw looked like it might detach and clang onto the ground like someone had placed a heavy anchor in it.

"No, you're winding me up again, Luke," said Paul.

"I told you, you wouldn't believe me," said Luke.

There was another satellite delay while Paul's brain processed the odds for and against Luke winding him up.

"Right, what's the real truth Luke" asked Paul.

"I've just told you it" said Luke.

Paul hesitated a few more seconds, "Alright, assuming you are telling the truth, what happened in the tunnel" asked Paul with the urgency of a ravenous person who has just been fed food for the first time in a month and just doesn't want to stop on the first mouthful.

"There was just more of the same in the tunnel, some guys trying to silence me, but I was lucky the Police saved the day, thank God," said Luke.

"And" said Paul, gesturing by rapidly rolling his right hand over and over again at chest height and lifting his eyebrows up, like someone who would collapse in the next few seconds if more information wasn't forthcoming.

"And that's really as much as I can tell you because of the trial, sorry Paul," said Luke.

"Do you know, you've been a great mate, but there are times..." said Paul.

"Yes, I know, you're right" said Luke "now, do you fancy another pint?"

"You can think about drinking at a time like this," said Paul.

"Well, I've had more time to adjust to it than you have. Same again, Paul" asked Luke. Luke looked at Paul who clearly wasn't thinking about a pint of beer, as he still had two thirds of a pint left in his glass. He had a faraway look as if immersed in his own little cloud. "Same again, Paul" said Luke, this time with a little more insistence in his voice.

"Ammm, ah, oh yes Luke, thanks," said Paul.

Luke collected the two pints from the bar and sat down again. "If it's any consolation, there might be more information released during and after the trial. Will that do, Paul" asked Luke.

"What's the other options" asked Paul.

"Anyway, did I tell you I watched a Goldeneye duck family several times this summer" said Luke trying to change the subject. "She started out with fourteen ducklings and about a month later, she still had twelve, so she did quite well, don't you think?"

"Ah, yes" said Paul who was obviously wanting to go back to the subject of the tunnel.

Luke though was equally determined to avoid any further involvement. "Have you seen any of our old rugby mates this year Paul" asked Luke. Without waiting for an answer, Luke continued "I saw Matt ironically in a shopping centre. There was a time you'd hardly have seen us dead in a place like that, or at least not unless we were kicking and screaming being dragged in by a wife or girlfriend."

Suddenly Paul kicked back into life, out of neutral and into first gear "Oh I meant to ask Luke, you said you have separated from your wife?"

"Yes, I had other things in my mind recently and we grew apart. She left me and took the kids and I got told to sell the house. Do you want to buy a house Paul?" asked Luke.

"Not so good" said Paul, not even thinking about the house question, "but anyway, look forward, new adventures, new friends and all that".

Shortly after that, the two friends drank up, left the bar and stood outside. "Don't go saying anything to anyone, Paul, about what I told you" said Luke to Paul.

"Well, you barely told me anything at all, just enough to leave me wanting more. And what could I tell anyone, anyway?" asked Paul.

"If you did tell someone, they'd think you'd just been wound up by me. They simply wouldn't believe you" added Luke.

"Well exactly", said Paul who now clearly was wondering if Luke had just been winding him up. They shook hands, said goodbye and departed their different ways.

## Chapter Eighteen – Retribution

The day of the trial arrived, and the ever-hopeful Mary had supporters with placards outside the court declaring they believed the Police had done a cover up on the death of AB (Dean McKenzie).

The baying crowd were moved further away from the courtroom, by a team of Policemen to avoid interrupting court proceedings and disturbing the people that needed to come and go. Even at an extra thirty metres away, they still caused a bit of a raucous noise. The protesting crowd was a good bit depleted, but the diehards that turned up did not lack enthusiasm.

Once everybody had settled in, including Luke at the prosecution table, the judge arrived in and the courtroom was asked to "all stand". When the judge had sat down, the rest of the courtroom followed suit.

Eventually, Luke was asked to take the stand. Luke ran his eye over the public seats at the back of the courtroom. There were a scattering of people sitting in the seats. Luke looked at the judge and said "Judge, do you mind if I speak?"

"Yes, what do you wish to say, Mr Walker?" asked the judge.

"These people in the public seats, can I ask that the Police photograph each and every one of them, to identify them. I believe some of them will be connected to the gangsters that were involved in the incident, your honour." A few people in the public gallery started to look uncomfortable, one actually rose to his feet and walked out. Luke tried unsuccessfully to get a view of him, which was difficult as he had turned his back and was walking away. Luke thought to himself “some of these people are dirty.”

“Mr. Walker, you will concern yourself only with the matters of this court and the questions that will be asked of you. Do you understand, Mr. Walker” said the judge assertively to Luke.

Luke appeared mildly embarrassed. “Yes, your honour” replied Luke.

The prosecution barrister stood up and asked Luke “so Mr Walker, can we ask why were you in the old railway tunnel, on that day?”

“A friend who is in the local area Bat group had asked me to check over the tunnel in case a colony of bats had moved in. There have been no bats for many years in the tunnel, but they asked me to check, just in case,” said Luke.

“Just to clarify, Mr Walker, the bats you are talking about are the small mammals with wings” asked the judge.

“Yes, that’s correct, your honour” replied Luke.

The barrister continued “so you entered this tunnel by yourself?”

“That is correct,” said Luke.

“So were you expecting anyone else, Mr Walker” asked the prosecution.

“Absolutely nobody or indeed anything else,” said Luke.

“So, when did you realise there were other people in the tunnel, Mr Walker” asked the prosecutor.

"I first got a clue when one of the men tripped on a small pile of rocks in the tunnel and was cursing because he had hurt his hand," said Luke.

"Can you describe what happened from there" suggested the prosecution barrister.

"Well, I was concerned that these guys may have represented trouble to me as I had witnessed a gangland crime, years ago and there had been a few attempts on my life in the intervening years. It turns out that I didn't see enough to convict anyone, but they didn't know that, so they just kept trying to kill me."

"Objection your honour, the witness should confine himself within this incident. That information could sway the jury" said the defence counsel.

The judge looked at the jury and said, "you will disregard that statement about being a witness to a previous gangland crime and previous attempts on the witnesses life."

Luke thought to himself "why the fuck am I here then?"

"Continue" said the prosecutor counsel.

"Anyway, I decided to be cautious and so I started to move away from the two guys coming towards me, but I soon found another two coming from the opposite direction. I therefore decided to go back to the darkest part of the tunnel. I covered my face and hair with the grey dust to minimise reflectiveness of my skin. I then went into the one of the tunnel shelters and did my best to stay out of sight. It almost worked as one of the guys passed me by without seeing me and carried on and joined his two compatriots coming from the lower end of the tunnel. I then decided to try and make it past the guy who had hurt his hand, but just as I drew close to him, his friends warned him they had seen my silhouette from their compatriot's torchlight. So, I hit him full whack with my metal torch. I then made a run for it but fell on a pile of rocks slightly further down the tunnel," said Luke.

"And what happened after that" asked the prosecution barrister.

"I was quite stunned and before I knew it the other three guys had grabbed me, pulling me up. One of them hit me across the right side of my face and I suffered a detached retina, from which I still have virtually no sight in the right eye. The guy who had fallen in the tunnel and whom I had hit with my torch, I think his name was Jimmy, was very angry and said for one of them to kill me. The guy he spoke to, took out a knife and was going to stab me, but I kicked the knife out of his hand, before hurting the guy who was holding me from behind by slamming my boot down his shin," said Luke.

"And what happened after that" asked the prosecution barrister.

"Luckily for me, the first three Policemen had arrived from the top end of the tunnel, and they shouted for them all to stop. But the guy who had had the knife, I believe he was referred to as AB, pulled out a gun and grabbed me saying he would shoot if they advanced any further. He then dragged me towards the lower end of the tunnel. We hadn't gone very far, when we came across three more policemen, so the guy holding me, fired off a shot down the tunnel towards the policemen. I knew there could be a fatality imminently, so I just grabbed the gun, twisting it away from his body. In the struggle, he fired another shot, I kicked the legs from underneath him and then kicked his tummy with my heel and kicked the gun away, all in very quick succession. Unfortunately, I ripped his Solar Plexus when I put my heel into his tummy, and he couldn't breathe. Despite attempts to help him, he died."

Next up was the defence barrister. "Mr Walker, if you hadn't hit Jimmy in that tunnel, I say to you that they wouldn't have attacked you in the first place."

"You are probably right. They only brought the knife and the gun along with them for a bit of shooting and knife throwing practice" said Luke with a facetious tone.

Two of the jury let out a little snorted laugh.

"I say again that it was only because of your actions that violence erupted" said the defence barrister.

"What you mean to say is that they were there specifically to bring violence and but for luck it could have been a lot worse" replied Luke in a terse tone.

"One of these guys died. Do you not feel that was a very high price for them to pay. You're still very much alive and healthy" said the defence barrister.

"I have lost the sight in my right eye. It was just their plans didn't fall into place and they came out worse for it. I regret that one of them died, but I believe their intention was to kill me that evening," said Luke.

"I have here character references on these guys which all say they were nice reliable guys. Is it not possible that they were there innocently, and everything just went against them to create this unfortunate set of consequential circumstances. Is that not a possibility, Mr Walker?" asked the defence counsel.

"Absolutely not, they were there on a gangland mission which was to beat me up or kill me. Full stop" replied Luke who terseness was beginning to concern the prosecution team.

"I put it to you Luke that it was your volatile nature which precipitated the whole sequence of lethal consequences and that nobody would have died that night if you had acted more responsibly" said the defence barrister.

Finally, it clicked with Luke, the barrister was trying to make Luke angry. He had been warned that once that happened, that the barrister would be like a shark feeding on an ever-diminishing bait ball.

"I was there on the most innocuous mission of checking for bats. I have no history of violence, but I knew they were there with evil intentions. I only did what I had to do. If I hadn't done what I did, and the Police hadn't turned up in the nick of time, I would most certainly not be here today. In fact, I would either still be in that tunnel decomposing or bagged up and buried elsewhere," said Luke.

"I say that you have a very overactive imagination and that these men are innocent and certainly shouldn't be here having their good reputations tarnished within this court simply because you overreacted on that evening" said the defence barrister.

Luke took a few seconds to hold back his reply which was just as well, as it might have been along the line of "go and fuck yourself, you cheeky bastard." With the defence barristers gaze fixed on Luke in an intentionally belligerent way, Luke reminded himself "cool it Luke, cool it". Luke broke the silence "your questions are not so much questions, as derisory falsified statements against my character. You should remember that these guys brought a fully loaded pistol and a long knife to their party. A shot was fired before it all really kicked off. That does say something, don't you think." The barrister backed off, obviously frustrated that his best efforts had not succeeded, as yet.

"No further questions, your honour" said the defence barrister.

Next up were the Policemen who were in the tunnel that evening. Their statements all closely matched the description given by Luke. It was obvious to all those watching or listening to the proceedings that there was no cover up by the Police and that the death was unfortunate but entirely because Luke decided to take action in the tunnel once the first shot was fired. Two of the Policemen did put the suggestion forward that if Luke hadn't acted the way he did, then there may have been other casualties, or fatalities, possibly either Luke or Police officers.

By the third day of the trial, Mary's crowd had diminished further and the placards had changed from referring to Police corruption to demanding justice for Dean McKenzie. After all the effort that Mary had put into the protest, she still wanted some sort of return on her efforts.

The prisoners were a mixed bag. Two were relatively compliant and said they didn't realise the mission was going to get very heavy handed. They suggested they thought it was just meant to be a mission to scare Luke. Jimmy though was less compliant and got shirty on a couple of occasions, demanding justice against Luke for breaking his ribs. When the prosecution barrister reminded him that he had demanded the execution of Luke in the tunnel, he declared that it was purely because he had got worked up because he had been in pain. Jimmy was expected to receive the heaviest sentence out of the three.

The trial passed surprisingly quickly and by the end of the week it was wound up, with only the sentences to be announced, at a later date.

One freelance journalist had sat in on the court during the trial. She ran a story which sold to several newspapers highlighting the fact that a civilian had intervened in the tunnel during the action and may have saved several policemen's lives. The initial reports did not have any real detail on why the whole incident had come about in the first place, but it certainly put Luke in a good light, even though he naturally shunned attention.

---

A couple of days after the trial closure, Shaun was talking to Robert, otherwise known as Rob, one of his most trusted untrustworthy thugs. "This fucking bastard Luke seems to get away with everything. I've decided to just have him shot, especially after he killed AB," said Shaun.

"I wouldn't do that boss, not a good idea at all," said Rob.

"Why's that" said Shaun with an irritated tone.

"Well for one, if a gun gets used, the Police will swoop down on each and every gangster's house in Glasgow that they know of, to search for that gun and find out who ordered the killing. That sort of thing really pisses off all the gangs. Floorboards will be being ripped up everywhere, dogs will be used. Bedlam, absolute bedlam, boss. Somebody will squeal something, maybe from a rival gang as revenge against you and before you'll know it, the Police will be banging down your door. At the moment, they know you're there, they're just not sure what your involvement is exactly. A shooting will give them the excuse they need. This fella Luke, if he had anything on you, the Police would have you in jail by now."

"Yes, your probably right" said Shaun "but I still want to get him for killing AB".

"Well remember, every time you send people to watch his movements or organise an accident, gives him and the Police more opportunities to catch you. My advice, if you want it, is forget him or you might live to regret it," said Rob.

Shaun grunted, pulling a face like he had just opened the top of a sewer lid and unintentionally breathed in the aroma deeply. He knew that Rob was right, but he still didn't feel happy about it. Shaun was definitely not the forgiving type.

Shaun thought for a minute or so and said to Rob "I know how we could do it without shooting involved. We can get Luke to commit suicide. Charlene and other people that have watched this guy Luke, have said he comes across as being somewhat depressed, possibly because of the death of Dean and with all the events that have happened to him."

Rob looked at Shaun as though he had suddenly grown two extra heads. "Well how could you do that" asked Rob.

"Simpler than you think, Rob. We use a motorcycle with a rider and the pillion passenger has a pistol. They ride alongside his car, get the pillion passenger to indicate to him to stop. Then when he stops, the pillion passenger gets into his vehicle, and they take him to the car park close to those cliffs where all the jumpers go. If done at night, they can walk him up to the cliff and make him jump," said Shaun.

"And what if he won't jump and you have to shoot him. Then you're back to square one, again," said Rob.

"Well, they won't tell him, just get him near the edge facing away from them and with a quick push and he'll be over the cliff, gone forever. As and when the Police find his body, he'll just show trauma damage from the fall, and they'll believe he just committed suicide because of depression" said Shaun.

"Brilliant" said Rob "that's why you're the boss".

"If it's done by reliable men, then I don't see how it can fail, can you, Rob" asked Shaun.

"No boss, it just need's reliable guys and picking the right time and place. Then it should go like clockwork. I'll go to work on picking the two men for the job for you," said Rob.

"That'll do nicely, I'll speak to you in a few days' time, and we'll set it up" said Shaun, who looked very pleased with himself for having thought of the plan within the restrictions recommended by Rob.

Far away, Luke was feeling quite down after the trial because he felt he had done everything as straight as he could, all along the process and yet he felt he was being blamed for the death of Dean. He hadn't received any thanks of any sort from the authorities, and he had been left relatively penniless by his previous employers black balling him. Only his closest friends seemed willing to stand by him, as they knew the real Luke, not the one seen by the baying mob worked up by the greedy lust of Mary. For all that, Luke still had a steely make up, which he was going to need in the next few weeks.

Shaun's men had started monitoring and looking at where Luke went in the evenings. Luke had not found the tracking device under his previous car after they had thrown the rock, smashing his sunroof, because it had been put in for repair. Now Shaun's men planted a tracking device again on Luke's vehicle and Luke had never regularly checked his car for devices. Using it, they could see, that on some nights, Luke travelled back to his home over quieter country roads rather than take the direct route. He did this to see the wildlife on the quieter hill road, such as owls, foxes, and stoats near the road edges as he went home.

Shaun told his guys to be ready to follow him when he looked likely to take one of these country roads home. That meant they would have to be available over several nights and to go on the mission with relatively short notice. They also needed to delay the manoeuvre until Luke's car was on a suitably quiet bit of hill road. It was autumn now and by the time Luke came out of the gym classes, it was always dark. A few weeks after Shaun had consulted with Rob, Luke took off in the opposite direction from the direct route home. He was obviously going the country road loop route. The motorcycle pair were told to go after him but to wait until he was in a quieter stretch of road, before trying to abduct him. They set off and were quickly behind Luke. Luke noticed the motorbike behind him, but he was not particularly suspicious. However, Luke didn't want any vehicle behind him, because if he spotted an owl on a fence post or a fox crossing the road in front of him, he wanted to able to safely stop to watch the wildlife without some irate driver nearly rear ending his car.

Luke planned to go by the hill road, so when he saw the motorbike near the bottom of the hill, he slowed down and opening his window, put out his arm to wave them past, but the motorbike did nothing except stay behind. Luke went further along the road with the motorbike still behind him, but by now, he had his suspicions raised. Luke tried the same manoeuvre again, but this time the motorbike stopped right behind him. Luke saw the pillion passenger start to get off the bike. Luke stuck on his rear red fog lights to see a bit more detail behind him and looking in his mirror suddenly realised the pillion passenger had a pistol in his hand. "Wow. Time to get out of here" he thought to himself. Luke raced away just as the pillion passenger reached his bumper, shouting abuse at Luke as he realised Luke was off. The chase was on.

Luke gained a two hundred metre start before the biker collected the pillion passenger and raced after Luke. Luke took the turn up the hill at record speed for him. He was going to have to drive recklessly to survive this situation. He realised that motorbikes were often used in towns to assassinate people as they were far nimbler and could get away between stationary vehicles or down alleyways. The motorbike would almost certainly ride up to the car drivers' side and the pillion passenger would shoot the driver at point blank range. In the country, the advantages were less obvious, with tight, poorly lit corners, mud on the road and narrower width, leaving more scope for error on a bike. Also, there were more trees to hit and verge potholes. Only the acceleration and manoeuvrability of a motorbike were left being the main advantages, but as Luke knew, that could be a disadvantage as well.

Luckily for Luke, he had anticipated this scenario because of his previous history. He knew what he would do. This hill road was a very narrow road, only just wide enough for two cars. He weaved and dodged a few times, but he knew that sooner or later the motorbike would come up his side. The motorbike even tried to go up the left side, but Luke quickly moved to crush him against the bank with its thorn hedges. The motorbike braked hard, dropping behind his vehicle and Luke could clearly hear him shouting "Fuck you, you bastard, we're going to get you" as once again Luke gained distance away from the bike. However, Luke needed to end this and to do that, he needed to act decisively and take a risk. As the bike accelerated toward the car edging towards the driver side, Luke waited a couple of seconds till the bike was lined up just to the right end of the car, he threw open his car door and at the same time braked as hard as he could. For all the skill of the motorcyclist, he still hit the end of the door very hard indeed and the bike rolled twice at speed before embedding itself into the neighbouring field after passing through the thick hedge. The two men on the back were cast in different directions, one went over the hedge, whilst the driver of the bike stayed closer to the bike, with it actually collecting and crushing him at speed against the hedge trunks as it went past and in one case through it.

Luke stopped as quickly as he could. His car door was crumpled totally out of shape and hanging against the road. He collected a small torch he always kept in his mid-compartment. He realised there may still be a live gunman, but he had little to fear that way. Sheltering behind the car, he phoned 999 and asked for an ambulance reporting his position and adding he thought it may well be a fatal accident. He then asked for police attendance to support him in the "accident zone". He wondered if he went up to the guys in the field would they still be alive and if so, would they be capable of firing shots at him. He needn't have worried. The mashed-up motorbike had stalled, deeply embedded in the mud and close beside it lay one of the men with horrendous trauma injuries. He was however, stone dead. Luke didn't know it, but his back had been snapped. The other guy was still alive but only just. Spitting blood mixed with broken teeth into an already sizeable congealing pool of blood within his helmet, he looked about to drown. Luke felt helpless to know what to do, but he knew if he didn't do something, this guy was going to die as well. He took off his helmet, despite the niggling doubt the man may have had vertebra damage. He stuck his hands in the guy's mouth to clear out the blood and broken teeth. Luke was worried that if he even tried to move the guy into the recovery position, that he may enhance the damage or accidentally kill him. Never had Luke felt so helpless as he saw this guy struggling to stay alive. He raced back to his car to get his coat and a rug he kept in the car to keep the guy as warm as he could, until the services arrived. The guy was virtually unconscious, but by now Luke was feeling a bizarre mixture of feelings - shame that he had deliberately caused the accident, horror at the consequences, fear at what might be likely to happen because of this and outright anger because somebody had instigated this attempt again on his life with unbelievably horrendous results. Luke tried talking to the man and asked him "who asked you to do this?" With his mouth so badly damaged, and his body smashed up, he was having real difficulty breathing, never mind speaking, but he mumbled what sounded distinctly like "Rob".

Just then, a Police car came racing along the road with three more service vehicles not far behind, all using their blue lights and sirens. Luke raced up to the car and waved to the

Policemen. "There's been a terrible accident. Two guys on a motorbike have gone into this field. One is dead for sure and the other one is in a very bad way. I think he might die as well," said Luke. The other service vehicles arrived at the scene, two ambulances and one more police car. Luke directed the paramedics to the still living man and then the dead man.

One of the Policemen asked Luke "what is your name Sir?"

"Luke, Luke Walker" answered Luke.

After asking his address and a few other details, the Policeman asked, "what exactly happened here, Mr. Walker?"

Luke knew this was going to be difficult to explain.

"First, I think you may need more Police here because I believe this was an attempt on my life. This is now a crime scene." said Luke.

"How do you mean, Mr Walker" asked the Policeman.

"I think you should have a look at this" said Luke indicating to the Policeman to come with him to his car. Luke pointed to the car door which was badly crumpled and twisted. "The motorcycle hit this door at speed before spinning out of control into the field. The two men on board ended up going over the hedge and through it with the bike."

"So did you have your door open in the middle of the road like this" asked the Policeman.

"No, this pair of guys were brandishing a pistol and were going to try to shoot me as they drove past." At this point Luke began to break down realising, not for the first time that explaining his position was an almost insurmountable task. "Look, you're not going to believe me, but I had stopped further back down the road to let the motorbike past me, but the pillion passenger got off and started walking towards me. At that point I realised that he was carrying a pistol, so I took off at max speed away from them," said Luke.

"So why did they not just ride up beside you and shoot you then" asked the Policeman who was looking at Luke as though he was standing beside the craziest person he had ever met in his entire working career.

"I don't know. I really don't know why but I wasn't going to wait around to find out. I took off as quickly as I could, but they chased after me and they were trying to get alongside me, presumably to shoot me," said Luke.

At this moment, the Policeman who had been weighing the odds of the truth being told to him, wheeled Luke around, handcuffed him and said "I'm arresting you until we get this matter investigated properly. I'm going to ask some officers to take you to the station where they can ask you for a statement detailing what happened here."

"But I have been telling you the truth" protested Luke. Luke's affirmations were not going to cut any ice with this officer.

Twenty minutes later, a Police arrest van arrived with two Policemen to take Luke to the station. Before he left, Luke said to one of the Policemen "make sure you find the pistol. It'll be in the field or hedges somewhere." The policeman grunted but in a way which suggested he didn't entirely believe what Luke was saying.

It was the first time Luke had ever been locked up in a Police van. He didn't like it at all. "I should have mentioned the recent trial about the tunnel incident. Then they might have believed me" Luke thought to himself.

Twenty minutes later and he was being processed by the police admin staff. He was taken to a cell and told he would be taken to an interview room in the next hour or so. He had time to contemplate his situation which was not good. He wondered to himself "how the hell does all this keep happening to me?" He remembered the grizzly sight of the dead man with the huge trauma to his body from the collision. He wondered if the other guy was going to make it.

It felt strange feeling concern about someone who had been prepared to apparently kill him only a few hours prior. The emotion and shock of the moment got to Luke, who spontaneously burst into tears and who cried like he wouldn't stop.

He had to stop though, because his cell door opened and in stepped a Policeman. "They're ready for you in the interview room, Mr Walker," said the Policeman.

As he walked in, he recognised DI Brough who said "I'm sorry this has happened to you Luke, but we have to ask all the details of what happened tonight. Luckily, when I heard it was you involved, I thought I better take over the questioning as I know some of the Policemen who had been at the accident scene were very upset at what they found there. One guy dead and the other likely to die in one incident can really upset people."

"The other one is likely to die" asked Luke who followed up with "Oh no, I was hoping that the second guy might survive."

"He hasn't died yet, but it's not looking good. Why are you upset if they were trying to kill you" asked the other Policeman who was with DI Brough. "Don't answer that just yet" advised DI Brough sharply, who then softened his tone and said, "sit down Luke, we just need to go through the evenings events step by step."

"First, I'll introduce Detective Sergeant John McIlroy who will be helping me with your statement tonight. Do you have any problems with giving us a statement?" asked DI Brough. "No, not at all," said Luke.

"Right if we start with what your movements were tonight, Luke," said DI Brough.

"I went to a gym class tonight between six and seven pm, then after I showered and changed, I decided to go home the long way over the hill road," said Luke.

"And why did you choose to go that way to your house as it's about three times longer than the direct route" asked Sgt McIlroy.

"Well as DI Brough knows, I'm interested in wildlife and if I go home that way, I sometimes get to see Owls, Foxes, Deer or whatever as they run across the road," said Luke.

DI Brough interjected "so come back to the gym, you set off for this hill road. What happened then?"

"I was getting fairly close to the turn off for the hill road when I noticed a motorbike behind me. I didn't want a vehicle behind me, in case I saw some wildlife and wanted to stop suddenly, so I slowed down and stuck my arm out to indicate it to overtake, but all that happened was it stopped behind me. I thought they were going to turn in somewhere, so I moved on, but the bike stayed behind me. When I saw them still behind me, I slowed down to do the same again, but this time the bike stopped behind me and the pillion passenger got off the bike. I could see in the rear mirror that he was carrying a pistol, so I took off as fast as I could. I know a lot of assassinations are done using a motorbike, so I just had to assume they were going to ride beside me and then shoot at me" said Luke.

"Well, if that was the case, why did they not just ride up to you the first time and do the shooting then" asked Sgt. McIlroy.

"I've wondered about that and to be honest, I really don't know why. All I knew was that it looked likely they were going to shoot me" replied Luke.

"Likely, but not certain," said Sgt. McIlroy.

"I wasn't going to take any chances. Would you have? The first time you find out you were right is when you've been shot," said Luke. "Anyway, they carried on trying to get up the side of my car on the hill road, so I eventually decided the only way I could protect myself was to fling open the car door and brake hard. It worked to save me as they tried to swerve but crashed into my door and ended up in the field," said Luke.

"Yes, with one of them dead and the other one probably about to die" said Sgt McIlroy adding "you realise we still haven't found this alleged pistol yet."

Luke was taken aback at this inference.

"So, what are you saying to me" asked Luke.

"We hope for your sake, we find the pistol, or you might be up on a murder charge," said Sgt McIlroy.

"What, how can this be, I saw the pistol as clear as day," said Luke.

"At night-time and I've been told you have only one eye that works anyway" replied Sgt McIlroy.

For the first time that day, Luke was stuck on what to say. His mind was rolling over on the possibility that he got it wrong. This news left him stunned. He began to doubt himself, how could he have got it so wrong.

DI Brough intervened "We'll have to keep you in the cell tonight, but I'm sure it will all be sorted by tomorrow, Luke."

Luke glanced at DI Brough with flared nostrils but only because he was still contemplating the suggestion of wrongful killing. His mind was not on what DI Brough had said to him.

A Policeman took Luke to the cell. A sinking feeling hit Luke as he sat down on the bed. Why was his luck never changing? Why were these things always happening to him? Could he really have misjudged the situation and two men may be dead because of it? For the first time, Luke seriously contemplated suicide. He didn't fancy long term jail. Once out, he could go to that cliff close by where people jump. What happens if he is kept in jail permanently, so by then that option wouldn't be available.

Luke couldn't sleep most of the night. But as the night progressed, his hope buoyed him up a bit and he decided not to follow up on this line of thought for now.

## Chapter Nineteen – Irredeemable

The next morning, Luke was taken in to speak with DI Brough.

"Luke we still haven't found a pistol. How certain are you that the pillion passenger had a gun?" asked DI Brough.

"I was just about 100% sure at the time. I had switched on the rear fog light and I saw it in that red light. The motorcyclist was very skilful, but the fog light might have meant he didn't see the brake light as I braked hard giving him no time to swerve. I'm sure if you send another team to check over the area, they should find it" said Luke.

"Well, we'll have to, because if there is a gun out there, we don't want it back in the wrong hands or even in children's hands" said DI Brough, who shivered at the possible thought of a kid finding a live gun.

"Have you been able to ask the second guy any questions as yet" asked Luke.

"Not yet, he's still in a pretty bad way" said DI Brough "I do hope he survives."

"So do I," said Luke. "One thing I forgot to mention was that I had asked him who had ordered him to do this whilst he was lying in the mud spitting out blood. I'm sure he mumbled "Rob"" said Luke.

"And you're just telling me this now" said DI Brough with a distinctly irate tone. "We'll be checking phone calls to see what call chains there are, so we can see if there are any Rob's involved," said DI Brough. "Is there anything else you may have overlooked, Luke" asked DI Brough.

Just then, a plain clothes policewoman arrived and handed DI Brough a note. It told DI Brough the pillion passenger had died. "Not good news Luke, the other guy has died too."

"Oh, that's definitely not good" said Luke who was beginning to realise that only added to his problems.

"We'll have to put you in the cell again until we get the report back on the team searching for the gun," said DI Brough.

"Get your team to check back the way from the original collision point, because when the pillion passenger came off, he went high in the air and he may have swung his arms in any direction, so the gun could have gone anywhere, not just into the field," said Luke.

By mid-afternoon, the search team reported back. There was no sign of the pistol. They would have found it if it was in the area. They reported that they would continue until it was dark, but it wasn't looking likely that a pistol was going to be found.

DI Brough realised this was not good news for Luke Walker. He called a meeting with his superior officers, and they all agreed that it looked like Luke had made a mistake and two men lay dead as a result of his flawed conclusion. They knew that he would have to be charged, but would it be murder or manslaughter. He had definitely killed these men, but his past history of being previously targeted by gangland people for either a beating or execution, could that be taken into consideration? They debated the pros and cons of which charge it should be.

The feedback on the identities of the two men showed they were gangland members with unclean records, robberies, lesser violence records, but no very heavy charges against them previously. This led the Police officers to think, could they have accidentally dropped the gun prior to the accident. They decided to extend the search area to roadside vicinity from where Luke had stopped the second time, right up to where the fatal accident had happened.

After another day and the search team still hadn't found the pistol. It looked like Luke had genuinely made a mistake about the pistol. But why were two gangland members riding so aggressively around Luke's vehicle. Could they have wanted to try to cause him to have an accident or was it pure coincidence they were there? After much debate, the Procurator Fiscal decided to press ahead with manslaughter charges against Luke, rather than murder as the feeling was, that it was too much of a coincidence that the guys on the motorbike were gangland members. They must have been up to no good, but Luke would still face years in jail as the result of the consequences.

Luke was devastated with the news as he felt adamant in his mind that he had seen a pistol. He wondered if there may have been some sort of cover up by the Police, but why would they do that? Because of the past record, Luke was given solitary confinement in his jail, but this had an erosive effect on his mental health.

One person that did go to see him in jail was Paul who was genuinely shocked to see his friend in this situation.

The searches for the pistol had come to nothing. Eventually, Luke put a proposal to his friend, Paul, to buy a metal detecting machine, which Luke would pay for, and sweep the area again where the incident had happened. Luke emphasised, with justifiable concern, that if he couldn't clear his name, he would be in jail for many years. Paul said he would order a good reliable make and spend a bit of time sweeping the area, just in case.

---

Once Shaun had found out about the situation with the motorcyclist's deaths, he got onto Mary and explained that the same guy, Luke, that had killed Dean, also caused the deaths of two more guys working for him. He explained that this must genuinely prove Luke was a killer and needed to be jailed and that she should ask again for a Public Inquiry into Deans death, because it all looked much more dubious now that two more men lay dead. Of course, Shaun also had an additional motivating factor in that jail might present a few opportunities to get at Luke through his contacts inside. Shaun was especially enraged with Luke as the death toll had risen and increasingly had presented more and more problems.

Mary felt certain she was almost guaranteed to get a very nice payment from her claim about being Dean's girlfriend, especially as the same guy had caused the deaths of two more guys. She looked upon it as just about in the bag, so she started to work up a mob on social media. She wanted justice, this guy Luke was irrefutably a killer and the whole thing stunk of a cover up. If the same thing happened again, then it would show the authorities were dirty. More and more people were hearing Mary's thoughts on the whole process and many people were determined to show their support for her when the trial date arrived. She had a very large baying mob ready to go to work when the day came.

The Police, though, had not been sitting on their laurels. They had determined that the two dead motorcyclist and passenger were both from Glasgow, had known criminal records and both had been in touch with Rob McFerran. He, in turn, had been in touch with Shaun McCready before and after being in touch with them. The Police now knew who Shaun was, but because of the circumstances in the upcoming trial, there seemed nothing they could do against him. He was going to get off with all the gangland activity they had traced back to him unless there was some sort of miracle.

The trial date arrived, and this time Marys placard wielding crowd was greatly enhanced from the last time. They made quite a rumpus demanding true justice for Dean, to the extent that the judge had to insist on the Police moving them even further away from the courtroom than on the previous trial.

On the trial date, a package arrived for Paul. It was the metal detector. Paul quickly assembled it and read the instructions. Paul had thought of going to the trial, but he knew that if he actively searched for the pistol, it would be time better spent for Luke's purposes. He set off to where the incident had occurred and got out. He searched up and down the hedges, within the adjacent fields and anywhere else that looked a possibility but to no avail. He had started furthest away and worked back towards the gate that the service vehicles had used to access the field. After several hours, with no success and hardly any beeps from the machine, he headed back up to the gate. Paul was beginning to wonder if the battery had gone dead, so he decided to hold the head near the fence and sure enough, off it went...beep, beep, beep. He made his way to the sludge of mud around the gate area to cross over the gate and get back to his vehicle, having failed in his mission. As he approached the sludge area of the gate, suddenly there was a strong reaction from the metal detecting machine. Beep, beep, beep, beep. Paul was taken aback, but thought it'll just be a spare bit of wire from the fence. It couldn't be anything else than that, surely. The thick mud didn't entice Paul to stick his hand in to check it out. He decided not to bother, as it'll be just wire or something equally useless. He climbed over the gate and walked the twenty metres to where he had parked his vehicle tight against the fence. He dismantled the metal detector machine and put it in the boot. He was just going to get into the driver's seat and head away when he paused, concerned that his reluctance to check out the signal because of the mud could be unforgiveable. He opened his car boot and took out the wheel nut bar, sighed deeply as he admitted in his mind that he should have checked it out the first time. He headed back, climbed the gate and proceeded the three metres to where the metal detector had indicated there was something buried in the mud. He stuck in the end of the wheel nut until he found something solid. Paul lifted up the end and the muzzle of a pistol emerged from the sludge.

"Fucking hell" thought Paul "this must be it. It must have been pushed into the slurry by the vehicles that night as they pulled in to attend to the two dead and dying guys. I had better phone the cops." He left it sticking out of the mud, without touching it.

Paul then phoned the police station, explaining the situation. He asked for Police attendance to collect the pistol. About twenty minutes later the first police car arrived. It was just two beat cops, who had a look at the muzzle sticking out of the slop and agreed it looked like a pistol. Eventually some detectives arrived and then DI Brough, who had been alerted within the courtroom, arrived.

He spoke to Paul "You've done well to uncover this, Paul. I can only think the ambulance reversing in that night of the incident must have just pushed it below the mud and because the search vehicles parked in here, they may have been right above the pistol. Nobody would have thought of checking under there. Thank God you found it, or Luke could have been heading to jail for many years."

The detective team extracted the pistol and took it away for examination and cleaning. The trial was postponed the next day, then dismissed the day after, Luke was released from jail, but he still had to give his account of the incident on a future date, but without the axe hanging over his head of a manslaughter charge. It was broadly accepted he had only acted in justifiable self-defence.

One person who didn't take the news well was Mary. She started a social media campaign, declaring that the authorities had conspired to cover up the truth. She still had a sizeable crowd following her case on social media, nearly all believing she had justification for her concerns. Mary found she enjoyed being an influencer on social media and kept her presence on the network. People began to approach her when they felt their case in a future trial needed some help.

Two guys who were very lucky and came out almost unscathed were Shaun and Rob. The presence of a pistol did not mean they could be charged with conspiring to murder, but they were lucky men. If not very careful, their time as free men could be running out.

Luke was very grateful to Paul for helping save him and the two became even stronger bonded friends. DI Brough joked with the pair of them that they should set up as a Private Detective

Agency and that they should call it "the Disciples Detective Agency" because of their names.

**Chapter Twenty – The Elimination**

One person who did read the article was Shaun who was by now incandescent with rage as he had lost so many men trying to rid himself of the Luke problem. He contacted Rob and asked for a meeting.

Rob knew what was coming next and anticipated Shaun's reaction. "Look Rob" started Shaun "I really need to get this fucking guy Walker because the bastard has killed several of my men and got several more jailed. Nobody, but nobody does that to me and lives."

Rob was somewhat more dispassionate. "Shaun, if that's what you want, we can organise it, but if he had anything on you, the Police would have had you behind bars by now. If you continue, you might just create a situation that turns your luck around or maybe, maybe a lot worse. It might just seal your fate behind bars. It would be safer to forget the whole thing altogether."

Shaun intervened "yes but he is making a mockery of me. All the other gangs will lose respect for me. I can't have that. I want him done, once and for all, understood." Shaun continued "go away and think of a plan that'll work. Use Mary to tempt him in, if necessary, whatever, just come up with a fool proof plan."

Rob knew there was no point in even trying to turn Shaun's attitude, it would only have inflamed him even more.

"Okay boss" said Rob "I'll have a think and get back to you in the next day or two with an idea or two."

"No ideas, just a solution" said Shaun very firmly.

Rob went away and mulled the options over in his mind. He knew that Luke was now separated and may have been susceptible to the charms of a woman, but he dismissed using Mary as she had been at trials and on televised interviews. He also knew that Luke would find her a little rough and smell a rat straight away. How could he do it? He didn't want to leave any clues which might come back to haunt him, so he immediately discounted a shooting or even a stabbing. Too many forensic clues could be left, far too many. If he hired a killer and they got caught, they might squeal, putting him and Shaun in jail for a long time. He'd seen it happen before. Rob was certainly astute for a gangster. He wanted to be successful, he certainly didn't want to be a jailbird. Maybe researching a novel or television programme might hold the answer, but no, within seconds he discounted that idea. Maybe he could research true unsolved murders on the internet, but then that could leave a digital trail back to him. There were no easy answers coming back to him, but he did know, somehow, he had to find a way to satisfy the wrath of Shaun.

He listed options on a wipeable whiteboard – honeytrap, suicide, accident and poisoning. Then he broke them down further with extra options below each method, such as fall, motor accident, mushroom ingestion, drink spiked, asphyxiation. He stepped back to see if anything rung as feasible, an option he could build a plan around. Nothing leapt out at him. Maybe he would have to resort to his last choice, the gun or knife option.

As he stood there, he suddenly realised that using just one option wasn't the way but using a combination of options may get the result he needed. He knew that Luke may have been susceptible to a honeytrap as he had been separated from his wife for many months, that he had been described by Charlene as sometimes sad, which may have left it open for suicide to appear as cause of death. If he could use an attractive lady option to get him up to the cliffs, then if Rob or Shaun came out from the woods with a gun, they might just be able to force him to jump to his death.

Could they use Charlene? Absolutely not. She certainly wasn't the right material for that type of set up. She would crack within two minutes of police interrogation. Could they use Mary? Absolutely not as her face may have been recognisable and she wouldn't have been the type of personality that Luke would be attracted to anyway. Pity, because she would have suited under police interrogation as tough enough to keep her mouth shut.

How would they get the honeytrap set up anyway as Luke would quickly smell a rat. He needed to be taken in completely for it to work. It couldn't be done, but then, thought Rob, if Mary played the catfish with her newly acquired digital skills and they used another ladies' photographs, Luke might just be taken in. Mary could use her best seductive digital skills to rope him in to a seemingly innocent meeting at the clifftop views, then Rob could take over with a pistol or knife and force him to jump. But how to hook him in first?

Charlene was the answer for that. Relatively innocent, she could be told to tell Luke about a beautiful lady looking for a nice man on a dating site and how to contact her. Rob was forming the plan in his mind, covering all the loopholes, making sure it was as watertight as it could be. It had to be perfect, leaving just about nothing to chance. Rob needed this to work and for there to be no comebacks to him.

Within a couple of days, Rob was in front of Shaun. They were reluctant to discuss delicate matters on the phone as the police may have had taps on them. Shaun was the first to broach the subject. “Well, have you got a plan to deal with Luke Walker?” asked Shaun. “I most certainly do, Shaun. We’re going to use Mary as a catfish to hook Luke on a dating site. We’ll get him up on the basis of it being a nice place to meet her at the top of the scenic cliff viewpoint and then I’ll come in and using a pistol, force him to jump,” said Rob.

“Ah well” said Shaun “from what I know about that cunt Walker, he’d be unlikely to meet a woman like Mary. I think he’s a bit of a snob, he’d be attracted to a level of refinement which would be beyond Mary’s normal behaviour.” Shaun continued “besides, Mary has been on television and protesting at the trials. He’ll just recognise her and that’ll be that.”

“Ah well, I’ve thought of that,” said Rob. “We’ll get her to do a proper catfish job, with false pictures and suggestions for tempting the guy into a meeting with her. It should be easy for Mary to do that, don’t you think?” asked Rob.

“Well, if it works, I want to be the one who forces him off the cliff. That bastard has done enough damage. I’m looking forward to it,” said Shaun.

“So, you really want to do the job yourself” asked Rob.

“Absolutely 110%” said Shaun unaware of his mathematical error. “You know, I think this plan might just work. Go for it” finished Shaun.

“Will do,” said Rob.

At that the two men parted and Rob headed away to plan the next stage.

“Mary, hi is that you” asked Rob on the phone a couple of days later.

“Who’s this?” responded a terse Mary.

“My name’s Rob, I work with Shaun, Shaun McCready.”

“Aye awright, so why are you phoning me” Mary questioned Rob, still in her broad Glaswegian accent and still with an abrupt tone.

“I want you to do a little job for me and Shaun, together,” said Rob.

“I didnae think Shaun was into that sort of thing, wi’ two women maybe, but I’d need to know you a bit better first” replied Mary, this time in a more matter of fact but surprised tone.

“No, no, I didn’t mean that sort of thing” continued Rob, “I need you to set up a false dating site profile and I want you to try to hook in a guy to meet you in the near future.”

“Why would I do that, all I’d have to do is appear in a bar he goes to, with my low cut, short dress and I’d soon have him like putty in my hand,” said Mary.

“Well, you probably wouldn’t Mary, not this guy,” said Rob.

“Why is he a poofter, does he prefer men?” said Mary in her typical non-PC way.

"No, not at all" replied Rob "it's just he might prefer a lady of a little more sophistication than you."

Rob didn't realise it, but he had begun to dig a very deep hole for himself with Mary.

"Oh yeah" said Mary very abruptly, "I'll bet you that if I set my sights on him, I could have him gaga for me very quickly."

"Well maybe, Mary," said Rob.

"No maybe about it" said Mary "it would pure dead certain."

"Look doll, I didn't mean to insult you, it's just that we need to get him at a rendezvous point without him realising he's walking into a trap" continued Rob.

"I don't like the sound of that" said Mary "who is he and what's he done?"

"It's the guy who killed AB in the railway tunnel and the two guys on the motorbike," said Rob.

"Oh, I see. Well, I suppose he deserves what's coming to him then" said Mary "but I could thank him for killing AB, dirty malicious bastard that he was".

Mary's face would have revealed only too plainly how she really felt about the thought of AB, if anyone could have seen her. She looked like she had just stood on something very squidgy and unpleasant, as well as receiving a highly repugnant smell.

"All right, what do you want me to do" asked Mary.

"Quite simple, Mary, we need to set you up with a false dating site account, I'll get photos of a suitably attractive lady for the site" said Rob "and then we'll get it out to Luke that he should get in touch with you. All I need you to do is reply as though you are interested but coy, sophisticated and reticent to meet until he is ready to take the bait. You need to build up a false portfolio of details about yourself and whatever you do, don't tell him anything true about yourself, so nothing can come back to you. You understand that don't you?' asked Rob.

"Yes, yes, I wasn't born yesterday, you know" said Mary in a slightly belligerent tone.

"Well, that's ok then" said Rob "I'll start the job and get back to you when we're ready to go, is that alright?" asked Rob.

"Aye, nae bother" said Mary "I presume I'll be well rewarded for my part in this?'

"Of course, Shaun will look after you on that score, nae problem" replied Rob.

"I'll speak to you soon doll" and with that, he rung off.

Within a week, Rob had the profile set up. He picked up a batch of photos of a Scandinavian model to use, with just enough images to do the job. He gave her the profile name of Emerald Eyes, because she had beautiful green eyes along with red hair. He set her details as Swedish but recently moved to Scotland and keen to see the local Scottish scenery and wildlife. She was in her forties and enjoyed socialising. Rob was guessing as to what Luke would find attractive, but he just about hit the nail bang on the head.

Next, he told Mary the details of the profile he had built and told her to prepare herself for pretending to be a redheaded Scandinavian beauty. Mary had already made up her mind on what she was going to pretend to be, so Rob's details threw her a bit and she had to start all over again. She had thought that Rob would make her a rich Glaswegian brunette, now living in Edinburgh. She was told to be prepared for a lot of guys contacting her but the whole purpose was to get Luke interested.

The next step was to get Charlene informed with suggestions of telling Luke about this beautiful lady but innocent of the true intentions. This wasn't going to be as simple as it might seem. Even Charlene could be suspicious, if things didn't quite fit. Rob knew Charlene's handler who had been asking her about Luke, was a fit looking young guy but he lacked finesse. Doing the setting up of Charlene alone would probably spell disaster. Rob knew he would have to pull in some help. He contacted a girl from Glasgow, good looking, relatively articulate, early thirties, called Fiona. She didn't need to do much except put a story across convincingly. Rob asked Charlene's handler James and Fiona to meet him in a quiet coffee bar near Glasgow City centre.

"Right, you two, I need you both to do a little job for me. You're a couple and what I want you to do James, is to contact Charlene in a few days' time. Tell her you've met this lovely lady called Julie, Julie Gray, that's you Fiona, and you want Charlene to check her out for you. Tell her you really think she may well be the one for you, but you'd appreciate if she would meet with you both and in a quiet moment, let you know what she thinks. Your role Fiona, I mean Julie, is to be as nice as you can to Charlene, win her over with your charm," said Rob. "What for though, where's this going" asked Fiona. "I'm just coming to that, Fi..., eh Julie. When you meet with her in a café just like this, I want you to tell her, eventually, after a suitable time, so there is no suspicion, that you have a gorgeous redheaded friend from Scandinavia who has only arrived about six months ago, living fairly locally and she's looking for a suitable boyfriend. He'd need to be someone who keeps fit and loves wildlife, about forty or fifty mark, unattached, fairly intelligent and interesting. Show her the profile of the woman and let her see how attractive she is. Ask her if she can think of anyone suitable that she could put onto her. The name in the dating site is "Emerald Eyes. Can you cope with all that?" said Rob. "What we want is for Charlene to put Luke Walker onto Emerald Eyes, but without Charlene realising she has been manipulated to that point."

"Aye that should be no bother," said James.

"Okay what's your girlfriends name then" asked Rob, looking at James, who had a befuddled look on his face and a satellite delay before answering.

"Eh, how'd'ya mean" replied James.

"Look, what's your girlfriends name" asked Rob.

"Patsy, why?" asked James.

"Look James, what's the name of your girlfriend" said Rob, pointing at Fiona pulling an exasperated face which reflected his feelings about James.

"Oh, right, Fiona" said James "Oh I mean, what's her name, ehhh, Julie, yeah Julie Black."

"Julie Gray. Eventually we've got there" said Rob "now don't forget the details, from now on, always call her Julie, Julie Gray." Turning around to Fiona with his eyes raised skyward in the hope that she might perform better, Rob nodded at her and said "perhaps it would be best if you do most of the talking. What's your name?"

"Julie, Julie Gray" answered Fiona.

"Correct" said Rob "and what's the name of the lady you want to find a new male friend for and her details?"

"Her dating profile name is Emerald Eyes, she's a Scandinavian red headed beauty as you plainly see by the photographs on the site. She's wanting to meet a fit guy in his forties or fifties whose interested in nature and the outdoors" answered Fiona.

"Full marks, Fiona, I mean Julie, Julie Gray, although I think you made up the outdoors bit, but that's ok, it fits perfectly. Well done, there's hope yet this plan will work. Right do you both know what you'll have to do in a few days when you've got it all firmly in your head" asked Rob doing a knuckle knock on the top of his head, emphasising the point.

"Yes, we've got it," said Fiona.

"Well make sure you both have, alright James," said Rob. "Once you've done it, let me know how it went," said Rob.

"And can we break up immediately after that" asked Fiona.

"Too right, I wouldn't blame you if you do, Fiona, I mean Julie" said Rob.

"I was hoping we could have gone on a world cruise together" chipped in James who had a soured face from Fiona's attitude about him.

“You’re not getting that well paid, James” said Rob “just don’t balls it up. Remember, let me know how it goes with Charlene.” With that he stood up, put a twenty-pound note on the table for the coffees and left.

A few days later James phoned Charlene “Hi Charlene, it’s James here, how are you doing?”

“I’m okay, how are you James” asked Charlene.

“I’m great, Charlene. I’ve met a lovely girl from Glasgow. I really think she could be the one for me,” said James.

“I thought you sounded rather bouncy. You’re not usually like this, James,” said Charlene.

“I was wondering, would you do me a little favour Charlene” asked James.

Charlene hesitated on the answer and wondered what was coming next.

“Alright, if I can. What do you want, James” asked Charlene.

“Well, I was hoping to let you meet her, say at a coffee shop, so you can let me know what you think of her, once you’ve talked with her for a while. Would you mind doing that for me, Charlene” asked James.

James was sure he heard a groan on the other end of the phone.

“I’m not sure that it’s my place to comment on a person I don’t know,” said Charlene.

James felt he was losing this request. "Oh please, please Charlene. It's just after a few of the girlfriends I've had, I want to be sure," said James.

Silence. James could sense this wasn't going the way he'd hoped. "Oh, please Charlene, I just don't want to be heartbroken again. Can you do this, just the once for me" asked James.

"Well, you've never struck me as the sort that had had his heart broken before, but okay, just this once" replied Charlene.

"Great, why don't we meet in McCaffreys Coffee Bar on Saturday at 11.00am," said James.

"Well okay, what's her name" asked Charlene.

"It's ahh, ahh, ahmm, Julie, Julie is her name, yes that's it" said James with a tone of relief he'd remembered.

"Well, I'm glad you two are on first name terms at least. I'll see you on Saturday." With that she ended the call.

Come Saturday and the three met in McCaffreys Coffee bar. Fiona (alias Julie) started the conversation. "Hi Charlene, I'm Julie, I've heard so much about you."

Charlene furrowed her brow and asked "all good, I hope?"

"Yeah, all very good, James was just telling me all about you. You go to the gym and like to socialise in the town. Sounds good and wicked to me at the same time. I've often thought about going to the gym myself but so far, I never actually get it together, for it to happen. I like dancing and other sociable forms of exercise, if you know what I mean" said Julie winking at Charlene.

"Yeah, I think I know what you mean. So how long have you guys been seeing each other" asked Charlene.

James and Julie blurted a reply at the same time "three weeks" said James, "three months," said Julie.

They both looked at each other. Julie intervened and said, "it's actually three months, James has just said to me how fast the last three months have passed." "Seems like three weeks instead of three months".

James added "yes, that's right, I was just saying that the other day, ah a week ago".

Charlene didn't pick up on the inconsistencies but liked talking about herself so she moved on to the next topic "yeah, the girls and I often go to Tiptoes nightclub. We have great fun there. If you move up here, Julie, you should come out with us sometime."

Feeling she had gained some ground, but a bit earlier than she meant to, Julie intervened, "You know Charlene, talking about moving into the area, I have a friend, a girlfriend from Scandinavia who has moved in close by recently. She's a bit older than us but she's keen to find herself a suitable boyfriend. I'll let you see her photos from the dating site she's on. She calls herself Emerald Eyes because she's got beautiful green eyes." At that, Julie opened the profile on the dating site and passed her phone over to Charlene.

"Oh, she is very attractive, isn't she" said Charlene "What's her real name?"

Julie and James looked at each other with sudden panic on their faces.

"Ah Jane" said James hurriedly".

"Yes, and she's looking for her Tarzan, is she," said Charlene.

"Aye, very good, very funny" said Julie dryly.

"You know, I think I might know just the man for her. In fact, he'd be perfect," said Charlene.

"Who would that be" asked James. "George, an uncle of mine" replied Charlene "except he doesn't go to the gym or is interested in nature."

"Oh no, I would say that friend of yours in the gym, you know, the slightly older guy in his late forties, would be really suitable," said James.

Charlene shook her head whilst looking straight at James, showing she was a bit bamboozled by his suggestion. "You know, oh what's his name, Luke, Luke Walker" said James who writhed a bit inside knowing he wasn't really supposed to prompt Charlene to that conclusion.

"But he's married, isn't he" asked Charlene.

"Well, I had heard that he's been separated for quite a while now," said James.

Julie intervened "do you think he might be a suitable candidate for Jane, Charlene?"

"Well now you mention him, yeah I think he would match her very well," said Charlene.

"Oh well, in that case, promise me you'll put him onto her, on her dating site. She was just saying how few men are even close to what she really wants in a man" said Julie looking straight into Charlene's eyes to reinforce the point.

"Well okay, I'll do that next time I see him at the gym, if that's what you really want me to do," said Charlene.

"Oh yes, that would be a great favour for me. Thank you very much. You won't forget, will you" replied Julie.

"No, don't worry, I won't forget," said Charlene.

James nodded at Julie acknowledging the success. Julie got up and said, "I'm just off to the ladies."

When she had departed, James leant over and asked Charlene "well, what do you think of Julie?"

"She seems very nice to me, she's attractive and smart" said Charlene whilst thinking "too smart for you, James. You're a bit of a muppet."

"If she moves up here, I'm sure she would fit in with the girls" added Charlene.

"Well, we shall see if that happens or not" replied James who now had a cold tone as he knew the work was done. A few minutes later, Julie came back, they paid the bill, made their excuses, thanked Charlene and departed. Charlene had only drunk two thirds of her mug of coffee and wondered to herself "what was all that about?"

A few days later, Luke and Charlene appeared five minutes before the circuits class started. Charlene went over to speak to Luke. "Hi Luke, how are you doing?"

“I’m fine Charlene” said Luke who was still a bit suspicious about the link between the tunnel incident and Charlene.

“I hear you’re divorced now. I didn’t know that,” said Charlene.

“Well not quite divorced yet but I will be very soon,” said Luke.

“I know a very attractive Scandinavian redhead that’s looking for a guy just like you,” said Charlene.

“What, for a one-night stand” replied Luke with a joking but hopeful smile.

“No, she actually wants a gym buddy who’s interested in the outdoors and wildlife,” said Charlene.

“Oh well, in that case, why didn’t you say so” said Luke who was thinking “well that’s fortuitous” and smiling infectiously like a Cheshire cat.

The class instructor intervened “right, lets get started”.

Charlene said “I’ll show you her details after the class, Luke.”

After an exhausting hour of exercise, most of the class dispersed either homeward or into the showers and changing rooms. Luke and Charlene went into the Lounge and Charlene said “I’ll just get my phone and I’ll show you this ladies profile.”

A few minutes later she was back and sat down beside Luke.

“Wow, she is pretty indeed. Scandinavian you say. Maybe, far too pretty for me” said Luke after looking at her profile.

“You’re probably exactly what she is looking for” said Charlene “you’re too modest, Luke.”

"Well maybe, but I'll certainly write to her and see how it goes" said Luke "thanks for letting me know, Charlene."

"No bother, by the way her profile name is Emerald Eyes but her real name is Jane" said Charlene.

"I didn't think Jane would have been a common name in Scandinavian countries, but maybe I'm wrong," said Luke. "Thanks again, Charlene, I better go and have a shower. I'm beginning to get cold."

"Me too", said Charlene.

At that, they went their separate ways.

Two days later, Luke sent off a message to Emerald Eyes, uncertain if she would reply. He was delighted when she wrote back saying she was glad that he had contacted her, that her friend Julie had been in touch with her and that she had said that we may well get on very well indeed.

Luke wondered who Julie was, as he certainly didn't know a Julie. He wrote back saying "I'm unaware of a Julie. Are you sure you're not confusing me with someone else?"

The reply read "Julie is a friend who knows of you, but she's never had the chance to meet you in person. She's going by your reputation as you seem to be a nice guy and when I said it's very difficult to meet suitable men, she said that you may well fit the bill perfectly."

"I hope she didn't tell you I was wealthy because I most definitely am not, much as I wish I was" wrote Luke.

"Oh no, of course not, but I'm sure you'll be wealthy enough for me" came the reply.

"Look Jane, by your looks I think you may well be outside my expense budget" wrote Luke, adding "if you're looking for somebody with a fair reserve of money, then I'm certainly not going to be that man, unless I win the lottery and that's very unlikely as I never enter it."

"Who's Jane, my name is Ingrid" wrote back Mary who had now taken over the catfishing account to write back, but who had been unaware of the proclamation of the name "Jane" by James to Charlene.

"Well, I was told that was your real name by Charlene, who says she knows you as a friend."

"Oh yes, Charlene, of course. She can be a bit dippy." stated Ingrid.

Luke knew that Charlene was capable of being a bit dippy. "Look, this all sounds like a bit of a mix up" said Luke who was feeling mildly concerned that it all didn't fit as a genuine link "much as I like the look of you, I think you've been given misleading information."

"No, no, not at all. I really have been told good things about you and I do want to meet and get to know you" wrote back Mary who was beginning to realise this fish may well throw the hook and all the hard work would have been for nothing. Plus, there would be the wrath of Shaun to face if it all went wrong. Concerned, she threw in an extra temptation "who knows what we might get up to after we first meet. I doubt if you'll regret meeting me" wrote Mary.

Luke was slightly bemused at this directness but thought maybe that's just the way Scandinavian girls communicate, as he honestly didn't know, never having dated one. The possibilities enhanced his curiosity and interest but ultimately succeeded in raising his suspicion levels enough that he wanted to cover himself, in case there may have been sinister intentions. The previous incidents were still far too fresh in his mind.

Mary continued writing "I know I wouldn't normally do this, but I'm going up to the Craigievoun viewpoint this Sunday morning to photograph the dawn sunrise with my brother. I would love to meet up with you at the viewpoint pillar. It would mean an early start to meet at 6.00am before the dawn, but I'm sure you'd love it. So, what do you think?"

Luke thought about it. Best scenario, it goes well, they get on like a house on fire and become great mates or more. It could be the best decision he has made in years.

Worst scenario, it's some sort of trick. Why had there been so many inconsistencies with wrong names and Charlene's involvement as well. Luke didn't think she had an evil bone in her body, but could she be being manipulated by someone else. Luke thought he smelt a rat, but he wasn't sure.

He wrote back to Ingrid "alright, I will come up to Craigievoun viewpoint on Sunday at 6.00am. I'll be looking forward to meeting you and your brother then. Hopefully we'll get a nice sunrise. See you then".

It all seemed very fast. He had hardly started talking to Ingrid but the meeting had been organised. Normally first dates take about a month of to and fro writing to get the trust built up on both sides, sufficient for the meeting. But here he was within a day or so of starting the communication. Why did he feel uncomfortable with the circumstances?

The more he thought about the circumstances of this development, the more mixed his feelings became. He was hopeful that she really was the attractive girl on the online site interested in similar subjects and pursuits. They could be absolutely right for each other. But then, previous experience had told him to be ultra-cautious as he might just be walking into some sort of trap. He decided to consult with Paul.

Paul's mobile rang. "Hello, Luke how are you doing? I was going to phone you anyway to see how things are with you."

"I'm well, Paul. In fact, I'm either very well or I'm going to have to ask for your help, because I could be up a creek with no paddle".

Paul frowned with confusion "how do you mean, Luke, what's happened since I last spoke to you?"

"It's a bit of a long story, Paul, but basically I've started talking online to a nice redhead from Scandinavia."

"Nice" said Paul.

"Well maybe, we've arranged to meet at Craigievoun viewpoint at 6.00 am on Sunday to photograph the sunrise," said Luke.

"That's a bit early, sunrise is about an hour after that," said Paul.

"Yes, I know that I did wonder why so early before the dawn" said Luke "but it's all the other inconsistencies that have got me worried."

"What like" asked Paul.

"Well, there have been names raised that I have no idea about, a Julie that knows me well enough to recommend me to this Scandinavian, but I don't know her. There was also a mention of Jane as the name of the lady, but she says her name is Ingrid" added Luke.

"Well, Jane doesn't sound like a Scandinavian name, there's probably nothing in that" added Paul.

"Yes, but the list goes on, it was Charlene that put me in touch with her and it was Charlene that said her name was Jane. Then there's the fact that I was only on talking to Ingrid for one day and she's already asking to meet," said Luke.

"Lucky you" said Paul "she sounds like a dream come true, she knows what she wants and just goes for it."

"I don't think you need my help at all, Luke," said Paul.

"Well maybe, but there is just something that worries me about this whole set up" replied Luke "What if it is a trap of some sort?"

"Ah, you're basing this on a couple of recent experiences, which admittedly would make me as cautious as you. So, what do you want me to do, just in case there might be ulterior motives for this lady to meet you" asked Paul.

"Right, here's the plan. Are you okay with meeting me at 5.30am at the main car park before we walk up and meet them, although we will split before then" asked Luke.

"Yes, no problem," said Paul.

"Bring your mobile with you and suitably strong pair of gripping boots," said Luke.

"Goes without being said, I gave up on bare feet quite a while ago" replied Paul cheekily.

"Great, I was just checking. What we'll do is when we get within 200 metres of the viewpoint, I will phone your mobile and keep it on open mic to you. I'll bring a Dictaphone, set it to record as well and put it in my other pocket. Then I'll go ahead of you. You go into the woods to hide your presence and follow me as closely as you can. I need you to keep an eye open for anything unusual or any obvious signs of evil intentions," said Luke.

"I'm quite sure that nothing is going to happen, but I'll go along with your plan just in case. So, what do I do if there is something dodgy does happen to you, Luke?"

"Well then you should call the Police, explain the situation and get out of there as quickly as possible" answered Luke.

"What and just leave you, Luke" asked Paul.

"Absolutely just don't forget to get the Police on scene as soon as possible."

"And if she French kisses you and is very friendly, what do I do then" asked Paul.

Luke laughed and snorted "with her brother there, I don't think so. She is a transvestite, so she won't be terribly shy. Did you not know that's what I am into these days," said Luke.

"No... What, she's a ....... Oh, very good, you had me there for a second again. That's two up, for you" replied Paul.

"Anyway, I don't want to score so many points over you that you refuse to turn up on Sunday morning," said Luke.

"There's very little fear of that. I mean I'm not going to turn up now anyway, after your attempts at humiliating me. I just have to even the score before we end the phone conversation," said Paul.

"Well, sorry to have to break this to you but I am going to end the conversation, you know, whilst I'm ahead and all that" said Luke "you are going to turn up though, aren't you?"

"Well, that's for me to know and for you to wonder why I didn't turn up" answered Paul.

"That sounds good enough for me" said Luke "I'll see you in a few days' time."

"Will do, see you then, …maybe" answered Paul mischievously.

At that they both hung up.

It seemed like no time before Sunday morning arrived. Luke was up at 4.30am, showered and dressed quickly, wearing practical outdoor clothes but tidy in case he would have to impress. He drove up to the main viewpoint car park which lay half a mile walk from the cliff top viewpoint. He arrived at 5.30am to find Paul there already fitting on his boots. Luke jumped out of his car and said "Morning Paul. You all ready for this. Phone and binoculars with you."

"You know, I knew there was something I forgot. I'll just have to go quickly back home and get them" said Paul with a solemn tone.

"Are you serious" asked Luke.

"First point to me. It could be a long day for you my friend" replied Paul.

"Lack of sleep you know. All down to wondering if you'd really turn up, knowing how unreliable you are" replied Luke.

"Seriously" asked Paul with a frown suggesting disappointment in his friend's lack of faith.

"That's one point each. Two can play that game you know" said Luke "I think though we better focus on the job ahead."

"I think whilst you've been unlucky in the past, I don't honestly think anything bad will happen today. In fact, it could be the exact opposite. It might be your lucky day" continued Paul.

"Well maybe, we shall see. Are there any other cars in the car park," said Luke.

"None at all, no cars, pickups, motorbikes, bicycles, nothing," said Paul.

"I wonder how they're getting up there" asked Luke.

"Don't know" said Paul "maybe they're going to stand you up. I hope your phone bill is on unlimited phone calls or you might run up a hell of a bill to me today"

Luke let out a laugh. "If they don't turn up, they don't turn up, nothing gained, nothing lost" said Luke as he tied up his boots.

"Right, you ready to go" Luke asked Paul.

"Ready" replied Paul.

"Let's go then," said Luke. At that, they locked their cars, crossed the road, went through the path gate and proceeded up the hill path towards the viewpoint. As they approached the last corner before they could be seen from the viewpoint, Luke said "right this is where we'll part. You go into the woods and follow me as close as you can, but make sure you're unobserved. That's critical, Paul. No using torches."

"There's no one about to observe me and nothing is going to happen, anyway" said Paul reassuringly.

"Hopefully" said Luke "but anyway, just humour me. Right, I'll phone you now and put the phone in my pocket. I'll see you at the other side, for better or for worse." At that Luke phoned Paul, put the phone in his pocket, switched on his Dictaphone, set it to record and walked on up the path, leaving Paul muttering comically "who the hell is phoning me at this time of the morning?"

It was still quite dark with a distant dawn glow in the southeast when Luke came to the viewpoint. Luke switched on the small torch he had brought with him. The metal circle on the top of the location indicated points near and far, from Ben Nevis to the more local mountains, Inverness, Aberdeen and even Iceland, the North Pole and Greenland. Nobody seemed to be about, but then a figure approached from within the woods close by. It was a man, reasonably tall and athletic looking.

"Are you Luke?" he asked in a broad Glaswegian dialect.

"Yes, and who are you" asked Luke.

"I'm Ingrid's brother" came the answer.

"Really, you don't sound very Scandinavian to me" stated Luke.

"No, well, I've lived over here for quite a few years and picked up the Glasgow accent" said the man "you'll be wanting to meet Ingrid, she's over there beside that old building right beside the cliff edge. It's only fifty metres away. Just head over and introduce yourself."

"Ahhh, thanks" said Luke who was wondering how the perfect copy of a Glaswegian accent had been achieved by a Scandinavian. Luke started to wander over. He was considering what he was going to say to make a suitable first impression. He had already temporarily forgotten about his questions concerning Ingrid's alleged brother.

As he approached the derelict building, Luke could see no-one about, so he let out a gentle call "Hello, Ingrid, are you there?" At that point, a woman with a big head of hair walked out of the empty doorway and said, "Hi Luke, follow me." She quickly turned and walked ten metres to the right. Luke asked, "where are we going?"

"Right here" came the answer in a broad Glaswegian accent as she turned to face Luke.

"That's not a Scandinavian accent" said Luke who finally realised with a shudder that he had been set up. Luke stopped and in the dull light of dawn looked at Ingrid. "I know you; I've seen you at my previous court cases. Mary, Mary is your name! You've gone to a lot of elaborate bother to get me here. What are you hoping to achieve here this morning, Mary?" asked Luke.

"She doesn't need to achieve anything more" came a man's voice fifteen feet behind Luke. Luke swung around to see two men standing together looking at him.

"Why have you got me here" asked Luke.

"You'll find out soon enough. You've caused me a lot of trouble. Now it's payback time. Right Rob, take Mary away to the car, I'll manage things from here, myself. When I get back to Glasgow, there will be suitable rewards for both of you" said Shaun who was still unrecognizable to Luke.

"Make sure that you do it right" said Mary "he has recognised me."

"Have nae fear about that Mary doll, I'll do it right, okay," said Shaun.

"Make it quick before anybody comes up here" said Rob "right doll, lets you and I go." With that they turned together and started to walk away to one of the woodland tracks away from the headland.

One hundred metres further down the track that Luke had come up, Paul had listened in to the conversation, disbelieving what he had heard. He wondered to himself "is this what's really happening, or could there be any other logical explanation?" After an initial thirty seconds of hesitation, he decided that he would have to phone the Police. He disconnected to Luke, phoned 999 and got emergency services. In a hushed voice he hurriedly explained who he was, where he was near the viewpoint on Craigievoun hill, that there were people about to possibly kill his friend Luke Walker and that he needed Police attendance immediately. The operator tried to get more out of Paul such as how many people were there, but Paul just frantically stated "Hurry" before hanging up.

One hundred metres further up the track, Luke watched Rob and Mary walk away and then turned to the last remaining man. “I gather you intend some harm to me, but there’s one detail you’ve overlooked.”

“Oh yeah, what’s that then” asked a belligerent Shaun.

“I’m quite handy when looking after myself. I reckon I’ll give you a little lesson you won’t forget in a hurry,” said Luke.

“Does this change the odds” said Shaun, pulling out a twelve-inch bladed knife.

“Ah. Probably” admitted Luke with a frown forming on his brow showing he had understated the odds situation. Shaun started to advance towards Luke. Luke knew his options were limited and backed off until he reached almost the very edge of the cliff. Luke peered down for a mere second over the cliff but even in the gloom of dawn he could see it was a fall of a hundred and fifty feet, at least.

“You can have it easy, jump and it’ll be all over in about three seconds,” said Shaun.

“Not a chance,” said Luke.

“If I have to cut you, the damage will only get blamed on fall trauma when they find your body” said Shaun “you’re going over alive or dead.” Luke was not going to say another word, he was fully focused on how Shaun was going to force him over the edge or stab him.

“Police, Stop, Police” came Paul’s shouted voice from forty metres away. This was heard in the distance by Rob and Mary who were two hundred metres away down the woodland track. They both turned up their heels and ran like their lives depended on it. Shaun momentarily was stunned by this announcement and whilst he was distracted looking towards the source of the shout, Luke saw it as possibly his only chance. He rushed in immediately towards Shaun and grabbed at the knife hand to minimise the risk of being stabbed. At the same time, he kicked Shaun's legs from underneath him, but Shaun had a hold of Luke as well. The two men fell heavily together to the ground. They wrestled and rolled away from the cliff and then towards the cliff as they tussled on the ground. Shaun was about to make another attempt at stabbing Luke, when Luke shifted the knife arm away to the side, moving their combined weight towards the cliff, causing them both to roll twice, just as Paul arrived ten metres away from the scene. The two men carried on rolling, but this time over the cliff edge and disappeared, causing Paul to gasp a long drawn out "nooooooo" with the horror of what he had just seen.

Paul stumbled and fell to his knees, shaking like a leaf with the shock of what had just happened. He shouted "no, no, no, no."

After about one minute he stood up shakily and moved gingerly towards the cliff edge. He was in shock and felt too unsteady to risk getting too close for fear of collapsing to vertigo. Still shaking, he stood for another three minutes disbelievingly staring over the cliff edge ten feet away just as the first Policemen arrived on scene and asked him what had happened. Paul collapsed to his knees and said to the Policeman "my mate Luke has just rolled over the cliff, whilst fighting off a guy who was trying to stab him with a knife. He didn't have a chance. The second Policeman, who wasn't affected by vertigo or shock, went right to the very edge, looked over and said, "does he have a greenish jacket on him?"

Just then a voice piped up from over the cliff "Oh, I can hardly breathe. I think I've knackered my thumb. Are you guys going to help me or just going to stand there looking at me in pain?"

"It's Luke" said Paul who started to make his way to the edge of the cliff.

"No, you don't, said the first Policeman "stay right there, we don't want you falling over the cliff."

The second Policeman said to Luke "don't move sir, you're on a narrow ledge only four feet down from the top of the cliff. Don't try to roll over or move as its very narrow. Do you understand, Sir?"

Luke muttered "I think so."

"Have you any pains, at the moment, that you're aware of" asked the Policeman. "Oh, I've got a whopper of a headache and my thumb is bleeding a bit. My left arm really hurts and I'm still winded a bit as well" answered Luke blowing hard as he spoke.

"Well don't move, we'll have some people to help you within a few minutes" said the Policeman.

As more Police and an ambulance crew arrived, they raised Luke up from the ledge and took him and Paul to hospital for a check-up. Both men were going to be fine in the long term, with only minor cut wounds to Luke, the most serious and painful damage to him was a dislocated arm and two broken ribs, which were the main cause of his winding.

Shaun was not so lucky. His mangled dead body was discovered at the bottom of the cliff. Rob and Mary got away that day, but it was only a matter of two weeks before Mary was picked up.

The recording taken by Luke proved the whole story, up to his roll over the cliff with Shaun. Rob evaded the law for a few extra days, but he too was certain to be entertained in a HM Prison for many years to come. Gangland members from then on referred to lucky Luke as "The Catman", as he had surely used up nearly all his nine lives.

Luke was visited by Paul a few days after they both left hospital. As Paul approached Luke, he looked around the room as though expecting an assassin to come jumping out from the furniture. "You know, you been living a very dangerous lifestyle recently. You're so hazardous to be with, that the next time I go out for a nature walk with you, I'm going to wear body armour and a parachute and I'm not joking," said Paul. Luke snorted a laugh and then said "Oh, Oh, don't make me laugh, it hurts my ribs."

Four weeks later and Paul took Luke out for an afternoon birdwatching down at a local estuary. After a walk about, both men stopped on a grass bank to take in the natural ambience of the place and the wildlife. Paul looked at Luke and asked "how are you doing now, my friend? Life has been pretty rough on you in the last few years?"

At that moment, a skein of geese came flying overhead, suddenly jinking away after noticing the two men on the ground. Luke turned to Paul and said "life is good now but like those geese, caution is now irreversibly instilled in me. But I do know one thing, without your help and friendship, I would either have been locked up in jail now or dead. You, my friend, have given me my life back and for that I will be eternally grateful."

"Well thank you Luke, it was quite an adventure. I wouldn't have missed it for the world" answered Paul.

At that both men turned and watched the geese landing out on the mudflats with the setting sun in the background.

Nothing more needed to be said.

After a few moments of quiet contemplation, the two men started to head back to the car.

Paul said "so what do you think of starting up The Disciples Private Investigation Agency?"

Luke wheezed out "what, are you nuts?"

"No seriously, what do you think" asked Paul.

"That's it, it's confirmed, you're completely nuts. And I'm trusting you as the driver back to my home. Woe is me! There's no hope!"

Paul had dropped behind Luke, so he shouted to him "I'm serious you know. I am."

Luke just walked on, shaking his head in disbelief.

## Authors Notes

If this fictional novel had been inspired by a true story, the law protects those involved, in that I would not be able to indicate the real names within the story. Criminals and rich companies are well served by the law. Innocent people who get caught in the middle of illegal activities are not so well served by the judicial system.

Organised Crime Groups are responsible for all sorts of criminal activity within Scotland and worldwide. Their activities include drug selling, prostitution, scamming people of their savings, robberies, illegal people trafficking, loan sharking, protection racketeering, corruption of government officials, pet theft to order, pet breeding farms, hare coursing, illegal gambling dens - you name it. If money is there to be made, they'll do their very best to get that money. If done successfully it can make a lot of people very rich.

However, the consequences of all this activity is a great deal of misery and death heaped on innocent people and animals. In Scotland, the death toll relating to drugs alone has been rising almost every year and is now well over a thousand people per annum. And yet that is probably only touching the truth. The true figure may well be much higher than that.

Recently, the real figure has been at a level nearly three times the number of deaths by the worst years of the trouble's death toll in Northern Ireland. Despite that, there is hardly any mention of it in the Scottish News, possibly because the deaths have largely been self-inflicted by addicts.

There are lots of long-term missing people of which some will have been taken out by OCG's. The latest methodology of

OCG's to get someone either to torture, re-educate or assassinate, is not normally to shoot the victim, which creates too much of a ripple effect, but to monitor long term until they have figured out a weak link in their movement chain. Once they know where and when they could be grabbed without raising attention, they will move on them.

So why do they do this?

It is quite simple, there are always people who will try to muscle in on a profitable market area for criminal activity or they may be someone who has spoken to the law as an innocent but concerned witness.

The drug trade, as one example is huge. Drugs are highly addictive but still normally a choice. When you live in poverty, they can seem like an escape from reality for a while. The trouble is once they become required, they cost money that is simply not there and so many people resort to crime or prostitution to fund their habit. This leads to a downward financial spiral which so many people find impossible to break out of. The whole thing spreads like a dry rot especially in the lower echelons of society. To a lesser degree, the richer professional classes often take drugs, but they have the financial resources to do so, at least initially.

To remedy addiction, the current thinking is merely to supply drugs free to addicts and at least have some control. In the first year it only caused a 1% reduction in the death toll. A better way may be to help the persons break out of their addiction habit and if achieved, reward them by writing off any reasonable outstanding debts, so they learn to better manage their lives, their finances and critically stay off the drugs.

OCG's can act with horrendous barbarity, using unbelievable levels of violence. There should be an absolute zero tolerance of that. Absolute zero should mean exactly that. In a recent case in Glasgow, some thugs chased a guy in a car chase through the streets of Glasgow doing over 100mph. When they caught him up, they beat him so badly that his lower jaw was only left attached to his head by a piece of skin.

These pieces of information are downplayed by the media as they know it is nauseating to the British public. People don't like to face up to the repugnant aspects of the violence from OCG's. Society doesn't seem to know how to deal with this totally unacceptable side of the OCG's, mainly because they don't want to see it or just avoid it, effectively brushing this unsightly dirt under the carpet, again and again.

In countries where OCG's thrive, they can be utterly ruthless, using bombs and machine guns.

But as OCGs become ever more successful and affluent, they are constantly striving for greater success. Drug cartels are now buying low profile, high power, sea going, vessels and even mini submarines to transport drugs. Gone are the days of traditional mules and donkeys sent over mountain passes, except in very remote countries.

Fortunes are being made in illegal trafficking of people as can be seen on the south of England coastline and the south side of the Mediterranean countries. That has been a major problem as it is organised by OCG's who run a very efficient system.

Most people have experienced scammers saying they are from Microsoft, the Police or their bank, trying to get access to their accounts. OCG's will always search for new ways to extract money illegally in whatever ways they can. The richer and more successful tier lords of OCG's can merge into respectable society, sometimes for most of their life. Police may know how some of these top gang lords operated and got there but if they have difficulty proving it, they may be unable to act decisively against them.

Which brings me to the Police and judicial system. OCG's barons that have been sent to court always seem to have no problem paying for the best and most persuasive defence barristers.

A defence barristers' job is to belittle the evidence, make a case that black is actually white and that there are huge holes in the evidence and integrity of the case against his or her client. Often, they take great pride in doing so, totally disregarding the ethics behind the case. Many a gangster deserving of a long-term jail term, has got off with no punishment because of "good" barrister work, but this is a misnomer. In many cases, they help murderers get away with just that. It takes a certain type of twisted mentality to suit that type of job and sleep well, unaffected by the morality. All to satisfy their ego and wallets.

When criminals start out, they often appear before the courts, but the smarter ones turn up less frequently as they progress up the hierarchical ladder and become more capable in court scenarios.

However, maybe a new idea would be to assign criminal life points, in that as they receive more convictions, it changes the outcomes of the court sentencing. The worse their record, the higher the points they accumulate. If they venture too far into criminality or become involved in violence, the point system should reduce or remove the possibility of probation and in the worst cases add a percentage to the sentence handed out or even seal them in jail for life, depending on how bad they've been.

As an example, a person handed out a sentence of three years jail but with up to eight points, would be entitled to the normal reduced sentence. Someone with between nine and fifteen points would not be entitled to a reduction of sentence and would have to serve the full three years. Someone beyond that would get an extra 10% added to their sentence per extra point. So a criminal with twenty points would have an extra 50% added to their sentence and to serve the full term.

In addition, above a certain point level, if out of jail, they should be fitted with tracking devices around their ankles, so that their whereabouts can be determined at any time, even retrospectively. This means beyond set certain points level, each case will be adversely affected by their previous record with life getting increasingly hard for the very worst criminal cases.

A disproportional level of crime is carried out by a small number of criminals, so this system would ensure they are the most affected by this scheme.

At the other end of the criminal leagues, young people who venture inadvertently into crime, should be assessed, coached and helped to adjust back to a more normal working life, if it is believed they have that potential. Any young criminal, outside of incorrigibly violent or potentially violent criminals, should be able to ask for this help to get back on the straight and narrow. This would surely be better than jailing unnecessarily.

There are young people, mostly starting in their teens, being trained by OCG's to be drug dealers. Invariably they get off because of the soft justice prevailing today in Scotland, but if they were given points and had it explained to them that they will inevitably be hit harder in the future with extended prison terms, if they continue in that line. Then only the stupidest or most arrogant amongst them, would be unaffected by the threat to their freedom.

Another useful aspect of this points system would be to harness those disruptive individuals in society that sail close to the wind and get away with it. Disruptive individuals literally abound within society and because they often don't believe the rules apply to them, they will bend the rules but try to avoid actual prosecution. As an example, if a building operating firm ripped out a long length of hedgerow during the nesting season in one day but made no announcements about it, they could be susceptible to having points imposed on the boss and contractor involved. In another example if a developer sent in contractors to clear fell an Oakwood SSSI, blatantly unconcerned about the consequences, they could have points imposed. These are just simple examples from real life cases. Usually nothing significant happens against these sorts of people. If complaints are made but the Police don't have the inclination or resources to prosecute, it could be referred to a small specialist group who examine these cases. If the case is irrefutable, then this group should be allowed to allocate points to the top person and responsible contractors. This means, if they eventually do overstep the mark, go to court and get found guilty of something else, their unethical behaviour in the past, will have cumulative consequences on their sentence. This may have the effect of making these types think twice before they deliberately overstep the mark, rather than just saying "we don't care" knowing full well that they will get away with their actions.

Using this system to cover current loopholes in the law may allow less chances of the abuser types getting away with all sorts of unsociable or unethical behaviours, without requiring the expensive resorting to legal proceedings.

As for the Police, it is necessarily a very secretive organisation, but this means they can become politicised and indeed considerably less competent without realising it because the true successes or failures go unnoticed.

Politicians ultimately are their bosses, who are frequently corruptible, dishonest by nature and self-serving. But if unacceptable party politics become acceptable to the Police, then that simply cannot be considered acceptable. The insular self-regulation of Police means that glaring flaws may not be highlighted and so left as normal procedures for many years.

By the very nature of the personality types who often become Policemen or women, there can be an arrogance which is not necessarily conducive to good detective work or indeed Public Relations.

Sorting out the truth can be a very difficult task and requires intelligent questioning, probing and intuition, not just a blind belief in themselves because they have an ego equal to any in the criminal world. When lives are at stake or in the case of high-level terrorism, agreed heavier handed interrogation methods should be allowable to get the information needed.

In England, there are different Police forces in different regions. It should be standardised that if criminals move from one area to another, it should be expected that the officers will move too, if necessary, at least until other suitable officers either arrive to help or take over. In other words, there should be no invisible boundaries for the Police. Criminals certainly don't envisage any boundaries, but they can be aware of boundaries applicable to the law enforcement agencies. The current set up can be a godsend for criminal gangs and should constantly be adjusted to allow the flexibility required to combat the criminal elements covering all the county lines.

OCG's will eventually become very powerful if the powers that be, keep brushing the problems out of sight or hiding them from public view or knowledge. In some countries they are more of a problem and represent a threat greater than any terrorism.

Politicians are ultimately the bosses of the Police forces. However, Politicians often have a very dirty house. In what other line of work would you be paid your salary but be allowed to work for other organisations and earn extra income which can sometimes be considerably higher than the MP salary. I would argue very few or none that I can think of. Politicians should either work for their salary or don't apply to become MPs. This sort of attitude facilitates immoral, selfish behaviour, which is contrary to the true code of politicians' very being. Similarly, politicians should not have access to bonuses paid by businesses of any sort, other than shares etc they have bought legitimately themselves. This type of behaviour facilitates unfair competition and corruption using the MPs with favouritism towards companies that have been paying back handers. It can also give criminally originated businesses or laundered money a legitimacy, which just should not be tolerated. Politicians will never agree to this though, because it would curtail the many benefits they have, unless the public can metaphorically bend their arms.

Final word is...

STAY ALERT. STAY SAFE!